THE JUDGMENT OF
YOYO GOLD

BY ISAAC BLUM

PHILOMEL

PHILOMEL
An imprint of Penguin Random House LLC
1745 Broadway, New York, NY 10019
penguinrandomhouse.com

Copyright © 2024 by Isaac Blum
Discussion questions copyright © 2025 by Isaac Blum

Penguin Random House values and supports copyright. Copyright fuels creativity, encourages diverse voices, promotes free speech, and creates a vibrant culture. Thank you for buying an authorized edition of this book and for complying with copyright laws by not reproducing, scanning, or distributing any part of it in any form without permission. You are supporting writers and allowing Penguin Random House to continue to publish books for every reader. Please note that no part of this book may be used or reproduced in any manner for the purpose of training artificial intelligence technologies or systems.

Philomel is a registered trademark of Penguin Random House LLC.

Edited by Talia Benamy
Design by Lily K. Qian
Text set in Adobe Caslon Pro

Library of Congress Cataloging-in-Publication Data is available.

First published in the United States of America by Philomel, 2024
First paperback edition published by Philomel, 2025

Manufactured in the United States of America
LSCC

ISBN 9780593525869
1st Printing

The authorized representative in the EU for product safety and compliance is Penguin Random House Ireland, Morrison Chambers, 32 Nassau Street, Dublin D02 YH68, Ireland, https://eu-contact.penguin.ie.

FOR ELSA AND HAROLD

PROLOGUE

HINDSIGHT IS SUPPOSED TO MAKE EVERYTHING clear. But when I think back, I'm still not sure how much of it was my fault. I'm trying to be easier on myself, so I won't accept *all* of the blame. But I have to take at least some of it.

Because I should have recognized what was happening to Esti. The signs were all there.

My father always says it's a slippery slope. That's why strict observance is so important: once you do *one* non-observant thing, you've taken a step down the slope, and that leads to more non-observant things, and before you know it you're sliding uncontrollably into a sick world of secular depravity. Or, in Esti's case, you're on a plane to Las Vegas, which I guess is kind of the same thing.

I, of all people, should have picked up on the signs. I'm the rabbi's daughter, and I'm expected to set an example, to help guide my peers. But maybe your best friend is a blind spot, like that space alongside a car that the mirror doesn't show. That's why they have those electronic sensing systems on cars. But they don't have those for best friends. There was no Esti-shaped warning light that flashed when she did stuff she wasn't supposed to.

Because it would have gone off when Esti cut her hair short and dyed it purple.

It would have gone off when she suggested that we find a

basement or parking lot that was "both dark and remote" in which to try marijuana.

It would have gone haywire when she kissed Ari Fischer in a field. That one set the whole community abuzz. Everybody was talking about her. My father was calling me into his office on a regular basis, asking me to fix the problem.

"Ari's tongue is very slippery," Esti explained to me. "I thought it might be more like a cat's tongue, you know? Where it's kind of rough and grippy."

We were having this conversation in the street. It was Shabbos, the Jewish day of rest, and we were walking home from our friend Shira's house. Our town is almost all Orthodox, and observant Jews don't drive on the Sabbath.

"Why would you think that?" I asked her. "Because, you see, Esti, you also have a human tongue. Is *your* tongue grippy, like a cat's?"

"That's a great point. You know, Yoyo, it's a good thing I keep you around."

And she kept talking about Ari, but I tuned it out, because we were supposed to be good Orthodox girls. And that meant that we didn't kiss boys. We didn't talk to boys. We made sure not to be alone in the same *room* as boys.

Suddenly there was a car coming. Esti was wandering into the middle of the road, lost in her thoughts of Ari. As the car blared its horn, I pulled her out of the street onto the sidewalk.

"See?" Esti said, coughing at the car's lingering fumes. "We'd all be roadkill if not for you. I'd just be a smear on the pavement without my Yoyo. Do you think Ari would still love my mangled, disfigured corpse? I think he would."

"Did you just say . . . 'love'?"

"Yeah," she said casually, almost matter-of-fact. "He loves me. And I love him. He's my bashert."

That's when my internal alarm system finally went off. I panicked. I scrambled. "No. No. Esti. You can't *know* that. You can't. Only HaShem knows that."

From the Torah, we know lots of the things God wants. He wants us to follow the dietary laws of kashrut and keep kosher. He wants us to do chesed and help others. He wants us to marry Jewish men and raise studious Jewish children. But these are all general things, the things he wants of the Jews, of his people. The Torah doesn't say anything about specific individuals. So we know what God wants of women, but we don't know what he wants from any given woman. The Torah is mum on the subject of what I should have for lunch, and it doesn't say a word about whom Esti Saperstein is supposed to marry.

"That's not for you to decide," I said. "That decision is reserved for HaShem."

"It doesn't feel like a decision," Esti explained. She kicked a piece of gravel along the sidewalk in front of her. "It just *is*. Your dad *said*."

"No, he did *not* say—"

"He said to think of the coming together with your bashert not as a union but as a *reunion*, right? You are two half-souls that have been missing from each other, so HaShem brings you *back* together."

"I know. I know. But who are you to just *decide* that he's your other half? Just because you *feel* something?" I dug deep and tried to channel my father's religious wisdom. "Tell me: In the Torah, did Yitzhak and Rivka make textural observations about each other's oral anatomy and *fall* in love? *No.* Eliezer, as a messenger of HaShem, arranged their marriage."

Esti just shrugged. She shrugged at her best friend. She shrugged at God and his Torah.

That's when I knew how bad it was. And I also knew that it was too late. Esti was too far down, and the slope too slippery.

"You don't understand. You've probably never had a feeling this . . . powerful," Esti explained. "I had my hand on his face, and I could feel his heartbeat, his *pulse*, and everything in the world was one big explosion, like a bomb, a big one. It's a good thing we were in a secluded area. Otherwise, there would have been casualties."

A few days later, Esti moved to Las Vegas to attend a boarding school.

And in those first few surreal days, when Esti was gone, but before the loss of my best friend really hit me, I kept thinking back to that metaphor, the bomb. Because it was a big bomb and there was at least one casualty.

Me.

Esti exploded my whole life.

CHAPTER 1

I WAS LATE FOR CLASS ONCE. It was calculus, and on the way I stubbed my toe so hard that the nail broke. I took a minute to fight back the tears and gather myself, and by the time I was gathered, I was late. I thought I'd be in trouble, but Miss Simpson said nothing about my tardiness. She saw my shoe in my hand and the blood coming through my tights, and asked if I wanted to skip class to seek medical attention.

That was the only time I'd been late to something.

Until now.

I stood at my front door, looking out through the frosted windows next to the door itself. I'd been there for five minutes. Maybe ten. I was just staring, expecting to see the Sapersteins' Toyota SUV appear at my curb, its form distorted by the glass.

Esti had left on Thursday. I'd tracked her flight on a Chromebook. So I knew she was about twenty-five hundred miles away. Still, now it was Sunday morning, and I was at the front door waiting for her to pick me up for chesed like she had every week since she got her driver's license.

Chesed is Hebrew for "kindness." For school, we had to do a certain number of hours of chesed. My friends and I did all of ours on Sundays, when we volunteered for an organization called JHR, Jewish Hunger Relief, which provided food to Jews experiencing food insecurity.

When I finally looked at the time on my phone again, I saw that I was late, and unless I smashed my foot against something, I wouldn't even have an excuse.

I reached for the car key on its little hook and shouted, "I'm taking the minivan."

At JHR, we started in a warehouse, where we packed food into boxes. Then everybody split up and drove around to different places, delivering the boxes. Esti claimed to hold all of the records for the fastest deliveries. I always reminded her that A) there was no such recordkeeping and B) actually, our chesed was tracked by the amount of time we spent, so it didn't behoove us, from a chesed accumulation standpoint, to do it faster. "I'll behoove you in the *face*," she'd say.

The parking lot was already full. I got out of the car and gave myself a quick once-over in the side mirror.

Your clothes are a way to express your identity. They tell the world who you are. My regular school uniform said that I was a proper Orthodox girl. The nice dress I wore for Shabbos said that I celebrated God's day of rest. Sunday was the only day to truly express myself fashion-wise. I wanted it to feel like a normal Sunday, so I dressed that way, in a normal Sunday outfit: tights under a gray skirt, a red-brown sweater paired with a dark blue blazer. It said I was tznius, or modest, but also serious and respectable.

"You look cute," said a voice.

I looked up. It was Chani Holtzman, in a loose turtleneck that said she cared more about mobility than style. She was leaning her head out the passenger-side window of the Holtzman van, which had just appeared at the curb. "Thanks," I said, though cute wasn't how I was trying to look.

Chani usually drove herself, so I looked across to see who was driving, and I felt my eyes narrow. It was a boy. Or a man. Or a male person in between those two. And he looked familiar.

He kind of looked like Shua Holtzman, Chani's older brother. He had the same upturned nose as Shua Holtzman, the same mouth that was a little too big, so you thought it might contain orthodontia, but didn't. He had the same dark brown hair that kind of swooped left to right across his forehead, like the Nike logo.

This guy was definitely Shua Holtzman.

Shua had been best friends with my older brother, Moshe, when they were younger. Then they'd gone off to different boarding schools.

But why was Shua here? He was supposed to be off studying in Israel. And if he was back, why had nobody told me? I always knew this kind of thing *before* everybody else.

"Just text when you're done," Shua said to Chani. He had one hand casually on the wheel, drumming with the tips of his fingers. He wasn't wearing a suit jacket or hat, just a white shirt and a black kippah.

"I can drive her," I said.

He looked up and noticed me. "Thanks," he said.

Chani got out of the car. She gave Shua a wave, and I turned to walk in with her, but Shua said, "Wait." I assumed he was talking to his sister, but then he said, "Yoyo," which was my name, and he was waving me over to the car. "You *are* Yoyo, right?"

"Yeah."

"Gold?"

"How many Yoyos do you know?"

"Right. Fair point. You've . . . It's just, you've grown since the last time I saw you."

"That's how it works." It came out snippier than I'd meant it to. And I actually didn't think it was true. I looked more mature. I'd lost the baby fat in my cheeks. But I hadn't grown vertically in like five years. He was the one who'd grown. He was taller, broader, and he had a patchy beard now that was somehow both neat and scruffy.

He was still drumming on the wheel. "I wanted to give you my phone number," he said.

I was about to tell him that was inappropriate—and surely he knew that—but he clarified. "I got a new number, so I was hoping you could pass it on to Moshe. I know he's away, but if he comes home to visit . . . I don't want to lose touch with him, you know?"

"That makes one of us," I said. Moshe was pompous, and whenever he texted me it was because he needed something.

Shua laughed, probably because it was the polite thing to do. Careful not to touch him, I handed Shua my phone, and he added himself to my contacts.

"*Such* a pain that he's home," Chani said, as we walked into the warehouse.

"Yeah?"

"Yeah."

"It's the middle of the school year. Did something happen?" I asked.

Chani looked around her and lowered her voice. "Yeah. Something . . . happened."

I was about to nudge for more specificity—any specificity—but we'd entered the warehouse and I cut myself off.

JHR was usually kind of festive. There's nothing fun about food insecurity, but JHR was a community event, a chance for community women to get together, talk, catch up, joke around. Being a Jewish woman was about caring and community, and JHR had both of those things.

There was a general buzz in the warehouse, but it hushed when I walked in. I could feel eyes follow me as I walked. I knew people were looking at me, but I didn't know what kind of looks they were. The only clue I got was when I caught a few people checking the time on their phone.

Chani grabbed a station at one of the long tables that ran the length of the room. I went to where my friends Shira and Dassi had left me my place at the head of the first table, but where Esti usually stood, at my right, Miri Moritz was in her place, standing very erect, looking proud and official.

Mrs. Gomes, our drama teacher, was at the other end of the table. She and her daughters were assembling the boxes, getting the process started.

We used the assembly line system pioneered by noted antisemite Henry Ford. We each had a little station. As usual, mine was the canned chickpeas station. I had crates of canned chickpeas stacked up next to me. A box started at the end of the table, and as the box was passed down, each person added their item. When I added my chickpeas, I closed the box and stacked it with the other completed boxes.

When we'd packed all of the food, I could feel people looking at me again. But these looks, looks of impatience, were easy to read. And I realized I'd messed up. I was in charge of organizing the distribution itself. Every week, I looked over the list of volunteers and the recipient addresses, and I paired the volunteers and assigned them routes. But where my usual printed spreadsheet would be, there was just the stained plastic tabletop.

I took a moment to stare at what appeared to be a coffee stain. Miri Moritz huffed. "Yoyo, who am I with?"

"I—" I began.

I looked across the warehouse, at the forty or fifty assembled women and girls, all looking at me, as they did every week, expecting me to direct them. It was like somebody had turned a spotlight on me.

I guess it had always been like that. I was always in the spotlight. I'd lived my whole life that way, and it was fine. I liked that people listened to me, relied on me, respected me. But today the spotlight suddenly felt different. It was bright, and hot, and I wanted to squirm.

"Did you just *forget*?" asked Miri.

I said nothing. I was as shocked as she was.

"You can't, like, *do* that," Miri went on. "The people we're bringing boxes to . . . They're *relying* on us."

I nodded. "I know," I said. "I—" But I didn't know what else to say.

Shira and Dassi appeared at my side with a pen and a pad of paper. I opened the spreadsheet on my phone and started scribbling on the paper. Everybody watched me work. And maybe

I could have read these looks, but I didn't have the time to lift my eyes off the paper, so I didn't know if they contained sympathy for a girl whose best friend had just moved away, or if it was disapproval at the rabbi's daughter who couldn't remember her basic administrative duties.

All I could hear was Miri mumbling under her breath as I worked, saying things like: "Now we'll *all* be late." And the one that really hurt: "What would Rabbi Gold say?"

Eventually I got everybody paired off and routes assigned. I realized only afterward that I'd forgotten to give myself a partner. It was inconvenient to go by yourself, because often there wasn't a place to leave the car when you made deliveries.

The warehouse was emptying out as people headed for their vehicles. I reached down, grabbed a couple boxes, and started carrying them toward the open warehouse doors. I thought maybe I could flag down Shira and Dassi. We could get two routes' worth of boxes into my minivan and the three of us could go together. The deliveries would take us longer, but they probably knew this day was tough for me and would agree anyway.

But when I got into the parking lot, they were gone. Everybody was.

I balanced the boxes on my knee, hit the button on the fob, and started loading the van.

It is a mitzvah—a commandment—to perform chesed, to love your neighbors through kindness. And usually I felt joyful and fulfilled when I did it, but today I felt neither of those things.

When I'd emptied the car and completed the route, I started driving home, hoping homework would bring joy. I got almost all the way home before I remembered I was supposed to pick Chani up at the warehouse.

I turned around and grabbed her. She stood alone in the dark of an empty parking lot next to a now-abandoned warehouse. But if she was upset, she didn't show it.

When we pulled up to the Holtzman house, I thought about Shua, and what it would be like if Moshe suddenly came home. "I guess it *would* be annoying if my brother moved back in."

"It's not his presence," Chani said. "He sleeps in the basement now, and only comes up to eat. It's that he's been so weird since he got kicked out of his—crap. I— Please don't tell anybody I said that. I'm sure your dad knows, but I don't want everybody to find out. People talk, and you of all people know what happens when people hear those off-the-derech stories. It was a really conservative place and it wasn't that big a thing, but before you know it people will be saying he was a drug-addicted prostitute or something, and nobody will date him, and my parents will—"

"Chani. Don't worry. I mean, I already texted a *few* people about it, just now, but I'll make sure they keep their mouths shut."

"Thanks, Yoyo," she said, unbuckling her seatbelt.

My curiosity pulled me momentarily out of my Esti-induced fog. "Will you tell me what he got kicked out for?" I asked. It was hard to imagine any friend of Moshe's as a rule-breaker.

Chani was silent for moment. She ran her fingers through her hair and dropped her voice to a whisper, even though we were alone in a car. "He got kicked out for internet-filter stuff. He was removing kids' phone filters. He was doing it for . . . money. Profit."

I felt my eyes narrow. "Why did they want that?"

"I don't know," Chani said. "To watch pornography, probably. What else do boys like? Sports?"

"What about video games?" I asked.

"Oh yeah. Video games. Those are the big three, I guess. I could ask," Chani said. "But I think it might be better not to know. It can't have been a good reason, so why would I want to know about it?"

Could it have been a good reason? I wondered. As Chani closed the car door behind her, I tried to think what a good reason might be.

I sat at the curb. I felt my fingers performing a Shua-esque drumming. I pressed my head back against the headrest, felt the cool spread out. I was trying to process everything, but it was a lot.

I could dress like it was a normal Sunday, but I couldn't fake it and make it feel that way. This was too much: all of the furtive looks and all of Miri's mumbling, doing the deliveries on my own.

Esti was the only person I could process stuff with, who I could talk to without judgment. With everybody else, I was Rabbi Gold's daughter, and nobody ever let me forget it. Wherever I walked, eyes followed me, with those hard-to-read looks of judgment. But with Esti, I was just me, just Yoyo. If she were here, I could leave my thoughts unsaid, but she'd understand them anyway, and she'd make off-color jokes about them, and just make everything feel less . . . heavy. It was like Esti changed the atmosphere so there was less gravity.

Suddenly I missed her so much I felt physical pain.

And the pain made me drive.

I'd thought I was driving home, but I realized I wasn't.

I'd thought I was okay, but I realized I wasn't. Something just wasn't right, and I didn't know how to make it right again. Something bad had happened, and I just wanted to wind the clock back and make it unhappen, but I didn't know how.

It was completely dark outside when I pulled up to Esti's driveway. I could only get halfway in because it was full of cars. The old house was split into three apartments, but the other two families each had two cars, so the driveway always looked like some kind of geometric puzzle.

I just sat there in the car, staring at Esti's third-floor bedroom window. The light was on. Maybe Mr. Saperstein was repurposing the room, turning it into an office or something, now that Esti didn't need it. His face appeared at the window. It was only there for a moment, but a minute later my phone buzzed.

It was my dad. Multiple people have called me. Come home and see me in my office. This behavior is unbecoming.

I didn't need anything more. Nobody did. If they got that sort of summons, anybody in Colwyn would have done exactly what I was doing now, reversing out of the driveway, following Rabbi Gold's instructions.

CHAPTER 2

"YOU CAN'T JUST IDLE MY CAR with half of it sticking out into the street," the prominent rabbi, Yosef Herschel Gold, told his eldest daughter, Yocheved. "It's not appropriate behavior."

I stood in my father's office. It was small and dark, the only light from this one bulb in his desk lamp. Around us shelves stood floor to ceiling, stuffed with leather-bound volumes whose spines glinted with gold and silver letters.

"I'm sad," I explained.

"There are ways to express sadness that don't block the street. And it's one thing if somebody else does it. But when it's you—well, you know this—it reflects on us, on *me*."

"How do you want me to express it?" I asked him.

Rabbi Gold was notoriously hard to read. I'd known him all my life, and even I had trouble sometimes. He wasn't very physically emotive, and he hid himself behind an enormous beard that covered all of the expressive parts of his face.

But this time, I knew what his silence meant: he *didn't* want me to express it. That might be fine for other people, but it was "unbecoming" for me, for his daughter.

"I miss her," I said.

"We all miss her."

But that wasn't true.

I was the oldest daughter of the rabbi. My father expected me to set an example: this is how a good rabbi raises his daughter, and this is how a good Jewish girl acts. And it looked bad if that daughter spent all her time with a girl who had purple streaks in her hair and kissed boys.

Rabbi Gold wasn't going to miss that girl, the one who raised eyebrows and inspired heated whispers all over the town. If he was going to miss her so much, he wouldn't have sent her away. Well, he claimed she wasn't *sent* away. He said it wasn't "punitive." Esti didn't fit in. She would be happier someplace else.

I believed him that he wasn't punishing her, or at least that he didn't see it that way. But it felt so much like he was punishing *me*. And I believed him that she might be happier someplace else, but *I* wouldn't be happier with her someplace else. She was the only person who didn't remind me every minute who I was, what was expected of me, what was "becoming" of my role.

My father reclined in his chair and scratched at his big red beard. "HaShem sends us nisyonos, tests of our devotion, of our faith," he explained to me. "We think, for example, of the Israelites in the desert. They wandered without water, and they had to simply have faith that God would drop food for them from the sky."

This must be part of rabbinical training: learning to talk in stories. When my dad has some kind of lesson to impart, he never just *says* it. He tells a story about Torah, or about some medieval rabbi, and then expects you to understand the meaning of the story yourself. It makes him seem more wise, I think, but it's also annoying.

"With nisyonos, HaShem gives us a beautiful opportunity to test ourselves, to show our dedication," he went on. But that was the end, and I had to fill in the blanks: I know this is hard for you, he was saying, but you are my daughter, and I know you will pass your test of faith, continue to make me proud, and continue to be a model for our community.

I *was* his daughter, but I wished, in moments like this, he would just treat me like that. I wasn't just another congregant asking for rabbinical advice. What I needed was a word of sympathy and a little slack. What I needed was the kind of big bear hug he used to give me when I was a little girl. But what I got was a Torah parable.

"I just need to talk to her," I said.

My father blinked his eyes, almost like they were watery. "I'm sorry," he said. "But you know that's not possible. Her boarding school doesn't allow phone calls in the first three months."

"I'm sure if you called . . ." I began, but I didn't finish the sentence, because he knew the ending of it, and I knew what his response would be.

He slumped back in his chair and changed the subject: "There's some kind of lasagna leftovers in the fridge," he informed me.

"I know. I made it."

"Right," he said. "Well, it's good. I recommend it."

I couldn't tell if he was joking around with me, or if he was earnestly recommending to me my own lasagna. Like I said, the man is hard to read. Either way, our conversation had ended.

As I walked downstairs, I considered his story-lesson. I

thought I could manage this. I could swallow it and push on, like I always did.

I took a gulp, tried to calm my body, and headed for the kitchen.

Nachi was sitting at the kitchen table. He'd just got home from basketball practice, and he was pretending to do homework while he waited faithfully for somebody—God or sister—to provide him with the sustenance to sustain him through his voracious adolescence. He was fourteen, and in that phase of growth where he was so frequently hungry that it was inconvenient for him to be far removed from the refrigerator. Like, if he ate a meal, by the time he got upstairs to his room he'd be hungry again and have to turn right around.

I have a large family, and while we're all different people, we have a type. Nachi is a typical specimen. He's a handsome brown-haired kid, but when he can grow a beard, it'll come in red. He's not short, but he's stocky. He has a low center of gravity. He'd be difficult to push over.

I went to the fridge and grabbed the lasagna. The laws of kashrut—kosher stuff—require you to keep dairy products separate from meat. My lasagna contained cheese, so I used the dairy microwave. "Are you fleishig?" I asked Nachi, double-checking that he hadn't recently had meat, so it was okay for him to eat dairy food.

"Nah," he said.

The microwave beeped. I removed the plate and placed it in front of Nachi. He grunted at me, said a quick blessing, and started eating. I placed a second slice in the microwave, for me.

My mother, the rebbetzin Chaya Ninah Gold, appeared in the doorway. She had just returned from . . . somewhere, and her bag was still draped over her shoulder. As always, she looked stylish, elegant, almost regal. She was wearing a long blue dress with a light jacket, and a scarf with a floral pattern. She wore a sheitel—a wig that some married Orthodox women wear—that perfectly matched Nachi's brown-gold hair.

She went to the sink and washed her hands, then pulled out a kitchen chair and sat down. I pulled the lasagna from the microwave. I put the plate on the table in front of my mom and got her a fork. "How was school?" she asked Nachi.

Boys had school on Sunday, extra religious education. I stared across the table at Nachi until he looked up at me. I pointed at his lasagna. The unspoken message was clear: you will thank me for the meal by absorbing this parental attention. "It was swell," he said.

"Yeah?" my mom asked.

"Yep. I . . . learned things. Did stuff. You know."

I gave him another look, trying to encourage specificity, but my attempted telepathy failed.

"I had classes in which I was the recipient of education," he said.

I went back to the pan, where there was one more piece of lasagna. There was no way I'd actually end up eating it, and sure enough, when I got it in the microwave I heard my mom's tone of voice change. "Get the little guys?" she said to me.

I looked at her, then at Nachi, who had not done his job. He gestured at his plate, and at himself. I'm a boy, his gesture said, and I'm eating, so you'll have to get them, like you always do.

I went into the living room, where Yoni and Yitzy were exactly where I'd left them, staring at the iPad. They were playing a game on there, and every few seconds Yitzy reached out and swiped at the screen.

They weren't supposed to use screens, but sometimes I just needed some peace and quiet.

I was sort of a back-up mom. I assume it's like this for elder sisters in most big families, not just Jewish ones. Whenever my mom wasn't home, I was in charge of the younger kids. I had to keep them fed, occupied, and—this is the hardest one by far—safe. It was tiring, but even though Yitzy and Yoni are almost objectively disgusting creatures—I think they're 90 percent germs—I love them entirely. They're adorable, special treasures, and I would step in front of any number of bullets for them.

"Eema's back," I informed them.

Nothing. They stared at the tablet. Yitzy tapped his finger on the middle of the screen. Yoni picked at the rug.

"She's in the kitchen."

They both looked up at that last word. I shook my head at them and pulled the tablet out of Yoni's reluctant hand.

"There's lasagna," Eema said when we entered the kitchen. She walked over to the microwave. She set the last plate of lasagna in front of the boys and walked them through the proper blessing.

I mentally ran through the contents of our fridge and pantry, thinking about what to make for myself. But I realized I wasn't even hungry at this point. My stomach was tying itself in knots.

I took the stairs two at a time up to my room, where I could be alone.

Or, not alone. Naomi was there. But being with Naomi was

just like being alone. I spent more time with Naomi than with any other person. We'd lived in the same room for over a decade. But I knew her the least of anybody in my family.

Naomi existed in books, mostly long fantasy novels with pictures of sorcerers and dragons on the covers. And that's where she was when I came into the room, in her own imaginary book world. She didn't look up. She just turned a page.

I lay down in bed and tried to turn a page too, a figurative one. I wanted to think about anything else, but all I could think about was Esti. I tried to picture her, but I didn't know what to picture. I knew what *she* looked like, but I didn't know what her surroundings might be. My understanding of Nevada was pretty basic.

When I tried to conjure up a mental image, all I came up with was a desert, a big empty expanse of sand and scrub, and Esti was there, walking alone among the cacti. And it made me think about my father's lesson, about the Israelites and their test of faith. I didn't like the way he'd presented it, so matter-of-fact. But he was the region's most prominent rabbi for a reason, and I had to admit what he said felt right. Esti was gone, and all of the little things that had once felt easy now felt impossibly difficult.

The Israelites had faith that God would provide for them, and he'd produced food that sustained them for forty years. If I did the same—according to Rabbi Gold—I'd be provided for.

I imagined myself in the desert with Esti, telling her about it. "I'm being tested," I'd tell her.

"You do great on tests," she would remind me.

"Calculus tests, maybe," I would reply.

"Yeah. Do some calculus for God. He'll be impressed."

CHAPTER 3

IT SEEMS TO BE COOL TO *not* like school. I hear girls complaining about it all the time. But I just can't get enough of it. There are so many things I don't know, and I get to go there, and they teach me those things. For example, because of school, I know that our bodies are 96 percent comprised of the following elements, in order from most to least: oxygen, carbon, hydrogen, nitrogen.

But as I walked to school on Monday, I felt like today was an exception. Today my body was 96 percent nerves, and I did not want to go to school.

It didn't help that I had halacha class first period. Halacha means Jewish law, the stuff you should and should not do. You should wash your hands before you eat anything that contains bread or bread-adjacent products. You should not sleep in your shoes. You should eat kugel, but not ham.

It's not that I don't find halacha interesting. But I feel like my whole life is a halacha lesson. I know surplus halacha. Like, not only do I know that gazelle is kosher—along with the other 145 species that make up the family bovidae—but I know the right blessing to say over my gazelle steak, in the unlikely event that they start selling it at Colwyn Kosher Grocery.

I was in my seat early, in my usual spot at the front row of the classroom. Shira and Dassi were there with me, at their desks on my left. Esti's seat on my right was empty.

Shira and Dassi were talking about the upcoming winter musical production. "I'm worried Mrs. Gomes is going to cast Miri in the lead—she always does. But the wife in this one isn't supposed to be glamorous," Shira was saying.

Dassi nodded in agreement. "And she doesn't have a lot of solo songs, so Miri's voice can be useful elsewhere. Maybe as the older daughter?"

Shira bristled at what she probably saw as a dig. She didn't like the suggestion that Miri had the better voice. "Yoyo, who should play the angry little boy without Esti?"

When Mrs. Gomes and I chose which musical we were going to do, I'd specifically looked for one with a good part for Esti. I didn't want to contemplate her replacement, and I was happy I didn't have to answer the question, because Rabbi Levin had just walked in.

Now that we were juniors, we'd moved past the basics and were discussing the connections between halacha and what my father calls "modernity." Some of Judaism's rules are clear, written directly in the Torah. But then some of them are *implied* by the Torah, and those rules have to be interpreted by different rabbis. But as we get further from Torah times, those interpretations get increasingly difficult, and we can't just rely on two-thousand-year-old Babylonian rabbis to tell us the rules, because those guys didn't exist in a world with television and the internet.

Rabbi Levin began class, as he always did, with a question that reminded us of the conclusions we'd reached the day before.

Today, he wrote the following question on the board: "You make a video of yourself singing. You text it to a friend. Why might this be a problem?"

Rivka Bloom raised her hand.

Rabbi Levin recognized her.

"I don't remember *exactly*," Rivka said. "But I guess it would be a problem if you didn't, like, *know* the gender of the recipient."

Shira raised her hand but didn't wait for Rabbi Levin to call on her. "Rivka, how frequently are you confused about the gender of your text recipients?"

"Well, I'm not, but . . ."

Shira kept her hand raised. "It's a problem, Rivka, because you don't know who the recipient will show it to. If I text you a video of me singing, you could show it to your brother."

"That's correct, Shira Birnbaum," Rabbi Levin said. "But maybe we could wait until our classmate is finished before we—"

"Why would I do that if—" Rivka began.

"I don't know why you would do that, Rivka. I can't account for your behavior. That's the point. It would be kol isha just like I was singing for that boy directly," Shira finished.

Kol isha literally means "voice of a woman." The idea is that women's voices are particularly alluring, so women shouldn't sing for men, so the men don't get over-allured. This exact idea is one of the reasons my father is so insistent about not using social media. Because it's one thing if Rivka Bloom's brother happens to hear Shira singing, but think about how many Bloom brother equivalents could be affected if Shira posted a video for the whole world to see.

"Enough," Rabbi Levin said. He adjusted his tie, then walked over to his desk in the corner and grabbed a book. He carried it back across the room to the shtender—his little bookstand—and changed the subject.

He started talking about negiah and yichud. Negiah means touch, and yichud refers to seclusion of a man and woman in the same room. The basic rules are that unmarried men and women aren't supposed to touch, and they aren't supposed to be alone in the same room together.

Rabbi Levin started asking questions about more modern touching, more modern room-like spaces.

He handed us a worksheet that laid out various "modern" scenarios that could present negiah and yichud issues.

"How long can a man and woman—unknown to each other—appropriately share an elevator?" Shira asked, reading from the paper. She then looked at me.

"Three minutes," I said. That was the generally accepted number, though of course it was somewhat arbitrary.

Over my shoulder, I heard Rivka parrot my answer to her partner.

"Aren't we supposed to look at the text?" Dassi asked, indicating the book open on her desk.

"Yeah, but Yoyo and the text are kind of the same thing, and she's so much more efficient," said Shira.

We raced through the next few questions. I answered them without really using my brain, which I used instead to consider Dassi's question about the text. I knew all the answers to the questions—or I knew all of my dad's answers. But suddenly I wondered what the different religious texts said about any of it. If I read them, would I agree with his interpretations?

Chani came by to get help with question five, which asked about men and women sitting alone together in a car. "Cars have windows," Chani noted, "so we were going to say it's okay, but I wasn't sure."

I took a deep breath and tried to muster my usual patience. "Cars do have windows," I said. "That's a great observation, Chani. But that doesn't help if there's nobody around who can see *through* those windows. So I know there are some rabbis who say it's fine if you're in a crowded place, but that it's a problem if you're in a rural setting. My dad would say it's better just to be safe, not to take the chance."

"Okay, thanks."

When Chani returned to her desk, Shira bent her head toward me and Dassi. "Did you hear about her brother?" she asked.

I wasn't sure how to respond. Chani had asked me to keep quiet, but that was about her brother getting kicked out of his yeshiva, not about his presence back in town.

"I heard he's back," Dassi said.

"I heard he didn't tell anybody," Shira said. "Not even his family. He just showed up in the middle of the night. He walked home."

"You can't walk from Israel," Dassi said. "There's this hella big ocean in—"

"From the airport. I don't know."

"I heard he got kicked out of his yeshiva. What do you think he got kicked out for?" Dassi asked, looking directly at me.

But Shira answered. "Probably for being too cute."

"Shira!" Dassi said. It was a scolding tone, but Dassi was smiling, a conspiratorial grin.

Shira had a lot of crushes, and Shua was one of them. She'd sung his virtues at various times. What exactly those virtues were, I couldn't remember.

It's a fine line we all walk. Our religion teaches us that men and women do not touch each other, or hang out together, until marriage. Your body is sacred and it's reserved for your soulmate, for your bashert. That's why we always wear long skirts, long sleeves, and high collars: to reserve our beauty for the men we'll spend our lives with. That's why we do worksheets like this one.

But that didn't mean we didn't *notice* the existence of boys. There was nothing *so* bad about noticing boys. It distracted you from God, but other than that it wasn't a big deal. You just had to wait before you moved *past* the noticing stage.

I didn't have any trouble waiting. I knew it would make the connection I formed with my husband that much stronger.

"Shira," I said, in my most scolding voice. "Were you not paying attention to the work we just did?" I thought the voice was just affect, like I was channeling my dad. But I found I was actually annoyed at Shira. After what happened with Esti, it was a lot less funny to joke about this stuff.

"I was paying attention. And I'm glad we have these safeguards. Don't worry. I'm not gonna get in a car with him. I'm not airheaded like Rivka, or cheap like Esti."

Now I was extra annoyed, because she was insulting Esti with one breath, while crushing on Shua with the next. And this was the first time anybody had mentioned Esti in the whole class. It was only the second school day she wasn't there, and the only time she was mentioned was to use her as some kind of cautionary tale.

I unzipped my pencil bag and used the sound to hide a deep sigh.

It made me want to turn to the seat next to me and talk to Esti about how Shira could be so casually callous, and about how Dassi never said anything about it because she needed Shira's social approval.

I guessed this was just another part of the test: Shira's words, the nauseated feeling it gave me in my stomach, the fact that I couldn't turn away from Shira and Dassi and tell Esti about my disapproval of Shira and its related nausea. I wondered how long the test would last, and if the nausea would always be part of it.

CHAPTER 4

AFTER SCHOOL, I STOOD OUTSIDE, SURROUNDED by the usual gaggle of girls, all in our matching uniforms: dark blue pleated skirt, dark blue sweater, light blue button-up shirt, the collar folded neatly above the neck of the sweater.

I wished I hadn't hustled out of last period so fast, because I was alone on the steps, and girls kept coming up and greeting me, and trying to have little conversations. Phones weren't allowed in school, but the day was over, so I opened mine to look like I was busy. I had a text from my mom. My dad's texts were all in full sentences. I think it took a lot of effort for him not to sign them "Rabbi Gold." But my mom's texts rarely exceeded two or three words, like the phone company was charging her for each of them. This one only said, "updated spreadsheet."

I had a grocery spreadsheet, and I opened it on my phone. I saw that my mom had moved a few items from the "need" column into the "urgent need" column. I looked them over, figured it was a small enough list that I wouldn't need the car, and turned back toward my locker to grab a reusable grocery bag.

Then I started the walk toward town. Downtown Colwyn was only a few blocks from school, down the hill.

Because it's mostly an Orthodox town, the stores pretty much all cater to Jews. The bookstore only sells Jewish books. The bridal shop only has dresses that meet the strictest standards of modesty. But don't get the picture wrong: from a distance, it looks like any other suburban town. There's a T-Mobile store, and one of those UPS locations where you can wait in line for thirty minutes to drop off a package. There are all kinds of different restaurants. It's just that the guy trying out a new phone at T-Mobile is wearing a black hat and tzitzis, and all three sushi restaurants are kosher.

The streets are always pretty busy that time of day, mostly with moms and little kids. There are as many strollers on the sidewalk as cars on the road. I dodged among them, saying "hi" to everybody as I wove my way along the sidewalk.

I ducked into the Colwyn Kosher Grocery.

When I had my bat mitzvah, I didn't suddenly feel like a woman. If you're a boy, after your bar mitzvah there are these signals of your sudden new manhood. You put on tefillin during prayers for the first time. You can help make a minyan, the number required for group prayer. The other men won't hesitate to fill your cup with wine.

For me, I first felt like an adult when I started doing the shopping for the family. I was really proud. I walked around the kosher grocery and the older women—college students, newlyweds, mothers—would nod and smile at me. I was one of them. We'd talk about how to find the best discounts, and what to serve to our little ones who were picky eaters, and how to make matzo balls with *just* the right consistency. It was a communal experience where I felt connected not just to the other women who happened to be in the store, but also to every woman in our community, and every Jewish woman who'd ever existed. Because even though the Jewish women in ancient Israel couldn't use an app to find manufacturer coupons, they still shopped with other Jewish women for their Jewish families and followed the same dietary restrictions.

Inside the door, I grabbed a basket. "I was hoping I'd run into you here," said a voice. I tried to guess the speaker by voice alone. It was pinched in a way that suggested Jacobs or Meisel.

"Hi, Mrs. Jacobs," I said, as a hand touched my arm—Mrs. Meisel was way more respectful of personal space.

"I looked for you after shul on Shabbos but didn't see you. I wanted to tell you how brilliant I thought your father's drasha was."

"Oh, *thank* you," I said with a practiced smile. I met Mrs. Jacobs's eyes to show that I was interested in her interest in my father's sermon.

"My dad, you know, taught at a grade school, so I know what it is to grow up with a learned father. But I think of you, and I imagine it must be something else to grow up in a home that just brims like that with knowledge and love of HaShem. What an honor that must be."

I gave Mrs. Jacobs a solemn nod, which I used to scan the aisles, thinking about which one was least likely to contain things on Mrs. Jacobs's list. This was a move my dad used all the time: the slow solemn nod to buy time. Along with the knowledge and love of God—and all of the honor, of course—I'd picked up some other tips here and there.

"Well, right now I have the honor of buying him mustard," I said.

Mrs. Jacobs chuckled. "It's the little things," she said.

But she didn't also express a need for mustard, so that was a win. "I'll see you on Shabbos." I said. "And this time I'll wait at the kiddush to hear your thoughts on the drasha."

I usually bought condiments in giant bottles at Walmart, but the Colwyn Kosher Grocery sold a lime-and-honey variety that Nachi loved. Plus, the mustard was off in a secluded corner of the store, so I headed in that direction.

I started at the mustard, and worked my way backward through the store, popping items into my basket. I was looking through the various tahini options when I heard the name Ari, and I froze. It wasn't unusual for somebody to say Ari—Aris were a dime a dozen—but it was the tone that got me, a kind of wistful sympathy that I recognized.

I peered over some boxes of Manamim wafers and saw Ari Fischer's older sister Bina talking with a friend. Bina was recently married, and she was wearing a dark sheitel that matched her natural hair color, but it was lush and perfect in that sheitel way that no natural hair could match—certainly not my hair, anyway.

I didn't immediately recognize the friend. She was about the same age as Bina, but looked more like me, in that she was unmarried and hoped the scrunchie she was using would keep her rebellious hair under control.

Bina turned a little in her aisle. I ducked back down.

"What does Ari say about it?" I heard the friend ask.

I was curious about the answer to this question. I doubted he told his sister that he loved Esti, like Esti had told me. But still.

"He wouldn't talk to me about it. But I told him I don't think it's his fault. Boys, I mean, at *that* age?"

They both giggled.

"And," Bina said, "you saw the Saperstein girl, right? Everything about that girl is prust. Even the way she *walks*."

Literally, prust means vulgar. But the way Bina was using it, it meant slutty. I tried to picture Esti's walk. I wished Esti were here with me, even if I was only allowed to watch her walk and assess its sluttiness.

"I'm glad she's out of town," Bina continued. "Now she can't go speeding around in her slutmobile, picking up my brother. Because with a girl like that, it was really just a matter of time. I just . . ."

"You just wish it wasn't *your* brother driving around in the—what did you call it—slutmobile?"

Bina paused to grab something from her side of the shelving. Then their footsteps started up the aisle toward the street-side of the store.

I followed quietly on my side of the aisle.

"Yeah," Bina said. "Really, they should have pushed her out of here faster. You know that kind of girl wasn't going to suddenly reform *herself*. But Rabbi Gold probably wanted to keep her around for his little daughter."

The "little" was shade at me, not an accurate assessment of size. I was bigger than Bina, and the friend.

The friend let out a humorless laugh. "Do you worry about Ari and his dating prospects?" she asked Bina. "Like, do you worry this situation will . . . follow him?"

"I don't think so. People know whose fault it was, right?"

"Maybe, but he did—"

"I mean, *right?*" Bina demanded.

The friend paused before responding. From her tone she sounded like she wasn't so sure. I tried to make out her words, but my heart was pounding and it was loud in my ears. And they were almost at the end of the aisle, and I didn't want them to come around the corner and run into me.

Without making any loud sounds, I walked as fast as I could back down my aisle and disappeared into the mustard corner again. I used the reflections in the freezer doors and the window glass to watch the two figures walk toward the counter.

I examined mustards for a while, long enough so they could check out and leave the store. I ended up swapping the lime-and-honey mustard for an extra spicy variety I hadn't seen before.

CHAPTER 5

THE WHOLE WEEK AT SCHOOL SUCKED. Friday was better, but only because it was half as long. We had shorter days on Fridays, and they were especially short in the winter, because Shabbos started at sundown. There was a lot of stuff to do to prepare the home for the Sabbath. We had to get everybody showered and changed. We had to clean the house both spick and span. We had to cook enough food to feed the whole family—and whoever decided to drop by—for the entire weekend.

When I say "we," I mean me and my mom.

I'd just tidied up the living room and the dining room, and I'd hidden Naomi's book and threatened Nachi with violence so they would do the upstairs. And now I was back in the kitchen, keeping pots from boiling over, making sure the kugel got in and out of the oven. Even in a time of turmoil, even when your best friend has moved across the country and nobody else seems to care, and the one person you rely on is the only person you're not allowed to talk to—*especially* under those circumstances—there's always peace in preparing the home for its rest.

Well, the preparation was almost never peaceful. It was an organized chaos, a mad dash, a frantic race against the sun. But we always won. And every week, when sunset arrived, there we were at the table, settings in place, candles lit, ready to go.

I always loved Shabbos supper with my family. I loved the soft candlelight, the way its shadows danced on my siblings' faces. I loved the rhythm it gave to the week, how it reset my life. I often wondered what gentiles did without it. How did they find structure in their lives? How did they decompress? How did they block out the deafening noise of the world to connect with God?

When we were all standing in a circle around the Shabbos supper table, and my father reached out, put his hand on my head, and blessed me, I didn't want to be anywhere else.

We almost always had guests for Friday night meals. My father was an important rabbi. His words carried a lot of weight in our community. The words he said over supper were usually "Yum" and "Mmmm," a lot of onomatopoeia, and the occasional "Can you pass that? No, that. *No*, the one I'm *pointing* at." I wasn't sure if it qualified as rabbinical wisdom, but it was something you could drop into conversation the next day at the synagogue or at a Saturday meal: that you had Shabbos supper with Rabbi Gold.

Our guests were a rotating cast. Sometimes it was family, but this week it was two young couples. There was Netanel Kornblatt and his wife, Yaffa, and then there was Bina and her husband. It was the same Bina I'd just seen—mostly heard—at the grocery.

My parents liked to invite young couples to our Shabbos suppers. The idea was to show them how to create a peaceful, loving, kosher home, to present them a model they could emulate in their own lives.

I didn't mind the small crowd, but I was seated only two seats down from Bina, with only Yaffa Kornblatt between us, and Yaffa didn't do as good a job blocking my view of Bina as the biscuit-covered shelves at the grocery.

Both of the married women were much closer to my age than to my parents'. They were in their early twenties, and they had similar vibes to them. They were both slim and had dark pouty lips. Bina accentuated hers with dark lipstick.

When he wasn't commenting on the food, my dad liked to talk about Torah at the Shabbos supper table.

The Torah is the Jewish bible, but the word "Torah" can also refer not only to other related holy documents, but also to all of the documents different rabbis wrote interpreting the Torah and other related holy documents. Being a Jewish man often consists of scratching your beard while you argue about Torah with other Jewish men while they scratch *their* beards.

My father used to prompt Moshe to start the conversation. Moshe knew Torah better than he knew himself. He dazzled our guests with his incisive and precocious analysis. But Moshe was in Israel, so now my father started the conversations with Nachi. Nachi was not as good at this as Moshe had been, because he was terrified of our father, and Nachi withered under his gaze. Like, Abba turned his gaze on him, and Nachi went straight from grape to raisin.

Nachi was in even worse shape when there were young married men around, and he knew he was supposed to impress them.

"So," my father began, putting his spoon down next to his soup bowl. "Menachem. What's still on your mind from your lessons this week?"

Nachi said nothing. He slid his spoon into his soup, remixing the oil that had settled on top.

I did feel bad for him. Moshe was named for our famous rabbi grandfather, while Nachi was named for a random uncle who died in a shoe factory accident. The O.G. Moshe received the Torah directly from God, while the biblical Menachem was best known for indiscriminately slaughtering pregnant women. Nachi was more loving and caring than Moshe, and eminently more huggable. But being a sweetheart wasn't going to impress Yaffa's and Bina's husbands.

"Nachi," I said. "Words, kid." When he still said nothing, I lowered the bar. "Word? Singular?"

"Calamity."

"Good word," I noted. "Polysyllabic."

"What *about* calamity?" my father asked. He was patient. He patiently chewed a piece of challah.

"Whose fault is it?" Nachi said.

The calamity of this failed conversation was Nachi's fault. I was growing impatient with Nachi's lack of speech.

This kind of Torah analysis didn't interest me. But the guests were looking at Nachi expectantly. Plus, I'd helped Nachi with his homework, so I knew what they'd been discussing. This, too, would fall to me.

"Well," I said, "the question it asks is about catastrophes, disasters, and—"

"Calamities," Nachi added helpfully.

"Are they all acts of HaShem? Or are some of them the fault of an individual?"

"Mmmmm," my father said, displaying the type of sharp

analysis he was renowned for. I actually couldn't tell if he was agreeing with me, or if he was just enjoying the roasted vegetables.

I didn't find out, because my father shifted the conversation to the biblical story that the discussion was based on. I reached for the salmon platter. This had become my signature dish: salmon with a thick teriyaki sauce. It was great for Shabbos because it was equally tasty hot or cold.

I passed the platter on to Yaffa, who was saying something in a low voice to my mother. I hadn't been paying attention to the women's conversation at all, but suddenly I heard "Saperstein."

"It must be hard on your daughter," Bina was saying.

My mom didn't look my way. She probably thought I was still working to save Nachi from drowning in a combination of Torah and embarrassment.

I noted that this time, at my family's Shabbos supper table, Bina allowed me to be a full-sized daughter, not the "little" one I was in the market.

My mom nodded at Bina.

"It's sad because I've been that girl," said Yaffa. "Not *that* girl, but you know what I mean. We've all done things that go against our teachings. And, *I* feel, anyway, that if you have the right support, you end up with stronger faith than you had before."

"That's so true," said Bina. "Because it isn't just the tradition that provides meaning. It's that community support we have. That's what I love about this community and this congregation, that we're all there for each other in difficult times. I've thought about this a lot, and I worry that we didn't support her enough, that we all bear some responsibility."

I almost spit out a mouthful of water. I couldn't believe what I was hearing. I tried to remember back a few years. Had Bina been in the school productions? She must not have been, because if she was this good an actor, I'd remember her performances.

This performance was working on my mom. "That's wise, Bina," she said. "But don't blame yourself. You'll see that when you're a mother. You do your best, but you'll never be perfect."

I wondered if my mom would make the connection I was making: we hadn't supported Esti enough, but maybe we *could* support Yoyo enough in Esti's absence.

My mom leaned around the two younger women and looked at me. She smiled, and my hopes rose. "The salmon is great, Yocheved," she said.

It was support of sorts, but not at all the kind I needed. And suddenly our peaceful Shabbos didn't feel so peaceful. But I maintained peace on the outside. I didn't do anything unbecoming.

"Yes, it's amazing," said Bina. "How do you get it so tender?"

Bina didn't deserve the secrets of my poaching method. I was quiet for a moment, like I was considering how to explain it. Then I said, "I'll text you the recipe."

You couldn't use your phone on Shabbos, so by the time I *could* text her the recipe, Bina would have forgotten about it. That was my hope, at least. But my salmon was pretty memorable, so maybe not.

"Send it to me too?" Yaffa said.

"Of course," I replied, and I put some of the aforementioned salmon in my mouth so I had an excuse not to meet her smile, because not even the sweet and tangy taste of my salmon—or its tenderness—could make me smile in that moment.

"How's Ari?" my mom asked Bina.

"I think he'll be okay. If somebody goes fishing, I suppose eventually they're going to catch something. And Ari got caught. It was a learning process for him, and he'll grow from it. It's like Yaffa said. I think it will bring him closer to us."

"Great," my mom said.

Yeah, that was pretty great for Ari. Good for him. Bina would just pull the hook out of his mouth and toss him back in the pond, while Esti was stuck in Las Vegas, which, being notoriously arid, probably doesn't have a lot of ponds.

I wished I could have recounted the supper conversation to Esti, so she could listen and help me process it. She would express earnest sympathy, but then flip a switch and mock each of the participants—even my father—in a way that made them seem small and therefore less threatening. And Bina's inconsistency and my mom's lack of support would feel manageable, because Esti would make Bina feel less sinister, and Esti's support would stand in for my mom's.

But I couldn't talk it over with Esti, so I spent all of the Saturday morning synagogue service sitting with the injustice of the night before, replaying the conversation over and over in my head, and feeling worse about it with each replay.

Esti wasn't here, and nobody but me even wanted to acknowledge her absence. At the beginning of shul, Shira and Dassi had stepped in right next to me, cutting out the space Esti always took.

Everybody expected me to just carry on as before, to do all of the same things with the same sunny disposition. Well, I don't think anybody would describe me as "sunny." But I was polite and friendly. A friend's mom had once described me as "stately." That felt a little too political, but I understood what she meant.

But I didn't feel that way now. I felt ornery, like something was just . . . off.

I skipped the post-service kiddush—even though I'd told Mrs. Jacobs I'd be there—and started walking home.

I walk a lot. Most of us over the age of one walk frequently. And generally speaking, walking is so easy that you can think about other things while you do it. For example, I can do calculus and walk at the same time, so long as the problem doesn't require paper. But if you actually *think* about the act of walking, it's fairly complex. There's the balance, the transfer of weight between feet, the synchronization of the legs with the swinging arms. Sometimes you have to adjust to uneven ground, step over curbs, carry smaller people in your arms.

It occurred to me, about halfway home, that that's how my life had been. It was complex, but it never felt that way. The many things that were expected of me, I just *did* them. I could do them almost subconsciously, in perfect synchrony.

But now it was like there was a sudden hitch in my walk. The whole thing was thrown off, and I was stumbling over curbs, tripping on cracks in the sidewalk, spilling the things in my arms out into the street.

CHAPTER 6

THE NEXT DAY, I WAS ON time for JHR. The parking lot was only a quarter full when I pulled in. I got out of the car, spreadsheet in hand, and stared at myself again in the side mirror. Did I look more put together than last week? I was trying, but failing, to feel that way.

The Holtzman van pulled up at the curb, and Chani got out. "Can you drive me again?" she called.

I nodded, and she nodded to the driver—probably Shua—and she followed me toward the warehouse. "But let me know if you're going to be late again, okay?" Chani asked.

"You don't want to get murdered in this parking lot?" I asked.

Chani looked around, as if appraising the lot. "Yeah, I mean, not really," she said.

This time I had everybody's roles and routes organized, and we moved through the warehouse process efficiently. I assigned Chani as my partner, so there was no way I could be late to pick her up.

Chani had disappeared out the door with our first two boxes when I noticed a strange new girl talking to Mrs. Gomes.

The girl's outfit left a gap between her pants and shirt. You didn't see a lot of exposed skin in the JHR warehouse, so her exposed stomach was . . . different.

The girl started heading my way.

There were a lot of questions I wanted to ask her. For example, she was wearing dark leggings, but I could see both the shape and pattern of her underwear through the sheer fabric, and I was curious to know if she was aware of this bit of textile transparency. She had straight dark hair and some features that seemed Asian to me, so I was curious to know her background. But questions about her underwear or her ethnicity didn't seem like the best icebreakers.

"She said I should talk to you?" the girl said. She indicated Mrs. Gomes with a nod of her head.

Mrs. Gomes was an adult, but she was deferring to me. She gave me a warm, knowing smile. "Do your thing. I can take Chani if you need."

I was always the one to welcome new people, to make them feel at home. I *really* wasn't in the mood to spend the afternoon with a weird girl I'd never seen before, and I didn't think she'd feel at home with me. But I handed the girl a box. "It's the white minivan. Should be unlocked. The back seat is folded down."

"Okay," the girl said. "Thanks."

Chani went off with Mrs. Gomes. The new girl and I loaded the car in silence, passing each other as we walked in and out of the warehouse with boxes.

When the car was full, I got behind the wheel and handed the girl my notes with our addresses on it. "Do you have Google Maps on your phone?" I asked her.

She looked at me like I'd asked her if she had skin. "Uh. *Yeah*," she said.

"Well, some phone filters—" But I didn't finish the sentence. She and I were clearly very different. She had many more piercings than I did. Her shirt's neckline was *way* below her actual neck. And I'd never once worn pants outside the house, let alone translucent form-fitting ones.

Statistically speaking, most people aren't Jewish. I knew that non-Jews existed in large numbers, and I saw them any time I left town. But I never interacted with them. In my eight months of licensed driving, I'd never driven a gentile before, and I was pretty sure I'd never been in a car alone with one.

I was really curious about how this girl had got to JHR, how she'd found out about it. Some of the people we delivered food to weren't Orthodox, but all of the volunteers were. "The best way to do it, I've found, is just to put the first bunch of stops in," I said. "Let it direct you from point to point."

"Okay," she said. She looked uncomfortable. Instead of looking at the sheet in her hand, or her phone, she was staring down at her puffy boots.

"I'm Yocheved."

I could see her trying to wrap her mouth around the name, maybe figuring out if there was a way she could acknowledge it without having to say it out loud.

"Everybody calls me Yoyo."

She looked up about halfway. "Mickey," she said. "Short for Mickaela. We both have nicknames."

"Yep," I said. She and I had *so* much in common. Both girls. Both had nicknames. What were the chances? We were going to be fast friends.

I'm kidding.

I think we were both actively wishing that a meteor would hit the car. "So, where to?" I asked, putting the minivan in gear, hoping the meteor could hit a moving target.

"Make a left out of the parking lot."

We were heading to the edge of Colwyn, where it met the city line. Colwyn was a relatively affluent suburb. It was mostly single family homes. Some of the bigger ones were split into duplexes and triplexes, but still, the people here were mostly doing fine.

But right across the city line, there were older houses with residents who weren't doing so well. The houses themselves sagged and leaned against each other for support. They were split into many tiny apartments. Interspersed among the old houses were a few decaying high-rises. They were gray and dirty on the outside. Inside, they were always too warm, even in winter, and the air had a thick, too-sweet scent, like something fermenting.

"So, this route is going to be mostly old Russian women," I told Mickey. "They're going to want to talk to you. If you're not careful, you're going to know a lot more about their grandchildren than you want to. They'll comment on your clothes, you *especially*. So whatever you do, *remain in the hallway*. Don't get dragged inside, because they don't respect due process, and you'll be held indefinitely, with neither official charges nor counsel. And you'll have to accept the Russian candies they give you, but do *not* attempt to eat them. They are so gross."

"I like all candy," Mickey said.

"Not these. Trust me. You can't even really *eat* them. You just embed them in your teeth, where they're stuck for literal days."

Mickey's phone directed us across the city line, past the nonkosher Chinese takeout place and the pawn shop, and into the parking lot of one of the high-rises. She consulted the list. "We've got Narinsky, Utin, and Dvornik. Dvornik gets two boxes."

"Need me to come up?" I asked. When it was just Esti and me, one of us idled the car while the other did the deliveries, but I felt like it was polite to offer.

"Seems self-explanatory," Mickey said. She popped out and grabbed four boxes from the passenger's side.

"Be careful of Mrs. Dvornik," I warned her. "She has a lot of grandchildren, all boys, so she has a ton to say about them. You've got to be assertive with her. You have to say 'No' very quickly and firmly. She takes *any* delay as consent. Do you want to practice?"

"Nah. I'll be good."

"Are you sure? It's tough if you don't have experience with pushy old Jews."

Mickey gave me a look, a kind of side-eyed glance I couldn't read.

"It's okay," I explained. "I can generalize about them. I'm Jewish."

Now the look was growing in its severity and side-eyedness and I wondered what I could have said wrong.

"I'm . . . Jewish too," Mickey said.

Now it was my turn to look at *her*. Maybe I'd seen her wrong the first time. But she still looked the same, like a gentile girl you'd see in a makeup ad. I knew there were Jews who didn't look like me—there were Ethiopian Jews, for instance. But I'd never met one, and this girl just didn't look like any Jew I'd ever seen.

"My mom's a rabbi," she said.

It wasn't a funny joke exactly, but I let out a polite laugh, and felt the tension release. She was just messing with me. Saying your mom was a rabbi was like saying that your cat was a fish. Or your toenail was also your liver. Or twelve was a prime number. It was hard to figure out a new person's sense of humor, especially somebody from a different background. All of the people I knew were Jewish, so maybe this was just how gentiles were. Maybe all these non-Jews just sat around shouting out different impossibilities and laughing hysterically. "This chicken finger is the queen of England!" one of them would declare, as they all guffawed.

I was clearly not reacting how she'd expected, because Mickey's voice grew quieter. "Really."

"Wait. So, *are* you Jewish?" I asked.

"Yeah," she said. "And my mom's the new head rabbi at Beth Jacob."

I'd driven past Beth Jacob synagogue. It was on the north edge of Colwyn, on the border with Tregaron. It was Reform, way less religious than my dad's.

All of the tension had returned, but it was much stronger, much thicker. I shifted my position in my seat as though my discomfort was from the way I was sitting.

I wanted to ask *how* exactly she was Jewish. Was she half-Asian, half-Jewish? Was she adopted? Did her mother convert? But each of those questions felt like a conversational land mine I didn't want to step anywhere near. "I'm sorry I . . . offended you," I said.

"I was just surprised. I figured—I don't know. It was just sexist."

I didn't see how it was sexist. It just . . . *was*. That was the Orthodox interpretation of the law: the rabbi is a man.

"I'm sorry," I offered again. "I know that less observant Jews have female rabbis. But I guess because I was taught that's not something—I . . . I don't know."

"I just figured . . ."

"What did you figure?" I asked.

"I thought maybe because you're Orthodox, and you're forced to—"

Now I was kind of glad she was pissing me off, because I could turn my discomfort into anger. "Maybe you shouldn't *figure* about people you don't know," I said. "What are you imagining? That somebody holds me down and puts a skirt on me every day?"

"Oh, come on. Like you didn't judge *me*. I saw the way you were looking at me when I walked into that warehouse." Mickey paused, took a breath. "Let me ask you a question. Are you on TikTok?"

"No. I don't use social media."

"Whose decision was that?"

It was my decision. Or, well, I thought it was. My phone had a filter on it, so it had a few basic apps and a very limited browser. No inappropriate content. No social media. And that decision had been made when I was younger. I imagined I could get around the filter if I tried. But if I didn't *want* to try, didn't that make it my decision?

"Did you hear my question?" Mickey asked.

"I did."

"So?"

"So I think you should go inside and give these olds their food."

Mickey got out of the car and disappeared inside. I left the car running in the loading zone outside the lobby.

While I waited, I looked on Amazon to see how much a puffer jacket cost, the kind this Mickey girl had, with the faux-fur hood. I realized that I'd seen a hundred jackets and a bunch of time had passed. Maybe ten minutes. Way longer than it should have taken to deliver four boxes in the same building. I was about to just leave the car and go in after her when Mickey burst out of the front door.

The girl was presenting a number of troubling symptoms. Her eyes were wide. She had a purple lipstick stain on her left cheek. Her right hand couldn't close because it was too full of individually wrapped candies. And most disturbing was that her left hand held an empty wrapper. Her chin was doing some kind of gyration, like she was trying but failing to chew.

When she opened the door, I was laughing.

And clearly it was contagious because her grimace slowly turned to laughter, and before we knew it we were both trying to hold back tears. It was the first time I'd laughed since Esti left.

When we'd calmed down a little, Mickey managed to speak. "You'll be interested to know that Daniel was on the honor roll *again* this past semester. And it's a good thing you're sitting down, because—wait until you hear *this*—Sacha got a job in *computers*, which is an exciting new field." Mickey had a finger in her mouth, scraping it around. With her other hand she reached out to me. "Candy?"

I accepted the candy, got out of the car, and deposited it directly into the trash can by the curb. Then I put the car back in gear, and Mickey took the cue to get us moving to the next stop. "You did warn me," she said.

"I'm sorry if I offended you," I said. "This isn't a *good* excuse, but it's been kind of a weird day for me."

"I get it," Mickey said. "You're probably used to doing this with your friends. My mom has her own congregation now, which *she's* really excited about. But it means she expects me to do more Jewish stuff, set an example. And since I'm not into the religion part, I thought this would be good."

I wasn't sure how to respond to that, the idea of not being "into" the religion. It made God's commandments seem trivial, like a hobby you could pick up or put down any time you wanted, like yoga or knitting. But she was fulfilling a religious commandment through chesed, and I knew *exactly* what that "set an example" thing was like, so I just asked her, "What do I do at this intersection?"

"Straight," she said. "Then right in half a mile."

We completed the rest of our deliveries in relative silence, and Mickey got much more efficient, popping in and out of apartment buildings, on and off porches. When the sun was just starting to go down, we were on our way back to the warehouse.

"Do you know about what time we'll be back?" Mickey asked. "I just need to text my mom to pick me up."

"I can drive you home," I said. "I just have to go back to the warehouse first to get Chani."

We grabbed Chani, who looked back and forth between me and Mickey as I drove.

Mickey lived on the edge of town, near the more secular, less

Jewish suburbs. It was a twin house with blue shutters and an inviting little sunroom. When I stopped in front of the driveway, she hesitated.

It felt like Mickey and I should say goodbye by tying some kind of bow on our day: That was weird, and you're different, but I don't hate you or anything—I merely hope we never meet again.

But that's not the kind of thing you say out loud.

Chani saved us by clearing her throat. "Um. Excuse me," she said to Mickey, "do you know that you have lipstick on your cheek?"

Mickey pulled down the passenger mirror and looked at her cheek, which still bore Mrs. Dvornik's distinctive mark.

"I just thought," Chani went on, "I don't know. If I came home like that, my parents would have questions."

Mickey laughed. "Mine would too. Different questions, maybe. But definite questions. Thanks, Yoyo, for letting me know about that, and making sure I didn't have it on my face all day."

I could tell she was kidding. Our eyes met, and we both smiled. "No problem. I got you," I said.

"And thanks for the ride."

Mickey shut the door behind her and walked up the driveway, hands stuffed in the pockets of her puffer jacket.

Chani leaned forward from the back seat. "I wasn't sure if I should even say anything. I thought it might have been a fashion thing, like the leggings or the belly-button ring."

CHAPTER 7

I HAD A CHEMISTRY CHAPTER TO review and annotate, so I drove home, with the Mickey girl's words ringing in my ears. "Whose choice was that?" she'd asked. She was talking about social media, but it felt like it could apply to everything. Did I choose to keep a distance from most of the girls at school, the way my father did in his congregation? Did I choose to take care of my younger siblings, run the JHR routes, do the fundraising for the production, and cook Shabbos supper? Were those all things I actively wanted to do? If I didn't fight them, did that make them my choices?

I took out my pens and highlighters and flipped to the correct chapter. Organizing my school stuff usually calmed me down. There was a system to it. Like the rituals that provided the rhythm of Jewish life, my system of studying helped me keep things in place. It helped me make sense of the material, but also of my world.

But I couldn't make sense of the chemistry right now, because I couldn't concentrate on it. And my world felt like it made a lot less sense than it used to.

I needed to talk to somebody. There was a limit to what you could hold on to alone. There was too much building up inside of me, like a swelling river pressing up against a dam. And that's basic structural engineering: if you don't cut a spillway, and relieve the pressure, the dam will burst.

I tried to force myself to concentrate by making notes in the margins, but the ink I was using started running as soon as it hit the page. Even the printed text was starting to bleed. And even if the ink stayed in place, I wasn't sure I could see it through the tears.

And even if I could see the page, there was Naomi, who was saying, "Hey, can you keep the wailing down a little? I'm just getting to the good part here."

I was crying in a way that I'd never cried before. I felt like, with each successive sob, I was going to be ripped apart along the seams, like an old stuffed animal caught between Yoni and Yitzy.

Because Naomi was "getting to the good part," I stuffed my head into my pillow and dug myself down into the corner where the bed met the wall. The pillow was more absorbent than the textbook, and it helped to muffle the sounds. Naomi did lift her head out of her book, just long enough to ask whether she could get me anything. But when I ignored her, she went back to reading.

I stayed like that, head in my pillow, weeping uncontrollably, then with varying levels of control, for what felt like a long time. When I was finally ready to pull my face out of the now-soaked pillow, Naomi was sound asleep, our overhead light was off, and the hallway was dark.

I hadn't eaten supper. I hadn't brushed my teeth.

I padded out into the hall. The house was dark and silent. The only light was a dim one, leaking out from under Nachi's door.

I went into the bathroom at the end of the hall, locked the door, and stared at myself in the mirror. My cheeks were swollen. My eyes were so red it looked like they were bleeding. As I breathed out heavily, the mirror started to fog. I just stood like that, staring into my own bleary eyes.

They said that women were naturally closer to God. That's why we weren't required to pray as often as men, or as thoroughly, or as intensely: because women were Godly in and of themselves. We were more spiritual. We didn't need ritual to bring us closer to God, because we were already there, right at his side.

So maybe I could talk to God. I knew how to *pray* to God, but I didn't think I knew how to *talk* to him. Given who I was, where I came from, I should have felt more naturally spiritual. It should have been passed down to me like my red-brown hair or the birthmark on my upper-right cheek, the same one both Moshe and Yitzy had.

I closed my swollen eyes and tried to access a more spiritual place. I tried to turn the bathroom into a forest. The whirring fan was the buzz of insects. The drip of the faucet was dew dropping from leaves. The soft knock on the door was the hoofbeats of a deer, making its way through its woodland home.

"HaShem," I said.

"Nachi," said Nachi through the door. The knocking was him. "You almost done?"

This from the kid who spent a full half hour in here every morning, playing music so loudly you couldn't get his attention.

I took a step to the door, so I could talk to him without raising my voice. "Nachi, because I love you so much, I'm going to say this very nicely: tonight, I will come to you like the angel of death and kill you in your sleep. I'll wake you up just long enough for you to know that A) death has come for you and B) it was me."

There was silence. "I'll use the downstairs bathroom," he said.

I gave up talking to God—the moment had passed—and I went and sat on the toilet.

I took out my phone. I stared at my own reflection in the black screen. My mind was doing this twisting turning thing it did when I was right on the edge of understanding something, like I was staring at a math problem and I could feel the solution coming, bubbling up, and I just needed to wait for it to break the surface.

Ninety percent of American teens were on social media, or so it said in an article I found. But it also said that social media was giving kids mental health problems. It was driving them to suicide. They were witnessing violence, drug use, sex. They were comparing themselves to others, seeing girls with implausibly flat stomachs in their underwear, and then asking themselves why they didn't look like that in *their* underwear.

Usually, I was thankful for Judaism. I loved that I didn't compare my body to others, that God loved me no matter my clothing size. I was thankful that I'd never once stood in front of the bedroom mirror in my underwear and examined my stomach. It might have been an interesting way to get Naomi to look up from her book, but I think that was the only purpose it would have served.

When everybody in the community started getting smartphones, my father endorsed internet filters, mandatory for kids, strongly recommended for adults. He was ahead of his time, really. Now there were name brands that would sell you phones with preinstalled "kosher" filters. One of them was called kPhone, so it was like iPhone, but k, for "kosher."

Get it?

So I could read *about* TikTok, about how these crazy gentile kids were burning down their own schools because of something that was "trending," but I couldn't actually watch the "trending" videos to see what exactly was so compelling about arson.

I tried to find the Mickey girl online, and I think I did, but when I clicked on the linked TikTok videos, it said that the page was blocked and downloading the app was prohibited as well.

And until that very moment, that fact had never bothered me. I had faith in God, of course, but also in the people who helped me stay close to him, by helping me block out the parts of our world that affronted God, that attempted to pull us away from his Torah.

But I needed an outlet of some kind. Any kind. Without Esti, without the support of my community, I didn't know where it would come from.

I pictured myself peeking over the internet firewall like I'd peeked over the grocery aisle, wondering if there was something for me on the other side.

Before I really knew what I was doing, I opened up my contacts, and typed in S-H-U-A.

Shua Holtzman.

Shua. It's Yoyo, I sent.

I took some deep, calming breaths. As I stared at my phone screen, willing it to light up, I reminded myself that I shouldn't be doing this, and it would be better if he didn't respond at all. And he could have been asleep. Or studying. Or engaged in one of the big three boy activities: sports, video games, or—

Gold?

I sputtered out a little laugh that echoed around the tile of the bathroom. `Can you get rid of my phone filter?` I asked him.

`$100`, Shua said.

I thought through my mental shopping lists, crossing off a few groceries, replacing them with cheaper equivalents.

`Fine,` I said.

`Walk. Don't drive. Take the basement stairs around the side.`

Did he know what time it was? Maybe he was like Moshe, and the rotation of the earth—and therefore time—was too secular a concept to concern himself with. Or maybe he just didn't have to wake up in a few hours and get five people ready for school.

I considered for a minute as I walked back to my bedroom. I laid back down in my bed to see what it felt like, but I was too tense to fall asleep anyway.

I quietly got dressed, padded downstairs, and slipped out the back door through the kitchen.

It was about a twenty minute walk to the Holtzmans', so that was twenty minutes in which to grow a combination of anxious and regretful. Twenty minutes in which to repeat to myself: If Abba asked, how would you justify this? Is this about the phone? Is this about Esti? You're failing your test. This isn't you, Yoyo.

Okay, maybe it *wasn't* Yoyo. But in an experiment, when you change the conditions, the reaction changes. And my life had a bunch of new conditions.

One of them was that it was cold. It was freezing out. As I walked, I ordered a puffer jacket.

CHAPTER 8

HAS THERE EVER BEEN A JEWISH ninja? I'm pretty sure the ninja is a Japanese phenomenon, so I'm guessing no. But I felt like a Jewish ninja that night, sneaking around the side of the Holtzman house.

The thing about it being dark was that, in the dark, it was harder to see. I didn't see a door or, really, anything, and I was about to just turn around and sneak away when my phone buzzed. Open the hatch, said Shua's text.

Sure enough, by my left foot was a metal hatch that opened up from the ground.

This was, low-key, how people got murdered. I was getting some serious murdery vibes. But here I was, doing it anyway. And on the positive side, if Shua murdered me, I'd never have to feel this anxious and conflicted again.

I reached down and opened the hatch. Its rusty hinges creaked.

Leave the hatch open, Shua sent.

?

Yichud. Unless you brought somebody with you.

Even with the hatch open, the concrete stairs were pitch-black. I couldn't even see my own feet. Are you going to kill me with an axe or something?

I don't think we have an axe. Leave the door open too.

I kept a hand out in front of me as I descended, and eventually it met a door. I fumbled around, found a doorknob.

I opened the door and paused to take in the scene. I was in the center of a long narrow basement room. Exactly half the room was carpeted. On the carpet were a bed, a coffee table, a beanbag chair, and Shua Holtzman, who was perched on the edge of the bed.

The other half of the room was "unfinished." The floor was uncarpeted, concrete and dusty. There was a door to what looked like a small bathroom. There was a washer and dryer—the washer was on, going through its spin cycle. There was a giant toolbox and, in the corner, a bunch of random yard and garden tools: a rake, a trowel, two snow shovels, a regular shovel, and an axe.

"So what's that?" I asked, indicating the corner with my thumb.

Shua smiled sheepishly. "I am imperfect, tocho k'baro, inside and out. Don't worry, I'll keep my hands where you can see them."

I noticed that he had soft-looking hands, scholar's hands. I felt like the girl in Little Red Riding Hood noticing things about her grandmother: My, Shua, what soft hands you have. I didn't think I'd heard the end of that story. I assumed it had a happy ending and Little Red got out of there unscathed with an unfiltered smartphone.

Shua kept his hands up in front of him.

I'd had no intention of ever entering a boy's bedroom until it was also my bedroom. I'd pictured that scene, after my wedding, exploring a room and a body that were both completely unfamiliar, yet somehow still familiar to me—that's how it was supposed to feel, that first night with your husband, as your two half souls became one whole.

But this room, with its dust and bare concrete, ripped the dreamy gloss off of both that fantasy and this reality. Everything I'd been taught said this was wrong. I felt a sudden wave of pure panic, the one you got when you were doing something you couldn't take back.

As if to punctuate that realization, the door behind me clicked shut.

"Keep that open," Shua said.

I did as he asked, but still I said: "In a room where other people aren't just going to pass through, especially a subterranean room like a cellar, yichud is prohibited." What I meant was that I didn't think it mattered whether the door was open or closed—we were still alone together in the same room. Which, as I'd been taught in class and in my home, was wrong. "I doubt your neighbors just pass—"

"That's why we're keeping both doors *open*, not just unlocked. Here, I think I have it down here." With his hands still held up in front of him, he got up and shuffled over toward the beanbag chair. Behind it was a bookshelf, filled with religious books, all dark and heavy, with gold- and silver-trimmed Hebrew letters. He grabbed one, brought it over to the coffee table, and opened it right to left, leafing through pages. "So this is by Rabbi Pinchas Eliyahu Rabinowitz. It's called *Toras Hayichud*."

There are different kinds of Jewish holy books. Some of them are God's law itself, and then some of them are rabbis *interpreting* God's law. This one was the second kind.

Looking back and forth between me and the book, there was an extra light in Shua's eye, brighter than the naked bulbs hanging down from the cracking ceiling. "I'm trying to find the part where he . . . Here," he said, his finger on the page. With his other hand, he waved me over.

I walked from the concrete to the carpet. He slid over and I knelt by the table.

I watched his index finger trace the text. "See?" he said. "The rabbi here says it's fine so long as you're in an external room, where the door opens to the outside."

He was using a holy book to justify doing something that was . . . unholy. "I don't know," I said.

"If you're worried," Shua said, "nobody's making you . . ."

"Yeah, I know," I said. I got up and pulled my wallet out of my bag. "Here's your money."

"I don't want your money. I wanted to see how much you cared. I don't think it's something you should take lightly. If it was just a phase or something, I wasn't going to do it."

I stood with my wallet in one hand, my other hand on my hip, trying to figure out this boy. Here he was directly violating my own father's rabbinical ruling by removing the internet filter on my phone. But then he was also worried about the religious laws regarding men and women, to the point where he had reference texts handy next to his bed to make sure he was doing it properly. It was like if somebody broke into your house and stole your jewelry, but they folded your clothes and washed the dishes before they left.

It was confusing.

I was not used to being confused. It was an uncomfortable feeling. I didn't know how Nachi handled it with so much aplomb.

"Phone," Shua said. "Unlock it."

I unlocked my phone and handed it to him. He placed it on the table, grabbed a laptop from his bed, and went to work. He worked methodically, his hands and eyes alternating between the two devices.

The washer completed its cycle and made a loud buzzer sound. Shua didn't notice. Boys didn't notice these things. I'll bet if I'd blindfolded him, he couldn't have told me any of the objects the room contained, or what color the carpet was.

The buzzer went off again. I walked over to the machine and opened its hatch so it would stop making noise.

When I got back to the carpeted side of the room, Shua was still working, so I took a seat in the beanbag chair. It was taking longer than I'd thought, but I didn't mind. There was a quiet comfort in watching him work, the way he furrowed his brow in concentration, the way he slowly rocked forward and back in that practiced rhythm all Orthodox boys have. It was like *most* of him was in this room, but there was a small part of him that was off praying or studying somewhere in his own head. Usually, I found that quality annoying and pretentious. But with Shua it was different. It was sincere, and I didn't think he even knew he was doing it.

When Shua finished and handed me my phone back, I was disappointed. I kind of wished I had another phone for him to unfilter.

"It won't send an alert out or anything," he said, "but if there's somebody really tech savvy on your plan, they could figure it out."

I got up from the beanbag. "You don't have to worry about that."

"Oh, and if you tell anybody about this, I'll kill you with the axe I totally knew we had, and I'll bury you with that shovel I was also aware of."

"I'm the only person in this whole town who can keep their mouth shut," I said bitterly.

It was time to leave. Our transaction was complete. Services had been rendered. But I hesitated. I was confused about something. Well, I was confused about a lot of things. "Do you regret it?" I asked.

"This?" he said.

"No. Well, kind of. Getting sent home."

There was a sudden change in him. A moment ago, he'd had a steady confidence, a self-assuredness. But now his shoulders slumped just the tiniest bit, and his whole body looked soft, like his hands. "I guess you heard all about that," he said. "I guess if you're Rabbi Gold's daughter . . ."

"I know almost nothing about it. And I won't pry if you don't want me to."

"I'll explain it if you don't judge."

I nodded. Who was I to judge right now?

"With the internet, it's just like . . . In *Yeshayahu*, there's this part about turning swords into plows, spears into pruning hooks, taking dangerous weapons and turning them into productive tools."

I knew the Torah passage he was talking about. Everybody did.

"Your plan is to turn porn into, like, a tractor?" I asked.

"No. I just think—I don't know. This new stuff. All of these things . . . we're told not to use them, because they're dangerous, like weapons, and they'll destroy our faith. And maybe they *are* weapons. I've seen some stuff on there I wish I hadn't." He gestured at his phone, the dangerous weapon resting on his pillow. "But if we toss all of these things aside, we'll never *know* if we can turn them into plows, or other useful tools."

He was looking at his hands as he said this. I could tell it pained him. He believed it, but he also knew it went against what was taught. And I knew that conflict. Or, I actually didn't. I was just beginning to.

"*Is* the plow a useful tool?" I asked with a little smile.

"I think the more important question is: What the heck is a pruning hook?"

"It's like a scythe," I told him, "but the blade is more curved. And I think the handle is longer."

"That would be a really helpful explanation if I knew what a scythe was."

I gestured toward the pile of yard tools in the corner. "Do you need me to identify each of these for you?" I walked toward them, pointing. "These two, for example—though they have superficial differences—are both rakes."

Shua produced a sheepish grin, which I tried not to enjoy.

"So have you found tools on there?" I said, now pointing at his phone.

"I'm not sure. But I have found people who have the same questions I do. And it's nice when there are other people who share your ideas, because otherwise you start to feel a little crazy, you know?"

I wasn't sure. I wasn't sure I was looking for somebody who

shared my ideas. I didn't know what my ideas were exactly. I was just looking for . . . somebody, period, somebody who would listen.

For a moment I wondered if that person could be Shua, but a cool breeze through the open door reminded me that it could not. You couldn't lean on somebody you couldn't share a room with. You couldn't lean on somebody you literally couldn't lean on.

Shua looked somber, wistful, like his whole face was on one of those dimmer switches, and somebody was slowly turning it down. I didn't want to leave him like this. When I walked back out into the night, I wanted to remember him the way he was when he was working on my phone: self-assured, capable, purposeful.

But I looked at my phone and did a double-take. It was *very* late. I buttoned my wool coat as fast as I could and hustled toward the open door. "Thanks," I said.

Before he had a chance to respond, I was up through the hatch. I'd just have to hope he understood what I meant: Thank you for the filter, for the distracting conversation, for sharing your thoughts.

Yeah, I'm sure he got all that.

I spent the walk home thinking about Shua. Sometimes it was a specific thought, like how he'd hacked my phone with an almost religious reverence. But then, sometimes it was just his name over and over again. Shua. Shua. Shoo-uh. Sometimes the name was accompanied by an image of his face, sometimes not.

It was gross. *I* was gross. I felt dirty. Both doors had been open, I reminded myself, as though that mattered.

I snuck back in the kitchen door and headed up toward my room.

CHAPTER 9

I ASSUMED THAT NAOMI LEARNED STUFF at school. There was evidence that she did, in the form of her report cards, which were solid if unspectacular. Her grades were just fine, but I'd literally never seen her pay attention in class. Every time I walked by one of her classrooms, she had her book hidden somewhere she could read it but nobody else could see. She nested it inside a religious book, or crossed her legs and laid the book sideways in the groove where her two legs met. I once saw her use a sandwich to block the teacher's view.

It begged various questions: Was she a Dassi Roth–type genius? Was she the world's best multitasker? Was she a cheat? I'd been meaning to ask her, but it really was so difficult to hold her attention.

But I found, this week in school, that I'd picked up a couple key tips from her. Because I spent most of my classes on social media, hiding my phone in my books and under my desk.

The first thing I did with my unfiltered phone was download social media apps. The main two I knew of were Instagram and TikTok. I started with Instagram, because it was mostly pictures so there wasn't much sound, but by Thursday I was blazing through TikTok with an earbud hidden in my ear, like some kind of secret agent.

And that's kind of how I felt: like I was spying on other people's lives. But unlike actual spying, these people were letting me do it. They were encouraging me to. They *wanted* people to watch videos of them talking about their personal lives. They wanted you to watch them cry on camera. They wanted you to watch them play pranks on their friends.

I texted Shua to thank him for unfiltering the phone, but I think I did that just because I wanted to text him. I wasn't actually so thankful. Because within the first hour on TikTok, I totally understood why it was prohibited. It was distracting. The time I should have been using to study Torah or math was now getting sucked up by videos of kids lip-syncing to songs with dirty lyrics. And then there was a lot of awful stuff on there. There was a lot of sex stuff. There were girls dancing in clothes that covered, like, two or three square inches of their bodies. I watched one where I thought this girl was wearing *only* a T-shirt, but then I could see she was wearing shorts, but they were so short you could see part of her butt hanging out the bottom.

I did stumble on some Orthodox videos, though. I found people talking about Torah. There was a rabbi explaining something about an obscure religious text. I found women walking people through their challah recipes, removing beautifully braided loaves from their ovens. There was a girl who was just listing all of the reasons she loved HaShem. I wondered which kinds of TikToks Shua watched, the ones with the butt-bottom or the praise of God.

I searched "Colwyn," and I found some videos filmed at ColTre Unified, the local public school. One of them had a bunch of girls dancing in a hallway lined with lockers. It was a synchronized dance set to a rap song I didn't recognize. One of the girls near the middle was Mickey.

I used that video to find Mickey's own account. There was one of her acting out some kind of scene in different accents in what appeared to be a home bathroom. There was one of her dancing in front of a mirror in what appeared to be a school bathroom. There was one of her putting on makeup next to a friend in what appeared to be a restaurant bathroom. I made a note to ask her why she only made videos in bathrooms.

My world had always felt big enough. But now it felt small. I saw the same people every single day: the same girls I'd gone to school with since we were in diapers, the same girls I saw at shul on Saturday and at chesed on Sunday. We were taught the same ideas by the same rotating cast of community adults we'd always been taught by. It was insular, like a circle or a polygon with all of its sides closed.

That closedness had always been warm and comforting, like a hug. And though my world itself had barely changed, it didn't feel like a hug right now. Or, it felt like a hug, but one where the other person was squeezing too tight. Social media was showing me just how big the world was, and as the week went on, I had this growing claustrophobia, as *my* world felt smaller and smaller. I stood by my locker on Friday morning, and the walls of the hallway felt narrower than they had on Monday. And I found I was desperately looking forward to Sunday, when I would see Mickey, the only person I knew who lived in that bigger world.

CHAPTER 10

I WOKE UP EARLY ON SUNDAY and drove to the JHR warehouse. When I got there, I parked and waited patiently at the curb. I tensed up as I saw the Holtzman minivan pull up. I held an internal debate about whether I wanted the car to contain Shua. The pro-Shua camp won the debate resoundingly, and I had to physically keep my mouth from smiling—like, I probably should have sewn it shut—when the window rolled down and revealed him drumming on the steering wheel.

He turned and looked at me, but Chani popped out quickly and slammed the door violently behind her. She grabbed me by the arm and started pulling me toward the warehouse. "He *insisted* on driving me here. He set an *alarm*. He's getting so . . . weird."

He'd insisted on driving her. He'd set an alarm. I repeated those two things to myself, before I tuned Chani back in. "Do you think it's inevitable?" she asked.

Inevitable? Only God knew what was inevitable. But maybe she saw something with me and Shua. "Maybe," I said.

"You know how *all* dads are weird? Maybe as boys approach that age, dad age, it's just an inevitable decline in that direction, toward weirdness."

She and I were not talking about the same thing. "I guess,"

I said. Shua would make a good dad. He was kind and thoughtful, and seemed like a patient teacher.

Mickey showed up on time this week. I thought she might hate me because I was "sexist" or whatever, but she came right up, said, "Hey, girl," and stood next to me in the assembly line, the boxed pasta to my canned chickpeas.

I was happy to see her, which was just bizarre, because our interaction had not gone so great last time. There was also the fact that she was basically dressed like a prostitute, or what TikTok said should properly be called a "sex worker." Her shirt was *very* low cut, and I could see her bra straps and parts of the cups as well. Was it still "underwear" if it wasn't really *under*?

The women across the table were looking at me and her and whispering to each other. I wondered what they were thinking: Maybe it wasn't Esti after all. Maybe this was just the type of person Yoyo Gold keeps around, the kind she draws into her orbit, like a pritzus moon to her tznius planet.

When the boxes were packed, Mickey asked, "Do we get the same route each time?"

"I can give us a different one if you want."

"I want the same one. I want to know if Mrs. Dvornik had a good Shabbat, and I want to know how Sacha is doing at his new job."

I did as she asked, and we hit the road.

While Mickey was catching up with Mrs. Dvornik, I tried to think of a way I could ask her questions without admitting that she'd . . . got to me. She was the one who planted that seed in my mind, when she'd asked me why I wasn't on social media, when she'd asked whose choice that was.

When Mickey got back to the car, she dropped a handful of candy into the cup holder, but I was happy to see that this time she hadn't eaten any. "I'm learning from my mistakes," she said. "Personal growth."

"I have a question for you," I said.

"Okay."

"What's 'dickeating'?"

"Oh my God." She started to laugh but I didn't think she was laughing *at* me. She put her hands over her face for a moment to compose herself. "That was the *last* question I was expecting. Like, if you'd asked me to make a list of possible questions, I would have died of old age before I guessed that one. Can I—can I get the context?"

"I was on TikTok, and there was one from your school, I think, and this girl was saying that a teacher is always 'dickeating.'"

Mickey nodded thoughtfully. "Probably Mr. Cooney. He's *always* dickeating. Yeah, I mean, literally it would mean he's sucking dick. But it's like there's some assembly, and you *know* it's going to be a stupid waste of time, but he's getting *so* hype for it, talking about how 'inspiring' it's going to be. Or Cassidy Dobbs turns in some poster project, and he just thinks it's *amazing*, so he's riding her dick nonstop, just dickeating, you know? Does that help?"

"No," I said.

We both laughed.

But I thought I did get it, or at least the right context to use it, not that I ever would. "One more thing. Why do you do all of your videos in bathrooms?"

"Okay, so, I look *so* hot in bathrooms," she said. "I think it's the light. And the mirrors. Also, I feel like it makes people think about the fact that it's . . . private."

"But wouldn't it also make people think about what people *do* in bathrooms? That's where you poop."

"When I can make it in time."

I must have looked a certain way.

"*Always*. Jesus, Yoyo. You should see your face right now. Okay. Okay. How do I explain this? My friend Kaden says the hottest thing he can think of is seeing a girl pee, but not because there's anything hot about peeing, though I guess some people are into that and that's fine. Kaden thinks that part is gross. He's not talking about *watching*. He's talking about a girl just trusting him enough to leave the door open. He says it's hot because you're showing him trust, opening up this private part of your world to him."

I double-checked the bathroom lock even when I was the only person in the house. If the nuclear apocalypse came and I was the last person on earth, I was going to lock the bathroom door in my fallout shelter. "Do you really want to share all that stuff with *the world* though? Do you want that much . . . attention to your body?"

Mickey shrugged. "Attention feels good."

"Is that something you've done, left the door open?"

Mickey thought for a second, like she was trying to remember, like that wasn't something she'd remember for the rest of her entire life. "No," she said. "I don't think so. It's good news and bad news, by the way," she went on, changing the subject. "Sacha likes the new job, but he's so busy and he hasn't been calling Mrs. Dvornik *or* his mother. Okay, take one," she said, and she handed me a candy.

"But—"

"We're each going to eat one and see who can keep a straight face the longest." Mickey took out her phone, and put it on the dashboard, facing us. "We're doing it for the attention."

She pressed record and we unwrapped our candies.

The wrapper had little Cyrillic letters on it, and the candy itself was brown, which is just not a great color for non-chocolate candy. I said the proper blessing and pressed the candy into my mouth. I had no idea what flavor it was supposed to be. It had an old country taste. It tasted like it *was* old, and it tasted like it came from an old place, a village with cobblestones, populated mainly by goats. I also couldn't tell if it was a hard or soft candy, because the outside was soft, but the inside was hard. Maybe it was a hard candy that had gone soft, or a soft candy that had gone hard.

It was like eating flavored glue.

"How you doin', Yoyo?" Mickey asked, her jaw moving up and down diagonally like a ruminant chewing cud.

I wanted to reply that I was doing bad, but the whole left side of my mouth was sealed shut. All I managed was a grunt.

"I agree. So delicious. What a treat. Who knows a good dentist?" she asked the camera.

Mickey stopped the video, spent a minute editing, adding music, then posted it. I drove.

We spent the rest of the ride just talking in a way that was surprisingly normal. It wasn't that different from talking with Shira or Dassi, or with Esti. Sometimes we hit topics that one of us didn't know about, like social media trends or streaming shows I hadn't heard of and would never watch. And I kept tossing Hebrew words around, some of which Mickey knew, some of which I had to translate.

CHAPTER 11

I WAS IN A DECENT MOOD when I dropped Chani off. Chani and Mickey were talking about something, and I got to stare off in the direction of the Holtzman basement and think about Shua. Then I dropped Mickey off at a friend's house and headed home.

But my mood shifted immediately as I realized that my route home was taking me past Esti's house. It was too late to turn around. I *could* have, but I would have had to turn around in somebody's driveway, and then go all the way around the block. So I just drove by. There was no rule that said I had to look at the house as I cruised past, or that I had to think about how much I missed her. But just as I was feeling her absence intensely, my eyes darted over her house and driveway, and something caught my eye.

I hit the brakes.

Her SUV was the last car parked in the driveway. The back tires were sticking out into the street. But on the back hatch there was something new. Somebody had removed the letters that said the model of the car and had written something different in their place. The red paint stood out on the familiar blue of the back hatch.

It now said "Toyota Slutmobile." It was shoddy work, but it was legible.

The point was clear.

I looked back and forth between the vandalism and a picture of Bina's face in my head: the bitterness on her lips in the grocery, her mock sincerity at our Shabbos supper table, eating my salmon with both sides of her duplicitous mouth.

I felt a feeling rise in me. I wasn't sure I had a name for it, but it was powerful, and burning, and all-consuming, and I thought I might cry out. It was like I was on fire, the flames searing my body, blurring my vision. Even with the car windows closed, I worried the whole neighborhood would hear me scream.

I hit the accelerator. The tires squealed. I blew through a stop sign. I made record time home, took the stairs two at a time. I thought I was headed for my bedroom, but instead I found myself in the bathroom, staring at myself in the mirror.

It was comforting to see that I wasn't *literally* on fire. That feeling hadn't subsided, but now I had a name for it:

Anger.

Anger at Bina specifically, and at the hypocrisy and unfairness generally. Anger at the fact that anger itself wasn't a feeling I was supposed to have, or allowed to have. And if I messed up and had some anger, I definitely wasn't supposed to express it.

Maybe it was more like rage than anger. It was all-consuming, and it wasn't something I could push down. This wasn't something even a well-constructed dam was going to hold back.

Before I knew what I was doing, I had my phone out on the vanity. I turned the camera on and trained it on my face through the mirror. I guess I could have just used the selfie-camera, and I'm not sure why I didn't.

"B said that we all need to support each other, because that's what makes a strong community. Did she think she was supporting E when she wrote 'slut' on her car? That's an interesting interpretation of community support. It's okay. I'm sure B is repenting right now, and searching for E, so she can ask for her forgiveness. But B won't find E, because E is all the way across the country, sent away by the people who said they cared about her. Okay, how do I—"

I stopped the video, then sat down on the toilet to edit. I remembered some of what I'd seen Mickey do earlier. I cut off the last part. Then I used a filter to distort my face. All you could tell was that there was a girl talking into a mirror. I replayed the video, remembering just in time that it still had my normal voice. I went into "voice effects" and made some changes. I didn't want to sound deep and distorted, but I also didn't want to sound like Yoyo Gold. I made some little tweaks so I still sounded like a teenage girl, just not *this* teenage girl.

My finger hovered over the button that would post the video.

I thought about the video I'd made with Mickey in the car, "for the attention." But I wasn't doing this for attention. I was doing it because I thought, if I didn't, I might explode, and I was the one who cleaned the bathroom, so who would scrub the bits and pieces of me off the vanity?

Some things have to be said, and I didn't have anybody else to say this to. I pressed the button, then washed my sweaty hands.

It was one thing to be curious about the world of the internet, a world that theoretically included almost every person on earth. It was one thing to ask Mickey about some slang I'd never heard. But it was another thing to *enter* that world, to send myself out into it.

It was such a strange and huge thing to do that I found I was staring at myself in the mirror, expecting to see some kind of new, changed reflection.

I turned away and walked back to my room to see what kind of reaction I got from the big world.

When Mickey had posted our candy video, the views, reactions, comments had started coming in immediately. By the time we'd finished our deliveries, three hundred people had watched it.

I lay in bed, anxious with anticipation, refreshing my video to track it. After the first fifteen minutes, nobody had watched it. After an hour, nobody had watched it. I got the little guys ready for bed and read them a couple books, and went to get myself ready for sleep, and still nobody had watched it.

I was disappointed.

But even with zero views, I felt like some small amount of pressure had been released, like a little bit of air let out of an overinflated tire, or a little bit of water released through a dam.

I could feel myself drifting off to sleep.

CHAPTER 12

AFTER SCHOOL THE NEXT DAY, I met up with Shira and Dassi in the hall, like always. They were talking about the school production. The production was a big deal for all of us. Half the school participated in some way. Every woman in the community attended. It was probably the biggest non-religious event of the year, and it was special because it was just for women, just for us. The men had their minyan and the kollel and rabbinical school, and they could read from the Torah at shul. But they couldn't attend the production—we didn't even *talk* to them about it.

"Miri just *keeps* forgetting her lines," Shira was saying. Miri had been cast in the lead role, and Shira was *not* happy about it.

Dassi made the *tsk* sound Shira expected. "She must have Mrs. Gomes under a spell."

"She has a magic voice," Shira said. "She could spit on Mrs. Gomes's shoes but if she started singing about it, Mrs. Gomes wouldn't even look down."

I was never *in* the production because I wanted to avoid this kind of drama, and the perception that I might get special treatment. But I worked with Mrs. Gomes on the business side of the operation. And I was me, so I was expected to weigh in here.

"Maybe Mrs. Gomes is attracted to her," said Shira.

"Mrs. Gomes is *married*," Dassi noted. "To a *man*."

"So?" said Shira. "I'm just *saying*. You never hear her talk about him."

"What's she supposed to say? And in what context? 'There is a husband in this musical. I too have a husband.'"

"Well, that would sound—I don't know—"

"Contrived?" asked Dassi.

"I hate it when you use words I don't know. Yoyo, Dassi's doing that thing again where she . . ."

I didn't hear the rest of the sentence. I was on my phone. I had a text from Shua. He and I had been texting a lot, sometimes about religious questions, sometimes about nothing at all. This text was a screenshot of a two-hundred-year-old pruning hook that was for sale on eBay. When's your birthday? he asked.

I had to stifle a laugh as I pictured him presenting me with a long, rusted blade. It would be a hard gift to wrap. Save the 200 dollars, I sent. That's too much to spend on a metaphor.

Is it too much for an inside joke though?

Then I got a DM on TikTok. It was from Mickey.

It was one thing to get a text from Shua, a boy, while standing in the hallway of an all-girls school. But Mickey's DM gave me a really odd feeling. It was like when you were eating and you encountered an odd flavor, like when there were two things on your plate that didn't really go together, but you took a mixed bite by mistake. It was strange standing in a hallway of Orthodox girls in skirts getting a DM from a girl whose profile picture showed her bare stomach on an app I wasn't supposed to have in the first place.

Hey girl, the message said, will you help me with math? PS everybody at my school is obsessed with our candy video.

I think it's gonna be a legit challenge trend. Hopefully it will lead to less lawsuits than the one where you were supposed to smack your teacher on the butt.

I had no idea what a challenge trend was. I was about to look it up when I heard my name.

"Yoyo. Hey," Shira was saying. "What do you think?"

I looked forward to the production every year. It provided this connection to all of the community women. But I found as I considered Shira's question that I didn't feel so connected to it right now.

"I don't know," I said, reading Shua's last message over again. "Miri has a great voice." I shrugged. "It's a musical. I guess that's the most important thing. I wouldn't read more into it, you know?"

"But the eldest daughter has just as many solos as the mother," Shira said.

"And you know Shira's more matriarchal than Miri," added Dassi.

Since neither Shira nor Miri was a mother, I didn't see how I could assess which of them was more matriarchal. But Shira was bossier, if that's what Dassi meant.

"Will you talk to Mrs. Gomes?" Shira asked. "She listens to you. You know that if you ask, she'll do what you say."

"I don't think that would be becoming of me," I said.

Shira, showing off her acting chops, winced like she was in a lot of pain. "Hey, Dassi," she said, "can you do me a favor? Can you check to see if there's a knife in my back?" And she turned around so Dassi could pretend to look at the back of her blue sweater.

"Oh my *gosh*," exclaimed Dassi. "There is!"

"I thought there might be. I can't believe Yoyo would do that."

"Me either," said Dassi. "I'll pull it out for you."

Are you around tonight? Mickey asked.

Shira and Dassi were giggling at each other, but the giggle was only for them. I wasn't included, because they really were disappointed that I wouldn't demand a role swap for Shira.

I have to go grocery shopping, then I have to make supper, then I have to put my little brothers to bed.

Holy shit.

I looked at Shira and Dassi, watched Dassi toss a couple binders in her locker. If I left school immediately, I could get the shopping and cooking done early, and my mom would survive if she did an extra bedtime routine.

Actually, I sent, I'll be around after supper.

My place or yours? asked Mickey.

Yours, I sent.

"Yoyo. You okay?" asked Dassi. "I ask because you're smiling for no discernible reason."

"Yoyo. Be normal," Shira said. "I need you. Dassi's being too contrived and . . . discernible for me to deal with her alone."

Dassi was the only one who laughed at this joke. But she laughed hard enough for all three of us.

I saw Mrs. Gomes coming toward us down the hallway.

"Hey, girls," Mrs. Gomes said. She gave Shira and Dassi a glance, then locked eyes with me. "Yoyo, I was hoping to catch you. I'm sure you've already talked to your regulars, but I've got some leads at the new Judaica store. I know you'll want to go over there at some some point soon."

I always used my dad's connections—and a few of my own—to

get sponsors to buy ads in the program. I had a spreadsheet that showed who had bought ads before and at what level, and their contact information, and any personal connections that I needed to remember.

But I'd completely forgot about it. I hadn't opened my spreadsheet once, let alone talked to any sponsors.

"Yoyo, don't you want to say something to Mrs. Gomes?" Shira asked. "It could be a response to what she said to you, or it could be about what we were talking about earlier, about, you know . . ."

I didn't want to go to the new Judaica store. I wanted to go to Mickey's and hang out with somebody who expected nothing from me. I wanted to find a new reason to go to Shua's. Maybe I could sell him an ad in the production program.

I ignored Shira. "Sorry. I was just making some mental notes. I'll try to get over there soon."

"You're the best," said Mrs. Gomes, and then she acknowledged Shira and Dassi, spreading her arms out wide, then turning them in the direction of the cafetorium where rehearsal would take place.

I watched the three of them disappear down the hall.

I went the other way.

CHAPTER 13

I MADE MY DAD'S FAVORITE MEAL so he'd be more positively disposed toward me, since I had to ask him permission for something. The way to a Jewish man's permissive tendencies is through his stomach.

Rabbi Gold's favorite is spaghetti and meatballs. I didn't usually make it this time of year. I liked to put fresh tomatoes in the sauce for taste, texture, and color—the contrast between the bright red of fresh tomato skin and the dark sauce added vibrance to the whole dish. But the only fresh tomatoes this time of year were greenhouse grown, and they were both more expensive and not as good. So I just went nuts with the garlic, and it seemed to work, because both Nachi and my father had their faces buried in their flat bowls.

Nachi's chin was stained bright red, like he'd painted on a goatee. I'm sure my dad's was too, but his giant beard was already red, so you couldn't really tell.

The two of them were engaged in conversation. Nachi looked uncomfortable, so maybe they were talking about Torah. It was hard to take either of them seriously when they were wearing tomato sauce on their faces.

"I just don't get it," Nachi was saying. "I try, but it—I don't know. When I play basketball, it's natural. I don't have to think about it. I know what I'm doing. My body just does it. But with Torah, it's not like that. I have to think about it."

"Thinking is good," my father suggested.

"It hurts," Nachi said.

I took a seat. "Maybe you should see a neurologist about that," I said. It wasn't a serious suggestion. I was just trying to provide some kind of diversion, so he wouldn't have to absorb full rabbinical scrutiny for the entire duration of my father's spaghetti consumption. "Or maybe you could take a Tylenol approximately twenty minutes before you think. What do you think, Abba?"

"I think of Rabbi Akiva at the creek."

"Of course," I said, and I gave Nachi a look, telling him to settle in. We both knew the story, but we also both knew we were going to hear it again whether we wanted to or not.

"I think of Rabbi Akiva at the creek, looking at a stone through which drops of water fell. Rabbi Akiva saw that there was a hole in the stone, but he didn't see how the hole had come to be. And he asked, 'Who made the hole in this stone?' After a while, he realized that the *water* had made the hole in the stone. As the water dripped on the stone, slowly, over many years, it made the hole in the stone. And Rabbi Akiva thought to himself, well if water can slowly, over time, make a hole in a stone, what kind of impression can Torah learning make in a man? Surely if he learns a little at a time, Torah will make him like the stone."

My father slurped up the last bit of spaghetti, put his napkin on the table, and rose from his chair.

Nachi looked confused.

"He's just telling you to keep trying," I said. "He's saying if you just let the Torah drip on you, it will erode a hole in you."

Nachi looked down at his own body, perhaps imagining what exactly that might look like.

"It'll be a figurative hole," I assured him.

"Yocheved," my father said, bringing an official end to our impromptu meal, "the spaghetti was amazing."

"Can I take the car out a little late tonight? I'd like to be able to use the car on weeknights. I need to help a friend study."

My father paused, then nodded slowly. "I'm glad to hear you're spending time with friends. I'm not surprised. I knew you would move on."

Then he moved on into the hallway and up the stairs.

I wanted to snarl at him, but that wasn't something I could do. Instead I snarled at Nachi. "Bus those," I growled at him, pointing at the dishes on the table.

He was about to protest, but he saw the look in my eye.

"That's what I *thought*," I told him.

I headed to the foyer to grab the key, messaged Mickey, and slipped out the door.

CHAPTER 14

WHEN I PULLED UP, MICKEY MET me at the curb and said, "Hey, I didn't eat anything. Will it be weird if we drive through McDonald's?"

"No. That's fine. But can we take a different car?"

"Sure."

We went into her driveway and got in a very small car. It had only two doors. "Do you not have siblings?" I asked.

"One older sister," she said. "She's in college."

Mickey turned up the music and drove.

I'd never been to a McDonald's. There was one at the edge of Tregaron, the next town over, where it bordered the town beyond it.

I'd said it was fine—not weird—without really thinking about it. Because usually I was fine with the existence of McDonald's. Every time we left Colwyn we passed all kinds of secular and non-Jewish places. And I didn't think much about them, what kind of food they served, what went on inside them. They were part of that other world. To me, they were just illuminated signs. I never stopped to wonder about them: Was there anything special about fried chicken from the state of Kentucky? Could the Hut be out-pizzaed? But as the neon glow of the McDonald's sign appeared in the distance, I suddenly had these questions, and I did feel uncomfortable. It *was* weird.

There are a lot of reasons that Jews create our own communities. A lot of times we aren't welcome other places. The rules of Shabbos make it important that we live within walking distance of our synagogue. We can take care of each other if we live near our people. If there are enough observant Jews around, we can support kosher groceries and restaurants.

But the insular community also keeps you sheltered from the outside world, and sometimes that's good. If they opened a McDonald's in Colwyn, literally nobody would eat at it. So we didn't have that bright sign, shouting at us in the night, asking, "Don't you wonder what I taste like?"

And there was the other issue, one that only occurred to me as we pulled into the parking lot. "Will it be weird if I duck down and hide?" I asked Mickey. "*I* don't care about going here, but if people see me, they'll talk. It'll be a whole thing."

"I'm sorry. I didn't realize. I wouldn't have suggested it."

"It's fine."

I reclined my seat and sank down so I couldn't see out the window. Mickey pulled us into the drive-through. She got some kind of combination platter with a hamburger, french fries, and soda. It came in a bag and smelled like grease. It was a big smell. It filled the whole car, though I guess there wasn't that much car to fill.

I must have been making some kind of face, because Mickey said, "When you're not hungry, it's the worst smell. But when you're hungry, it's *incredible*. Don't worry. I'll eat fast."

She pulled into a parking space and put the car in park. She was not lying. It was like she was inhaling the food. I tried to decide whose meal was grosser to watch: Nachi's or Mickey's. Mickey had less of it on her face, but the noises she was making were more disgusting. I decided that Mickey was the winner when she started talking with her mouth full of hamburger. "So I'm thinking we should ask Mrs. Dvornik where she gets those Russian candies. That way we can get them in bulk. Then we can get everyone to try them and put it on TikTok. I've never started a legit trend before, but I think this could go viral, at least at my school, so, like, low-key viral."

"Okay."

"I think we could even use it to raise money for JHR, you know? Or recruit more volunteers."

I actually thought that was a pretty good idea. "Okay. I like it," I said.

"Also, unrelated, but my friend Kaden watched our TikTok and said you looked like a, quote, 'sexy field hockey player.'"

Instinctively I reached toward my collar. It was high, starched, buttoned. I ran my hand down my ponytail. I didn't know how to feel about being called sexy. The outfit was designed to be the opposite, to be simple and modest. But I guess most boys made everything sexy in their minds. I wondered if Shua did too. He saw me in the same outfit. What did he think? Did he know what field hockey was?

"I've never played field hockey," I said.

"You're not missing much. Wait, holy *shit*," Mickey said. She was looking out the driver side window. She did a kind of nod in that direction.

"What?" I said.

"Do you know this girl?" she asked.

Out of the sliver of window I could see, I could make out exactly two things: a tall light post and the top of a tree.

"Nobody's looking," Mickey said.

I sat up a bit, but it was hard to see past Mickey. Staying low, I climbed into the cramped back seat. With my knees on the floor, I peered out the window. There was a car next to us, a big SUV. In the driver's seat there was a girl eating fries out of a greasy McDonald's bag.

The girl was Miri Moritz. She was still in her school uniform, just like me.

Rabbi Moritz taught at the boys' yeshiva in Tregaron. Her mother taught in our elementary school. Her brother played basketball with Nachi. And here she was, her mouth full of treif fast food, her face illuminated by the glow of the McDonald's sign.

"Do you know her?" Mickey asked again, gesturing at her with a fry. When I was still silent: "Yoyo?"

"Yeah," I managed to say.

But I didn't know *this* Miri. She was dancing in her seat, singing along to music I couldn't hear. She was bouncing up and down, holding her soda cup up in front of her mouth, using it as a pretend microphone. She grabbed a french fry and waved it around in front of her, to emphasize some important part of the song, before sliding it into her mouth. It was a whole performance.

I had a million questions.

How long had Miri been doing this?

Why?

Was this the *only* commandment she was breaking, or was

this one of many? But I didn't know who these questions were for. Were they for Miri? Were they for God?

"So," Mickey said, "what's the first letter of her first name?"

"M."

"So is your next TikTok going to be like, 'M and I saw M eating McDonald's french fries in the parking lot of the Tregaron McDonald's.' Or will that be too confusing because me and her both have M names?" Mickey had a look of mischief. "Or do you not want to put yourself in there, so you'll say, 'M was seen'?"

I didn't know how to process any of this. I was like a Chromebook when you were trying to do too many things at once. I was freezing up. Somebody was going to have to turn me off and back on again.

I reached back into the front seat for my phone. I pulled up TikTok and looked at my only post. It had one view.

"I'm finished eating if you want to buckle up again."

I slid back into my seat. I took one more quick look at Miri, just to make sure I'd seen right.

We drove the few minutes to Mickey's house in silence. We took off our shoes in the sunroom and walked into the main part of the house. Her parents were on the couch. They both had laptops on their laps, and there was a television on in the background, but it didn't look like either of them was watching it.

Her dad was white. Blond hair. Blue eyes. He looked like he would sunburn very easily. Her mom was definitely Asian. Their feet were sharing an ottoman, and her dad's feet were nuzzling her mom's feet.

Mickey saw me looking at the ottoman and whispered,

"I know, they're gross, but also cute." Then she raised her voice. "Mom. Dad. This is my friend Yoyo."

Was I her friend? What made us friends? But I guess you don't introduce somebody to your parents as an "associate that I don't really understand but am curious about."

They both looked up in unison. "Hi, Yoyo," they said, also in unison.

Her dad looked back at his computer, but her mom made eye contact with me. "Mickey tells me you're involved in running things down at the JHR."

"Yeah. I've been doing it for a couple years now. We all do chesed as part of school."

"Hey, Mick, you should start that at your school."

Mickey rolled her eyes.

"That's something I want to reestablish at my congregation," Mickey's mom said. "Chesed, it . . . helps build *community*. Right, Mick?"

Her congregation. A female rabbi was like some kind of foreign animal—a rhinoceros or a bird of paradise. You knew they existed, but never thought you'd see one in person. But her words didn't sound foreign. They sounded just like my dad's when he "suggested" I should do something community-related.

I saw Mickey eyeing the stairs. I also eyed the stairs. Her mom noticed us eyeing the stairs. Now it was her turn to roll her eyes. "Okay, okay," she said, and waved toward the second floor.

"Does your dad do that to you?" Mickey asked as we climbed the stairs.

"What?"

"I don't know. She passive-aggressively suggests that I upend my life to be her rabbi's daughter."

It was hard to say if my dad did the same thing. I didn't have some other life for him to upend.

"She was an assistant rabbi at our old synagogue, and it wasn't like this. But now she has her *own* congregation and it's a whole thing. Every Saturday now she wants me to dress up like a princess and, like, hold court with all these girls I don't know. They try to talk to me about Jewish stuff, and I just don't know what to say to any of them. I like being Jewish, but I don't have that much to *say* about it."

I wasn't sure how to respond, so I made a show of looking around Mickey's room. I'd seen the inside of all the bathrooms she used, but I hadn't seen her bedroom until now. It was way more pink than I'd thought it would be. It wasn't that Mickey wasn't *girly*, but based on her room you'd have expected a girl who wore frilly dresses and tried on sequined tiaras in front of an oval-shaped vanity. The girl who lived in this room shouldn't have had any trouble acting like a princess.

"I know, I know," she said, sounding just like her mom. "It's from when I was little. I was very into princesses."

There was a princess—well, one of many—on top of a dresser. I picked it up and turned it over in my hand. "Now you don't like princesses?"

"Not as much. All those princess stories, they're a little—"

"Sexist?"

"Yeah! Are you saying you agree, or—"

"I'm saying that's your favorite adjective."

"Has anybody ever told you that you're—I don't know what the right word is. Biting?"

I put the princess down on top of the dresser. Nobody had ever used that word before, but I guess that was how I came off sometimes.

"I like it. It's not a problem. Don't be offended."

"I'm not offended." I turned around and leaned against the dresser.

"Hey, look," Mickey said. "Do you have any—I don't know—tips? Tricks?"

I didn't know exactly what she was looking for. Did she want to know how to deal with rabbinical passive-aggression? Did she want to know how to sound wise even when you didn't feel that way? Did she want to know how to get people to leave her alone?

Maybe I could show her how to do that last one—if Mickey suddenly became *another* person relying on me, I would walk straight out of her house. So I just stood there a moment, silent, like I was considering her question. Then I gave her a single, solemn nod. "You said you wanted help with math?"

"Okay. I see," Mickey said. "That was pretty good. I feel . . . politely dismissed." She grabbed a Chromebook, a pen, and a notebook, and brought them over to her bed. I joined her, perched like a pretzel on her pink comforter.

Two things became clear immediately: Mickey was not good at math, and she had no interest in doing it. What she was doing was Algebra 2. I could have done it in my sleep, in Ancient Hebrew, with my foot. Her notebook, which was labeled "math," was completely empty, except for a collection of doodles that depicted faces in varying stages of anguish and despair. Mickey placed her phone on top of the open notebook and started scrolling through TikTok. We were jolted from image to image, voice to voice, song to song.

I was going to protest, but this was one of the things I missed most about Esti: doing nothing, just being together, just existing comfortably in the same space.

"If you want to get views, you need to play along with the algorithm," Mickey told me. "So, the app's algorithm decides what people see, right? Sometimes it feels random, but there's stuff you can do to influence it. You should use hashtags. And then you could look for trending music and use it in yours. Like, here's my best one."

By "best," she meant the one with the most views. The video was three seconds long. At the beginning, a song was playing and Mickey was wearing all black. Then the song changed and it cut to Mickey in the same spot, but now she was wearing all white. That was it. A few thousand people had watched it.

"See? Nothing crazy. But it follows a trend and it uses the right audio. If you don't have a lot of followers—you have *one*, and I'm only going to keep following if I like the content—you have to get the algorithm to show it to other people."

"You know algorithms are just math, right?"

"I did not know that. But thank you. See? You're teaching me so much." She flashed a smile. It was a little guilty, but mostly not guilty. She closed her notebook and reclined on the bed. With her foot, she closed the Chromebook. "Here. Look at this."

I had to lie back next to her to see her phone. We spent the next hour laying back on her bed, scrolling through TikTok.

There was an awkwardness we'd had in the car that faded away.

When there was a McDonald's sign, it was this huge reminder of how different we were, how we couldn't *really* be friends, how I had to think about every word I said in a way I never had to—had had to—with Esti. But when we were just lying on her bed cackling at people making intentional fools of themselves on their phone cameras, I forgot all about the fact that this girl ate bacon and probably kissed boys, and wanted to pee with the door open.

Mickey walked me out, which I was thankful for. I didn't want to have to walk past her parents alone. She leaned on the minivan and stuck her head through the passenger window. "See you Sunday?"

"Yeah."

CHAPTER 15

I DON'T THINK I'D EVER SEEN an Orthodox Jew eating non-kosher food, so I should have been fixated on Miri. But instead, as I walked to school the next day, I was thinking about the other M: Mickey. It had felt so good to just lie on her bed and scroll with her, and I didn't really understand why. Did I like her? She could be funny in a kind of caustic way, and she was friendly if not warm. She had an appealing confidence, like she had her beliefs all figured out. And there was the rabbi's daughter thing. It was pretty different for each of us, but it was still a pretty small club.

Maybe I just liked her because she was the only person on the planet who'd watched my TikTok.

I was still turning those questions over when I sat down in halacha class. As class started, I watched the Russian candy TikTok again, looked at the goofy half smile half grimace on my face.

Rabbi Levin introduced the latest topic: the job interview. He explained that the Torah says that Moshe was the humblest of all men, and from his example it's clear that people should practice humility. You should not brag about yourself. You should never sing your own praises. So situations like a job interview presented potential contradictions.

Rabbi Levin wrote the following question on the board: "With regard to middos, why might you say 'who cares?' when it comes to getting the job?" He wrote the sentence in English, but the word "middos," character traits, was in Hebrew.

Rivka raised her hand. "Well I'm not really *sure*," she said, "but I guess if you show you're not a good person, or you *are* a good person . . ." Her voice trailed off.

Rabbi Levin encouraged her, motioning at her with his hand, as though trying to pull more words out of her.

Rivka quieted.

Shira jumped right in, as usual, without raising her hand. "'One who is arrogant will be excommunicated,'" she said, quoting our text. "So, let's say you're arrogant in the interview, saying how wonderful and great you are, and how you're better than everybody else . . . So what if you get the job? It's more important to serve HaShem than to have a certain job."

Rabbi Levin nodded. "Well put, Shira. Now, let me ask you about the other side of the coin. You are in a job interview. Are you required to reveal your *negative* middos? Must you divulge information that would make it less likely for you to get the job?"

If a rabbi's question began with the words "must you," the answer was usually "yes, you must."

There was general mumbling around the classroom, but no clear consensus.

Rabbi Levin cleared his throat. "Yes, you must divulge negative information about yourself in a job interview."

Rabbi Levin opened the book in front of him, found the page he was looking for, and started quoting to us the religious text that made this ruling clear. I opened my book on my desk, nested my phone inside, re-read my latest conversation with Shua, and watched Mickey's morning lip-sync TikTok from her school bathroom.

After school, I went to the cafetorium to tell Mrs. Gomes that I wasn't going to help with the production anymore this year.

For performances, the lunch tables were folded up and pushed against the walls, to make way for folding chairs. But for rehearsals, the cafetorium was more cafe than torium.

I was early. I was hoping I could talk to Mrs. Gomes alone before the rehearsal started. But there were already two girls there. Shira and Miri. They were standing off to the side of the stage, talking to Mrs. Gomes.

Mrs. Gomes turned and waved me over. I walked to where the three of them were talking by the stage-right curtain.

"This is exactly what you should expect from Shira Birnbaum," Miri was saying.

"What's *that* supposed to mean?" Shira said. "My only point was that the two parts are equal, and I feel like I fit the mother better. I think it would improve the production overall."

"Oh *sure*, of course you do. Good thing this has already been decided. Good thing this isn't a job interview, so you don't have to tell Mrs. Gomes about all of your negative middos."

Mrs. Gomes was authoritarian during rehearsals, but she was clearly worried about this rift between her two best thespians. "Miri, do you think there's any truth to what Shira is saying in terms of the *fit* for the two roles?"

"No," Miri said forcefully. This Miri stood in such stark

contrast to the version of her I'd seen the night before. French fry singing Miri had been so . . . loose, almost wild. This Miri was stiff, and proper, and put together. Her hair was parted perfectly, not a single strand out of place. Her collar was perfectly even, and she held her chin exactly level, like it was resting on some kind of invisible support. "I think you gave me the part because I'm the best singer in the school, but also because the lead in a production is about character, and Shira—well, she's the kind of person who tries to beg her way into what she wants, and tries to get her powerful friends to pull strings for her. I know she asked Yoyo to ask you to switch parts. I'm the better singer *and* I have the middos that make the kind of role model you want in the lead part."

"Yoyo?" Mrs. Gomes said, turning to me.

I wasn't sure which part I was supposed to respond to. Did she want me to confirm or deny Shira's string-pulling, or did she want me to vouch for Miri's superior vocal and personality traits?

But before I had a chance to answer either question, Miri jumped in. "Yeah, Yoyo. How many program ads have you sold?" she asked me.

I didn't say anything. I wanted to tell Mrs. Gomes that I wasn't really in a place to be a salesperson right now, but this wasn't how I wanted it to happen.

"See? Everybody gets fooled by this group. If my last name was Gold, we wouldn't be having this conversation."

Mrs. Gomes looked back and forth between the two sides. By instinct, I'd made the mistake of standing next to Shira, so it looked like I'd chosen a side. "Either way," Mrs. Gomes said, "we have to work with each other, girls, so why don't we talk about ways that we can get along with—"

"We can act," said Miri. "Or, *I* can. And I think Shira can too, because she's been so sweet to me, and then I find out she's been talking to you behind my . . ."

Her voice didn't trail off. I was just walking away, and I couldn't make out what she was saying. I didn't see a quick end to this conversation, and I didn't want to pile on Mrs. Gomes—I'd have to find another time to disappoint her.

I had to get out of the room. I couldn't be in the same space with Miri, acting like she was all holy perfection when I'd just seen her dance her way through a violation of one of the most important commandments.

As I walked, I seethed at Miri, and I texted Shua. Are you at home? I sent.

Naomi was standing out on the front steps of the school, looking at the sky. "I was waiting for you," she said. By way of explanation, she pointed at the horizon, where the sun was heading down. Now that she had a spotter, she slipped her book out from her bag. "Make sure I don't walk into anything?" she asked.

She extracted her phone and turned on its flashlight.

We started walking.

I'm always home, Shua replied.

A question for you: Is there a halachic rule against hypocrisy?

Why are you asking?

There has to be, right?

I don't know if text is the
best way to discuss it.
I'll come over then, I sent.

I didn't mean to be so forward. I wasn't sure if I should take it back and uninvite myself. I wasn't supposed to go to his house. That was clearly the wrong thing to do. But the Miri situation was enraging. It was something I would have talked over with a friend, or a rabbi, but I didn't trust those people right now. Strangely, or horrifyingly, depending on how you looked at it, I did trust Shua.

That's fine, he sent.

Fine. I repeated that word to myself. Fine. Not amazing. Not wonderful. But also not horrible.

Fine.

See you in a minute, I sent.

I stopped walking. "Naomi," I said. "Naomi. Naomi. Naomi."

The way to get Naomi's attention was to say her name numerous times. I think the first couple times you said it, she thought it was part of her own inner narrative, like it was embedded in the text she was reading. But if you said it enough times, she usually realized that there were no Naomis in her story, and she'd wake back up to the real world.

This was not one of those times. She just kept walking, tripped on an uneven piece of sidewalk, and lost her phone, her book, and her glasses. She remained standing, so that was a win. "What the *heck*, Yoyo?" she said. She left both her phone and glasses on the ground and, with the light from a passing car, tried to find her place in the book.

"I'm sorry. You're right. That was *my* fault. But I—I have to go."

Naomi snorted at me, but she gathered her glasses and kept walking toward our house. I doubled back down the block, then turned left toward the Holtzmans'.

CHAPTER 16

SHUA DIDN'T APPEAR TO BE THERE. The lights were on, but I didn't see him. For a quick moment, my rage mixed with disappointment.

But then I heard the flush of a toilet, the sink running, and Shua emerged from the little bathroom on the concrete side of the room. He was wearing pajama pants. On top he was wearing a white undershirt and tzitzis, the ritual strings hanging down below his waist.

He looked surprised, embarrassed, and weary. I think it was the weariness that made him look good in that moment. There was something beautiful about a Jewish boy who was exhausted by his own devotion, who put his energy into Torah, and had so little left for the material world.

He could have been weary for any number of reasons. Maybe I'd just woken him up from a nap. But I was going to tell myself that it was his commitment to Torah study that had worn him out so.

"I didn't realize you'd be here that quickly." He had a couple button-down shirts hanging from the foot of his bed. He grabbed one, sat down, and started buttoning it from the top down. He did the buttons absentmindedly, with only his right hand, each in a single practiced motion.

Then he got up and stood in front of his bookshelf, his eyes searching. Eventually, he reached for a book and brought it to the table. There was another book on the shtender, and he picked it up, put it aside, replaced it with the new volume. He flicked his fingers through the pages right to left, and I watched the Hebrew and Aramaic letters fly by. Near the center of the book, he slowed down. He found the page he was looking for, and he gave himself a small encouraging smile.

"Now," he said, and he held up a single finger, like a rabbi leading a discussion. "You asked whether hypocrisy is against Jewish law. Let's take a look here. The Rambam says hypocrisy is a 'desecration of the name of HaShem.'"

I nodded, vindicated by the Rambam, one of history's greatest rabbis. "Okay," I said. "Now I have a follow-up question."

"Can I guess the question?" he asked, looking up from the book. There was a little spark in his eye. "The question is: Okay, you encounter hypocrisy. What are you supposed to *do* about it?"

"That is the question." I needed to know if there was an acceptable way to channel my rage.

"Okay." He traced his finger over some text. "It says here that you're supposed to just chat about it in a basement."

"There's no way it says that."

"Here's what it says: 'They are wicked but they present themselves as righteous. If there is someone who recognizes the true nature of the bad actions, it is a mitzvah to bring them to light.'"

The holy text—or Shua quoting it—gave me a rush of adrenaline, and my anger at Miri surged again. I jumped up from the beanbag. I knew what I had to do.

"What're you doing?" Shua asked.

"Nothing. Going home."

"But you just got here." He looked put-upon. "I put a shirt on and—"

"I'll take it off for you if it's *that* big of a—" I stopped myself. I didn't mean it like that. But now we were both looking at his shirt, and I wondered if we were both imagining me taking it off. "I didn't mean . . . I was only saying, like, if you were concerned about the labor it took to put the shirt on and didn't want to have to exert yourself again by—"

When he imagined this scenario—me unbuttoning his shirt—what did he feel? Did he only think about the sin of it? Or was there a part of him that wished it weren't that way, that he could flip to another page and find an ancient rabbi who said it would be okay for a girl to take off the shirt of a strange man.

I was hoping he'd meet my eye, show me somehow—in his facial expression or body language—how he felt about it. But he just flipped to a different page in the book, put his finger down on the page, and started tracing the text, moving his lips in a silent chant.

I started doing the buttons on my coat, which took way too long, and made me think of his buttons again, and also reminded me that I should track the shipment of my zip-up puffer jacket, which would solve at least this one button-related issue.

I walked quickly up the stairs. "Goodbye. Thanks. See ya," I said, trying to sound casual.

"Bye."

"Bye."

We were both still saying "bye" as I headed up the stairs, a stream of monosyllabic awkwardness.

CHAPTER 17

BACK HOME, IN THE BATHROOM, IN front of the mirror, I took out my phone.

When I thought about Miri, I didn't really picture the scene at the McDonald's. That scene was more interesting than disturbing. I was curious about *that* Miri. But I wasn't curious about the cafetorium Miri. When I thought through that scene again, I felt that feeling again—anger, rage, whatever I was calling it—and I let it flow out of me, into the bathroom mirror.

"M was seen driving through a certain non-kosher fast food restaurant. Coincidentally, it also starts with M. Did she enjoy her cheeseburger? Will she be singing its praises in the musical? She brags about how perfect and righteous she is, then turns right around into the drive-thru."

I added the same distortions to the video that I'd added last time. But I also took Mickey's coaching to heart. A video with one view wasn't much of a release. If I wanted to talk through my lonely anger with Mickey, I could just call her.

I hoped I was doing this because I needed to, not because I wanted attention. If it was for the attention, I wouldn't have blurred myself, right?

I searched through different Orthodox TikToks and checked out the hashtags they used, picking the ones that were most common and that fit my content best. Then I grabbed some ominous music that was "trending" and laid it over in the background.

I replayed it. I was satisfied. Or, I'm not sure if I would call the feeling satisfaction exactly. It was like a building of potential energy, or like a balloon rapidly filling. And I knew when I pressed the post button, the balloon would burst in a way that felt good.

CHAPTER 18

WHEN I WOKE THE NEXT MORNING, my video had one view. I didn't even get to imagine that it was a stranger, because Mickey had also commented, a single heart emoji. Pressing the post button had been *some* kind of release, but it was more like a little bit of air had slipped out the bottom of the balloon, less like it had burst.

So I texted Shua and apologized for cutting our conversation short, telling him I'd been rude, and I'd be willing to finish it after school. He said cool, and I ended up in his basement again.

When I arrived, he was bent over his book, swaying up and down fairly rapidly, like he was only doing it to keep himself awake.

I stood on the stairs for a moment, just watching him. Not in a creepy way. Well, whether it was creepy or not, I was doing it anyway.

His finger moved over the text. He mouthed words as he read.

"You're not in school," I said.

Shua looked up and gave me this big toothy smile of his that I was getting used to. Or, actually, I *wasn't* getting used to the smile. I was getting used to the way it made me feel. It felt like a special look he was saving just for me, and it made me want to pause that moment in time and just live in it. But that was yet another feeling that I was not supposed to have. It was the wrong feeling. I actively did not want to have it. It made me want to turn around and run right back up the stairs and out the open hatch.

"That's correct. This basement is not a school."

I stepped into the room and collected my thoughts by looking at the parts of the space that weren't Shua.

"I mean you're not in school in general."

I was afraid he'd look offended—I was bringing up a sensitive subject. But he didn't look that way at all. He wasn't smiling anymore, but he didn't betray any of his thoughts. He kept his finger on his place in the text but met my gaze.

"So why are you studying?" I asked.

Would I have kept studying if I didn't have class to go to? Maybe it was just the spartan nature of Shua's study area, but there was something a little bleak about studying alone in a windowless room. I didn't know that I would have had that level of dedication.

He motioned to the beanbag chair. I walked over and sank into it.

"Why do you take care of your little brothers?" he asked.

Typical Jewish male behavior: answer a question with another question, bonus points if it appears to have no relation to the one you were asked.

"I—I don't know. It's complicated. I care about them and I love them, but also it's just . . . expected that I will. Nobody even tells me to, I guess. It's just *understood* that I will, you know?"

"That's my point. I always liked studying Torah. Or I thought I did. But how much of my studying was because I liked it, and how much was because it was just the thing I was expected to do, because if I didn't study it, and I was sitting around with Moshe and your dad, I'd have nothing to say? Jewish boys study Torah. And I was a Jewish boy."

"*Was?* You're not a Jewish boy anymore?"

"I'm a Jewish *man*, Yoyo. I have my own place. I can grow what I think might qualify as a beard. I mean, look at this," he said, picking at the hair on his chin. "Behold!"

I did look at his beard, though if it met the technical qualifications, it did so . . . barely. It looked like it had been painted on by somebody wearing a blindfold, so there were parts that were extra dark, and others that were completely missing.

"Your 'own place' is a basement where your mom comes down to do the laundry. I wouldn't get *too*—"

"Chani does the laundry." Shua looked up at the washer and dryer, then back down at his book. "I study now because I'm tired of taking other people's word for stuff. No offense, but I don't want Rabbi Gold to tell me what HaShem says. I need to know for myself. I need to know what I believe."

"So. Okay. What *do* you believe?"

"It's a work in progress."

"Like the beard?"

He reached his hand back to his face and pouted. "Don't shame me into shaving my beard."

It hadn't occurred to me that I could have that kind of power. I enjoyed it, but was also terrified by it.

I never thought of myself as having a particularly vivid imagination. Naomi was the Gold who wandered in fantasies. Esti was the friend who cooked up ideas and schemes.

But my imagination was doing things. I was imagining Shua shaving in his bathroom, with the door open. I was imagining his face stubbled and rough. I never thought I could vividly imagine something tactile, but here I was, imagining what that roughness might feel like on my fingers or palm, or even a brush with the back of my hand.

I tried to shut it down. I forced my eyes to look away from Shua, and I searched the room for something appropriate to focus on. I found a spider on the wall behind the washer. I watched its slow progress across the concrete.

"Honestly, I think that's the thing I like most about Judaism," Shua said.

"The beards?" I asked. "It is a solid beard religion. I know Muslims do beards too, but a lot of theirs are tame and trimmed. We go *hard* with our beards."

"Yeah, just look at your dad."

"Yep. Say what you will about Rabbi Gold, but you can't deny the beard game. You can barely see *any* of his facial features. I only know it's him in there because other bearded men don't live in my house."

"When I said I don't want Rabbi Gold to tell me about HaShem, I didn't mean anything personal against your dad. I was just trying to say that Judaism encourages you to think for yourself. Like, you're supposed to read for yourself, study the text, learn it, and use it to argue and convince other people."

"Not if you're a girl, though. 'It's better to burn the Torah than teach it to a woman,'" I quoted from one of the books my dad kept on his office shelf.

I was still spider-watching, but I saw Shua shake his head in my peripheral vision. "'A woman's sins can be erased if she is learned in Torah,'" he quoted back from a different spot in the same book. "That's *exactly* what I'm saying. Both are written. But they contradict each other, and you have to figure out which one is right, or which you want to follow, or which makes sense to *you*, because otherwise you're just—"

"Stuck?"

"Yeah," Shua said. "Stuck. Are you stuck? Is that why you're down here?"

I was still staring at the spider wall, but in my peripheral vision I saw Shua turn toward me, and it was like I could feel his look of concern.

I was stuck, definitely. But was that why I was down here? Was it because I thought Shua might unstick me? Or was it because he looked at me this way, with this look of genuine concern that I just didn't get anywhere else?

I felt like I should share something. I should answer his question. Or I should say something profound about the fundamental nature of our Jewish tradition. Or at the very least I should share my favorite thing about Judaism. But I had never considered what my favorite part of it was—there were a lot of good choices—and I felt rushed.

I was saved when the door at the top of the stairs opened.

My heart jumped into my throat and Shua jumped up off his bed. "I'm naked!" he shouted.

"Ew. *Why?*" said a confused but not yet visible Chani.

I wondered the same thing, why he'd had to use that exact excuse, because now I was both panicked *and* trying to avoid picturing Shua naked.

"I'm not waiting. The laundry basket is heavy."

"Just leave it at the top of the stairs. I'll do it."

"Fine. You're just . . . ugh," Chani said, her footsteps retreating.

Shua went up the internal stairs. I rose from the beanbag chair and moved toward the external ones.

CHAPTER 19

WHEN IT HAPPENED, I WAS PLAYING Hearts with Nachi, Naomi, and my mother. It was Friday night. Shabbos. Our supper guests had gone home. My father was studying. At first he'd roped Nachi into studying with him, but my mother convinced him to loan Nachi to us for the game.

I looked at my hand of cards.

We were playing in low light: candlelight from the dining room and a lamp by the couch we'd left on. But it was a warm light. Or maybe everything just felt warm and cozy on Shabbos. It was the only time we got the whole family in the same room.

The card game played out the same way it always did. The leader went back and forth between me and my mom, based on whoever was less distracted by the boys. Right then, I was winning, because my mom was reading and singing with them. They were doing the *613 Torah Avenue* book and song for the thousandth time.

To be clear: I mean the thousandth time *that night*. On the five-hundredth rendition, Naomi had threatened to blow her brains out, but we'd kindly reminded her that the use of a firearm was prohibited on Shabbos, so she'd have to wait until tomorrow night.

When one rendition ended, they began the next one:

> *It's time to learn Torah right now*
> *Follow me, I'll show you how*

This time through, the song was accompanied by a tapping sound, like somebody was drumming along. I ignored it, because I was trying to decide which suit to lead with so I could avoid picking up this trick.

> *If every one of us tries*
> *We will grow up great and wise*

But now the tapping was more persistent and the drummer had lost the beat. It sounded like someone tapping on glass, but the only glass in the room was the coffee table. My father was sitting there, but he wasn't tapping. He'd fallen asleep slumped forward on his open book.

> *The Torah is our guide*
> *By its mitzvahs we abide*

It'd gone from tapping to banging, but I was right that it was glass. Somebody was knocking on the window. Hard.

My mother put her cards down. "Yosef," she said. "Yosef." My father did not stir, so she got up and shook him. "Yosef. Wake *up*. Somebody is breaking into our house."

The boys heard the urgency in my mom's voice and stopped singing. In the relative quiet, I could think.

The thing about burglars was that, traditionally speaking, they didn't knock before entering. Ideally, burglary is a quiet activity.

Naomi and Nachi were cowering on the floor, where the couch shielded them from direct view of the window. The little boys were still standing, looking around, confused and scared.

I got up and went to the window. It was dark outside, so it was hard to see. I had to put my face right up against the glass. "Get back!" my father shouted at me.

But I immediately saw that the situation was non-threatening. I called over my shoulder, "It's okay! Everything's fine. Nobody's breaking in."

There was a person knocking on the glass. Well, now she stopped because she saw me. Mickey still had one hand in a knocking-fist, and with her other hand she was waving her phone around trying to show me something.

I opened the window a crack. "What are you doing?" I whispered. "Go away."

"But you—"

"Kitchen door."

She tried to say more, but I slammed the window down.

My mother still looked flustered. "What is going on?" she asked.

"I don't know," I said, "but nothing threatening. A . . . girl I know was just knocking on the window."

"Someone from school? I don't understand. Who would—"

"Just excuse me for a minute, please? Abba, can you play for me?"

My dad eyed the game and shook his head. He turned back to his book, like he couldn't play because his reading/napping was simply too urgent to permit a break for cards. But it was probably just because he didn't know the rules.

I left the room and shuffled to the kitchen, where Mickey was waiting outside the back door.

"You went totally viral," she said.

I stepped outside onto the slate of the back patio, felt the shock of the cold through my socks.

She was trying to show me on her phone, but she was so excited she couldn't hold it steady. "Like, *viral*."

Mickey kept saying words, but I wasn't really processing them. I was about to grab her wrist so I could hold her hand steady, but then, I really shouldn't have been looking at the phone screen. I hadn't turned the screen *on*, so I could have argued that viewing the already illuminated phone wasn't a violation of the Sabbath. But it certainly wasn't in the spirit of the day. "Why didn't you knock on the front door?" I asked.

"I did. Nobody answered. But I just *had* to show you this. It's *crazy*."

What was crazy was her showing up at my house unannounced, waving her phone in my face like it was a winning lottery ticket. "Can we adjourn this meeting and start again tomorr—"

"One hundred *thousand* views, Yoyo." Mickey said this quietly. And repeated it: "One. Hundred. Thousand."

It was like somebody had flipped a switch, which you're not allowed to do on Shabbos, but that's what it felt like. Somebody had flipped a switch in me and suddenly I felt different. My whole body was numb, but my mind was laser-focused on Mickey. "What number did you say?"

"One hundred thousand. The comments are amazing too, though some of them are— Well, just look."

I wanted to look. I wanted to look so badly. But I didn't. I turned back to the house like I'd turned to Shua's wall. It took what I thought was an impressive amount of willpower. I expected praise of some kind, but Mickey didn't seem impressed and offered no praise.

I scanned the wall for spiders but couldn't see any. It was too dark.

It was hard to wrap my head around the idea that so many people had watched my video. "How?" I managed to say.

"Well, first I should get a lot of credit for telling you about the whole trending audio thing, and also some of your wording was *eerily* similar to what I drafted for you in the car. But the whole singing thing was a clever turn of phrase by you. And really, I think it just resonated with people, you know? Like, you're seeing something you don't think is right and you're speaking truth to power."

I didn't think Mickey really understood that expression. I didn't speak truth to *power*. I spoke truth to myself, to my mirror, to a void of internet nothing. Except now it wasn't nothing.

Mickey was still talking. ". . . don't exactly understand what the issue is with a cheeseburger once in a while, but there are two issues there, right? Because if you're raised that way, maybe it *is* a huge deal, and then if you're telling people *not* to do it while you're doing it yourself, then that's messed up. So I don't know this M girl, but if that's what . . ."

I tuned her back out. I needed to get back inside. Because, if I didn't, I was going to grab the phone out of her hand and start scrolling through the comments and reactions. It would be painful enough trying to make it through the rest of Shabbos knowing this was going on. I didn't need somebody holding a phone in front of me. It was too tempting. I needed to walk back into my house. "I'll text you when there are three stars in the sky tomorrow."

Mickey was nonplussed. "Three stars? We're too close to the city to see *any* stars. And it's very overcast, so how could you possibly know when there are three stars?"

"It says so on the calendar."

"But you can't use your phone, so how would you look at the calendar?"

"The calendar is on paper. Paper is kind of like a screen but it's made of trees, mashed up and soaked and treated with chemicals. Good night. Thanks for stopping by."

"Man, that was—"

"Biting?"

"Yeah. Good night. I didn't mean to disturb your Shabbat. That's on me." She patted her chest in a gesture of personal responsibility. "I was just excited."

"I'm glad you . . ." but I didn't finish the sentence. Glad wasn't the word. I was not glad that she came by, interrupted my game, made my family fear for our lives, told me that thousands of people were reacting to my video and I wouldn't be able to see their reactions for a full day.

Instead, I just went inside.

CHAPTER 20

THE GENEVA CONVENTIONS WERE AGREED UPON in 1949 and ratified by 196 countries. They set out rules for the proper, humane treatment of prisoners of war. Basically, they're the international laws that say it's illegal to torture people.

I thought I had a strong case against Judaism for setting up this situation where my video went viral on the *one* day of the week that I wasn't allowed to use my phone. As soon as Shabbos ended, my first phone call would be to The Hague.

The most distracting thing I could think to do was homework, but you couldn't really do homework on Shabbos. The problem was that you weren't allowed to write, and I didn't really read without writing. That was the way I processed all the knowledge: I contextualized it by condensing it and reorganizing it in a way that made sense to me.

So instead of doing homework, I spent my Saturday lying on the living room floor reading book after book to the boys. When I'd read them the thirtieth book, they started to get suspicious. It was like when Naomi got her appendix out, and everybody else was at the hospital, and I just kept feeding them ice cream. And they were so torn, because while abundant ice cream was their wildest dream come true, the unlimited nature of the treat also sent a signal that something was different, off, wrong.

As soon as Shabbos was over, I went up to my room and got my phone from my bedside table.

We used to have the room set up so the two beds were parallel and Naomi and I shared a bedside table, which sat between us. When we were little, we were close. We played together. We read the same books, sometimes out loud to each other. When Naomi had a nightmare, I'd reach across the space between us and hold her hand.

But right around my bat mitzvah, I started doing more in the family and the community, and Naomi went the opposite way, into her books. The hand-holding stopped. Like, I'd still hold her hand if she *asked*. I wasn't a monster. But I wanted to feel more like I had a private space, and she seemed to find all the comfort she needed in her books anyway.

So now our beds were on opposite walls. We still had just the one bedside table, but it was mine now. She kept a pile of books next to her bed and it worked just as well. It didn't have a drawer, but it was just as good at supporting phones, keys, and beverages.

I flopped down on my bed and turned my phone on. My fingers were trembling as I opened TikTok and checked my latest video.

It had 120,000 views now, and hundreds of comments. I scrolled through them, stopping every so often to read. The comments could be sorted into three categories. They were:

1. Randomly but deeply antisemitic. There was this one, for example: *U say it u dumb k1ke bitch.* This one confused me because it was an interesting combination of strangely

encouraging and horrifically bigoted. I was guessing he—I thought it was a safe assumption it was a he—used a 1 instead of an "i" in "kike" so he could avoid it getting censored. But then I felt like the filter should definitely have caught "k1ke." Like, what was the non-hateful purpose for that combination of characters?

There was another one in this category I won't even repeat. It said if I hadn't blurred my face, the commenter would have found me and force-fed me non-kosher food while committing sexual violence against me. When I read it, I literally threw up a little bit in the back of my mouth, more at the assault threat than the food one, because while he didn't specify what treif items he would feed me, the threats about what he would do to my body were specific and *really* graphic.

It had taken me a long time to believe what people told me about antisemitism. It was a common thing I heard from my dad and other Jewish leaders: "Careful. Everybody hates Jews." But I'd always been like, "No they don't. Everybody in the world is Jewish, and we don't hate *ourselves*." Everybody I knew was Jewish. Everybody *they* knew was Jewish. But then I got older, and saw a little more of the world, and then I got a phone and a driver's license. And I saw that not only was most of the world non-Jewish, there was a small but vocal portion of it that really hated Jews. People had been hating the Jews for over two thousand years, and in the age of the internet, they continued to innovate, like in the comment that called me a J3w3$$, which was equal parts clever and dehumanizing.

The silver lining, at least, was that under each of the antisemitic comments was a bunch of replies calling out the hate speech.

2. Supportive but confused. My guess was that these were mostly from old people. Old people were often confused. These comments were also written in full sentences. with punctuation, another hallmark of old people—punctuation is like catnip to an old person. These comments said things like, "Thank you for calling out this person violating HaShem's mitzvahs. It is a shame that M does not love HaShem as HaShem loves her."

Which missed the point. I didn't care if Miri had a cheeseburger. I cared if she had a cheeseburger, *then* claimed to be perfect and shamed others for their lack of perfection.

3. Supportive, just *so* supportive. There were people *thanking* me. There were people telling me I was courageous, even though I'd blurred my face and distorted my voice. There was one commenter who said she "needed to hear this in the worst way." When I went to her profile, I saw it was another Orthodox girl. But she wasn't from the Philadelphia area, because there were palm trees outside her bedroom window. "People act like we only have yetzer hatov and forget we all have yetzer hara too and I'm so tired of it."

Yetzer hara was the evil inclination, the thing that all these people throwing the K-word around had in such abundance.

Yetzer hatov was the inclination to do good, the one I'd hoped I was using when I'd posted the video. And this girl's comment made me think it was.

Before I knew it, it was the middle of the night and Naomi was asleep, but I was still re-watching my TikTok and reading comments and watching the videos of the commenters. Part of me wanted to put the phone away and go to sleep. But part of me was enjoying it too much. Or, I wasn't sure I was *enjoying* it. It was exhilarating. It was thrilling, like I was driving too fast but I didn't want to slow down. I still wasn't sure Mickey was right when she'd said that attention felt good. But whatever feeling attention gave you, it was one that grabbed hold of you and didn't want to let go. Just like I didn't want to let go of my phone, or my consciousness, despite how tired I was.

As I finally drifted off, I wondered about Shua, as I usually did. But this time it wasn't a general picture of him or a stray thought about whether he ever had trouble sleeping. It was a specific question: Was Shua one of the 120,000 people? And if he was, which category would his comment fall into?

CHAPTER 21

"YOU WERE SUPPOSED TO TEXT ME last night," Mickey said as she slid into her boxed pasta space at the JHR table. "Did your paper calendar glitch up?"

"I got distracted," I said.

Mickey seemed legitimately angry at me, or at least upset. I felt like my excuse was a pretty good one. Going viral was *very* distracting. I wanted to try to explain myself further, but Mickey kept her head down, her jaw clenched shut.

Plus, I hadn't got any sleep, and my head was all foggy. I could feel my hands placing cans of chickpeas in cardboard boxes, but I wasn't thinking about it.

Maybe it was the weather—there was a steady cold drizzle outside—but everybody seemed a little out of it. Most of the time, we all talked while we loaded up the boxes. But today, nobody had anything to say, at least not to the whole table. Mrs. Silverstein and Mrs. Singer were whispering heatedly back and forth, but I couldn't make out any of their words. Shira and Dassi were talking to each other in low voices too, and every so often one of them stole a glance at Mrs. Gomes.

Mrs. Gomes was a colorful, animated person, exactly how you'd expect a theater teacher to be. But today, she looked like she'd just seen a ghost, or become one.

I kept my head down and did my job. Mickey and I loaded the car in complete silence. But it was going to be hard to drive around together all day like this. "Hey, I'm sorry," I said. "I didn't realize it was such a big deal. It was a lot to process. I went from thinking it was wrong to *have* TikTok to having thousands of people watch my TikTok. I didn't mean to upset you."

"You didn't. It's not you."

I pulled the car into our first apartment complex. "Do you want to talk about it?"

"I don't know if you'll get it."

That stung. It was a little mean, and I thought it was probably also true. Mickey and I might have found a few square centimeters of common ground, but we spent most of our lives on opposite sides of a line neither of us had ever crossed. When we each woke up Monday morning for school, she wasn't going to suddenly decide to say the Modah Ani prayer—I wasn't sure if she knew the words. And I wasn't going to spend five minutes picking out the "cutest" underwear.

Mickey seemed frozen in her seat. "Maybe Mrs. Dvornik will understand," I said, giving her a hint. But she didn't seem to have heard me. So I unlocked her door. She didn't notice that either. I put her window down. She looked up when the cold rain started splashing on her arm.

Mickey was pulling her fingers carefully through her shoulder-length hair like she was looking for split ends. "So on Friday I went and got frozen yogurt with a bunch of kids, including the boy I like."

"Kaden?"

"Ew. No. *God* no. So my best friend Tess takes a picture of me, her, Kaden, Nick, and Jayda."

"The boy is Nick?"

"Yeah. And then Tess tags everybody *except* me. I was pissed, but I thought it was a mistake. But then on Saturday there was a party at Kaden's, and . . ." At this point Mickey's voice cracked a little, like this part was hard to say. "I got there late, and she's hooking up with him in the middle of the room, on the couch."

I wasn't exactly sure how scandalized I should feel about this, since I wasn't 100 percent clear on the meaning of the verb-preposition combination "to hook up." There were lots of different parts of the body that could "hook up" with parts of other people's bodies.

But the details didn't really matter. The point was that Mickey felt betrayed. And that's a feeling I did know.

"And she knows. She *knows*, Yoyo. She knows how I feel about him."

"I'm sorry," I said. "That sucks."

"I tried to talk to her about it. But she kept avoiding me. She was like, 'I have to go to the bathroom,' like we don't usually go *together*. So then I text her this morning and she's like, 'Oh, sorry. I was pretty drunk, so I didn't really know what I was doing.' Of *course* you knew what you were doing. And then she has the balls to say, 'It didn't even *mean* anything.' Didn't mean anything to *who*? So she hooks up with the boy I've liked all year—who we've *talked about* constantly—and then instead of apologizing, she just denies my feelings *and* my reality. And now obviously it's over for me with Nick."

Mickey was definitely right that there were *some* things about her situation that I didn't get. But the rules of friendship were universal. "I'm sorry," I said again. "That's brutal."

"Yeah," she said. "I thought Nick liked me too. But maybe he just thought Tess was too much of a baddie for him. I'm not as hot, so I guess I was just a backup plan or something."

I looked at her. It wasn't something I spent a lot of time thinking about, but she seemed really pretty to me. There was a fierce darkness in her eyes that was appealing. She had the kind of slim figure all of the models had in fashion ads. And she carried herself with her chin up, like she knew who she was, or who she wanted to be.

"It's his loss," I said.

"Thanks." She took a deep breath and got out of the car. "You're a real one, Yoyo."

When Mickey reappeared, she was in a visibly better mood. The red around her eyes was gone. She had a whole grocery bag full of Russian candies. "So," she said, "we have to plan your next move. Your new followers will expect content. And if you want to stay relevant, you have to post regularly."

"Are you saying we should just drive around and look for Jews eating non-kosher food?"

"Is that a possibility?"

"No," I said. "I'm not even sure if I'm going to do another one. It's exciting, but I was doing it for *me*, and now that so many people have seen it, I feel weird about it." But as I said it, I knew it might be a lie. I'd been looking at my TikTok all morning, hoping that I would have more views. But the video had slowed down.

There were only a few new views in the last couple hours. Every time I opened my phone I tried to will more comments into existence, and I felt disappointed every time there weren't any.

It made me feel less lonely, less overwhelmed, to share with so many people. And what about that girl who said she "needed" my video? She probably "needed" more, right?

"Is it easier to just not think about boys?" Mickey asked me.

Mickey and Esti had a lot of similar qualities—high energy and low inhibition, for example—but it was moments like this one that made them so different. Mickey was quiet and subdued. She'd clearly thought carefully about this question. Esti's questions burst out of her *before* she thought about them.

Mickey continued her line of questioning. "Is it *easier* to just not worry about who's dating who or which boy likes you, or whether this guy is following you, or what it means when he comments on your stuff?"

When she asked the question, Shua immediately popped into my head. Maybe I was worried about him in a different way, but it was impossible not to think about him. I thought about him constantly.

"It isn't that we don't think about boys. That's the *reason* for the separation: because we *do* think about them. And they think about us. That's why we dress modestly. Think of your body like a diamond. It's beautiful, flashy. It shimmers."

Mickey looked down at her body, which was damp. She was dressed mostly in black.

"You don't just go waving your fancy jewels around. Yeah, it's hard not to have those feelings. But if you want to follow God's mitzvahs, you just put yourself in situations where those thoughts aren't going to come up as much, where you aren't going to see all those flashing diamonds. If you keep yourself away from boys, you aren't going to be as tempted to—I don't know—hook up with them or whatever. So yeah, I think about boys, but I try not to put myself in situations where I might do more than think about them."

A few weeks ago, I'd have said the exact same words and felt no guilt, shame, or irony. But now I felt all three of those, because there was no way, when I walked down the basement steps of the Holtzman house that I was "putting myself in a situation where those thoughts weren't going to come up as much."

Mickey was quiet for a minute. Her eyes were closed. A small smile appeared at the edge of her mouth. "But it's fun," she said. "That's the problem." I guessed her eyes were closed because she was imagining the "fun" she'd had with boys.

"Maybe you can run into trouble when you spend your time thinking about what's fun, instead of thinking about what's right?"

Because sometimes God likes to make me feel silly, at the end of the drive, we passed a convenience store along the border of Colwyn and the city. It was still raining. Even though the sun wouldn't set for another hour at least, it was dark outside, the parking lot illuminated by the yellow light of the store's sign. There were two figures at the corner of the building. One of them was pressed against the wall, out of the rain. The other person was getting wet.

His kippah was soaked. The wearer was Ari Fischer. His tzitzis were tucked in, so the kippah was the only thing announcing him as an observant Jew. When you're not in a Jewish area, kippahs stand out. Usually, if I was in a non-Jewish place, I looked around for them. They were a sign of familiarity. They were comforting.

But I did not feel comforted. Because there wasn't a good reason for Ari to be there. He seemed to be handing the other guy some money.

"It's really obvious you're watching if you slow down like this," Mickey said.

I had almost stopped. I hadn't realized.

The car behind us leaned on its horn. Ari looked up at the sound, did a little jump, and took a step backward into the shadows.

I hit the accelerator. The car lurched forward.

"Don't worry," Mickey said. "I don't think he could see us through the rain."

I drove in silence for a minute, trying to get my nerves to calm down.

"It's convenient for your content," Mickey noted.

"Yeah," I said, letting out a long breath. "But with Miri I knew what was going on. With this, I don't know what it . . . was."

"Drug deal."

"Drugs . . ." I said, turning the word over.

"Non-prescription medication," Mickey clarified.

"I get it."

"I'm going to guess that the Torah, and therefore Yoyo Gold, disapproves of drug use," Mickey said.

The Torah, yes. It was pretty clear on that, though there were certain drugs, like alcohol, that were a big part of Jewish rituals. As for me, it wasn't the drugs that bothered me exactly. It wasn't the non-prescription medication that made my anger return, that made my hand itch for my phone, that made me want to describe this scene to the whole world.

I thought back to what Bina had said about Ari. She'd implied that Esti had somehow duped poor Ari into kissing her. That he was a good Jewish boy who'd been tempted into transgressing, just that one time. That his mistake had only brought him closer to his faith.

Was Bina just putting on a good face for my parents, or did she really think Ari was the perfect Jewish boy? Was it worse if Bina was the hypocrite or if Ari was? I passed the rest of the drive home debating back and forth, and settled on the idea that it didn't matter. I hated it either way.

By the time I got home, I was in a blind rage, but I still managed to find the bathroom. I didn't bother to compose myself, or plan what I was going to say. "A was seen on the edge of town, exchanging his cash for . . . something. I'm going to guess he wasn't buying a new kippah. A and E messed up *together*. She had to move out west, but A is still right here, so he can share his new medica—sorry, kippahs?—with his classmates."

After I posted the video, I stayed in the bathroom for a minute. I told myself it was just because I wanted to towel my hair dry—it was wet from the rain. But really I wanted to stare at myself in the mirror, to see myself better, to adjust to this new version of me who posted TikToks about people and felt a strange relief when she did it.

CHAPTER 22

FUN FACT: A PERSON WILL DIE of sleep deprivation before they die of hunger. Personally, I try to sleep *and* eat, so I don't die of either. I'm pretty good at both activities.

When I'm awake, I've got a lot on my mind. I really savor the lack of consciousness that comes with sleep. When I'm asleep, nobody asks anything of me. There's nobody to take care of.

So it really sucked when I found myself awake at four thirty a.m., with TikTok open on my phone, unable to fall back asleep.

My new video hadn't gone viral in the same way. A few thousand people had watched it. There were the same types of comments. Somebody said that we Jews were always transacting business, drug deals and otherwise. Anytime there was money being exchanged, you were going to find those money-grubbing Jews around. But somebody else thanked me for reminding everybody that the rules were not always applied fairly, especially when it came to men and women.

And then there was a whole conversation going on in the comments. A bunch of Orthodox girls were talking to each other. "This this this," one of them said. "None of us are perfect, but y'all act like we're supposed to be."

"'Even a high priest transgresses,'" another quoted, "No 1 is a 😇"

"Torah full of confused people who mess up. But we're never supposed to?"

I had a couple DMs. One of them kindly requested that I send unblurred photos of myself, preferably in a state of undress. But another one was from the same palm-tree girl, the one who'd commented before about how she'd *needed* my previous video. She only sent one word: "Shkoyach."

I loved that word, because it meant both "have strength" and "thank you," and I needed to hear both of those messages.

I was smiling at my phone when it rang. It was four forty a.m., still pitch-black outside.

I stopped smiling.

I knew who it was without looking, and what the call would be about. I answered and didn't try to hide my annoyance. "Do you know what time it is?" I asked Moshe.

There was silence on his end. He'd been in Israel almost a full year, but he still hadn't figured out the time difference. The spinning of the earth in relation to its sun was too secular an idea for Moshe to pay attention to it.

"Uh . . . no. I don't wear a watch. You know that."

The guy didn't even know what time it was where *he* was.

"I guess I could look at the phone, but I'm *talking* on it."

"Oy," I said, and waited for him to tell me what very basic problem he wanted me to solve for him.

"We got a flat tire."

When I said that I knew what the call was going to be about, I meant that I knew what *kind* of thing it was going to be. I knew he wasn't calling to say hello and ask me about my REM cycle. He was calling because there was something simple and practical that he didn't know how to do.

He'd once called me at two a.m. to ask me how to use a toaster. I'd told him to "push the thing down, then wait." He'd then asked me—and this is a direct quote I'll remember for the rest of my life—this follow-up question: "How much toastiness is appropriate for the average toast?"

I had so many questions here, but I had to get up for school in about an hour, so I knew to limit them. "Okay," I said quietly, trying not to wake Naomi, "so you got a flat tire, and instead of calling Israeli AAA, you called your younger sister who is six thousand miles away, even though it's four forty a.m. her time?"

"Well, when you put it like that—"

"Who gave you a license to drive?"

There was some murmuring on the other end of the line, and then: "The consensus here is actually that I'm *not* licensed to drive. And it's a borrowed car."

"All right," I said. "First step: grab the spare tire."

"We didn't bring one. It's a small car."

I hoped he could feel me rolling my eyes through the phone. "It's like you make an *effort* to not know things. What color are your own eyes, Moshe? Don't worry. If you don't know off the top of your head, you can probably use the reflection in the car window."

"I'm with friends," he said. "Are you going to help me or ridicule me?"

"Both," I told him. "Now go open the trunk. The trunk is the hatch in the back. Sometimes people use it to store luggage."

When Moshe discovered the little doughnut tire, car jack, and tire iron hiding under the trunk fabric, he marveled at the continuous wonders of God.

And I thought about the time Esti and I got a flat tire. She got the road and sidewalk confused and drove into a very high curb, exploding the tire. We didn't know how to change it either.

You know what we did? We figured it out.

It took Moshe almost an hour to get the spare tire on, and when he was done, he forgot to thank me and had to be prompted.

When I went to rouse the boys, I made sure they thanked me for waking them, and as I helped them get dressed, I explained in detail how to check tire pressure, how to use a penny to ensure proper depth of tire tread, and how to change a tire without the help of somebody in a different time zone. They were pretty interested. They loved cars almost as much as Moshe loved God.

CHAPTER 23

REMEMBER WHEN I SAID I LOVED school? It wasn't a lie.

And I still loved calculus, because math was, as Moshe might put it, "a continuous wonder of God."

But suddenly I was having more trouble with my religious classes. In halacha class, Rabbi Levin was still talking about how to present yourself as an adult: in job interviews, in the workplace, out in the world. He was citing all of this Jewish law, telling us how you had to be honest about yourself, how you had to make sure you weren't too boastful, and how you had an obligation to reveal your negative qualities.

But it made me wonder if he followed his own advice. There was nothing about him specifically that seemed dishonest. It was just, recently, I'd started wondering how good *anybody* was at following that particular advice.

When Rabbi Levin interviewed to work at the school, did he reveal the commandments he'd violated in the past? If he skipped a prayer one day, did he go into the office and tell his boss about it?

In the hall after halacha class, Shira and Dassi were talking about Rabbi Levin's tie. This was a conversation I was usually pretty invested in. It was the culmination of a painstaking, yearslong investigation into his clothing.

He wore what *appeared* to be the same outfit every single day, a black suit with faint gray pinstripes. Sometimes it looked a *little* different, but was that because he sometimes rotated his shirts, creating an *appearance* of difference, or did he have multiple very similar suits?

Dassi and I had made a spreadsheet earlier in the year to track his ties. Based on the data we'd collected, we decided that he probably had more than one of each tie. But now there was new evidence.

"Did you notice the stain—oily, like from mayonnaise—near the bottom?" Shira asked.

"Of course," said Dassi.

"Yeah," I muttered. I hadn't noticed.

"It was there yesterday too, *and* the day before," said Shira. "But today it's bigger."

"So we're thinking it's the same tie, and he just keeps spilling mayo on it? *Or*, he has two ties that have mayo stains on them, in the same location, but the sizes of the stains are different."

"Hmm," said Shira. She tapped her foot thoughtfully. "I'm thinking the tie got stained two days ago, and he figured it wouldn't come out anyway, so he just kept wearing it."

"Oh my *goodness*," I said. "Just *ask* him if it's so important."

They turned their bodies away from me so they could give me side-eye. "It's not *important*," Shira said. "It's just funny."

"So funny."

"You thought it was funny, like, a few weeks ago."

I didn't have a good comeback—that was objectively true. So I just shook my head and turned away. Dassi and I were going to the same class, but I walked ahead of her, my eyes following the black rubber streaks on the blue and white floor tiles.

I spent math class thinking about Shua. When I pictured him, he was bent over a religious book, studying. He was rocking back and forth, his lips moving with the words on the page. In this particular daydream, he was wearing his undershirt and tzitzis, but no shirt, and just boxer shorts. The lack of pants was *only* based on that stereotype of the religious yeshiva boy: too wrapped up in thoughts about scripture to think about silly earthly things like whether he was wearing pants.

Moshe took it to an extreme, to the point where he couldn't make toast without live instruction. Shua seemed to have that studious quality but without cutting himself off from the world he was currently living in. He could quote obscure scripture, but he could also remove phone filters and do laundry. He was a double threat. Triple, if you included the fact that his neck looked scruffy in a way that would probably be nice to touch. Quadruple, if you factored in the fact that he had a quiet sense of humor, where when he smiled at a little joke, you knew the smile and the joke were only for you. Though maybe I should have deducted one, because he was distracting. I couldn't focus.

As I twirled my pencil between my fingers, I pictured his fingers tracing the text, his eyes laser-focused on his book. I felt a little of my anger—the anger I was sending out into the world—rise up again. This boy had been sent home from Israel in shame. And for what? For having a different interpretation of the rules?

Dassi and our math teacher, Miss Simpson, were talking through different approaches to a particularly tricky problem.

I could never keep up with Dassi—nobody could—but usually I at least tried. Today I gave up early and unlocked my phone under my desk. I started typing out a text to Shua.

Missed you on Sunday. Chani said you had a meeting.

The problem with my text was that the verb "to miss" had two meanings. One of them was just missing, like an arrow missed a target. But then one of them was *missing*, like feeling regret that you were not in the presence of that thing or person. I didn't want him to get those confused. And I didn't want him to know that when he hadn't been at the wheel of their car on Sunday, I'd panicked and interrogated Chani for five minutes about his whereabouts.

I deleted that text and started again. It was easy to text Shua about garden tools, but impossible to just tell him I missed him and needed to go to his basement.

"I don't get it," Leah Rosen said, rubbing at her eyes.

"Do you want me to repeat the last step?" Dassi asked.

"Not on my account," said Leah.

Should we have another study session soon? I typed to Shua.

I liked this text better. But the problem was that we'd never really *had* study sessions exactly. I'd needed something from him. I'd needed a question answered, or I'd needed him to do something for me. The way I worded it felt too open-ended. Without a clear purpose, it felt like it was just an excuse to spend time together.

I deleted that message too.

At least with Dassi showing off at the board, the Shua distraction didn't keep me from learning something. As Chani explained to Dassi at the end of class, "It doesn't matter how many times you repeat it. The rest of us just aren't going to get it."

CHAPTER 24

BACK IN THE HALLWAY, I TRIED not to think too hard. I wrote out a text and hit send before I could change my mind again: Do u know how to change a tire?

A split second later my phone rang.

It was Shua. I looked around for him, like he was going to be there, but that wasn't how phones worked. All I could see was a mob of girls in blue skirts. Still, I felt like somebody would know who I was talking to.

My heart was pounding and my eyes were darting back and forth. "Hello?" I said, in a hushed tone.

"Are you safe?" he asked.

"Yeah, of course."

"Just get safely to the side of the road. You matter more than the car. I can pick you up, and we'll get Heshy to change the tire. You can just wait at our house and Heshy will bring the car . . ."

I was probably smiling pretty widely. I kind of wanted him to just keep talking. How did he convey this combination of calm and urgency at the same time?

"Shua. Shua."

"Yeah?"

"I'm fine. I don't have a flat tire."

"Oh. I guess I just— I'm sure you'd call somebody else if you did. I guess I just didn't really think about it. I just kind of— I don't know."

"I know how to change a tire. I was just curious. My brother called me this morning, at four forty a.m., because he didn't know how."

Shua laughed. "That's the Moshe I know. Brilliant mind, but not all that connected to his body."

I snickered a little, because that was the *perfect* way to sum up Moshe. His was the kind of brain you wanted to preserve in a jar for future generations to study. But sometimes he forgot that he still needed to use it to send important signals to the rest of him.

I was laughing out loud in the hall, and I looked around self-consciously, but I was the only one there. Everybody else had gone: home, to rehearsal, to story club.

"Would you really come get me if I had a flat tire?" I asked, leaning back against a locker.

"Of course. I'd do that for any of my—"

He cut himself off. I desperately wanted to replay that last second of my life, so I could try to listen more carefully. What was that last word going to be? Any of his *what*? I felt like he was starting to say an F sound. "Friend" starts with that sound. But so does "Friend's sister," and he was—or had been—friends with Moshe.

"I'd help any of my study partners too," I said. I knew I was taking a leap, and I definitely questioned my own motivations, but I said the next thing anyway: "Can I come over again? Maybe on Shabbos?"

He didn't answer.

There was silence on the line, and if it continued, I would collapse and die on the floor.

"Shua. Shabbos. Yes or no."

"Oh! Sure. Yeah. Of course. I—yeah, sure. After shul? Or were you thinking—"

"Either. Gotta go," I said, and I hung up. I'd text him later to apologize, and to confirm a time.

But right now, Miri Moritz was running toward me at an impressive speed. She walked with a composed elegance. But she did not run that way. With every stride, she swung her legs out to the side like she was trying to kick over invisible traffic cones.

She was crying audibly, and as she ran she made a rhythmic sobbing sound, like an ambulance over a series of speed bumps. When she saw me, she ducked her head down to the side, leaning away from me, and covered her face with her arm as though, this way, I wouldn't see her. Or, I'd see her but not recognize her.

"Miri," I said. When she didn't stop, I said it again. "Miri."

The hallway wasn't that wide. She slowed down so she didn't run into me, but she kept her arm draped over her eyes. She looked like the boys when they played hide-and-seek, where they just covered their eyes and thought that constituted hiding. It was less cute when Miri did it, and it was made worse by all of the anguished sounds she was making.

I was used to girls at school coming to me for help or advice, but not like this. This mid-hallway charge was unusual. I wasn't sure if she even wanted me to say anything, but when I stepped aside and gave her a clear path past me, she stayed where she was, heaving into the crook of her elbow.

"Are you okay?" I asked.

She didn't answer. I guess the answer was self-evident. People who were okay didn't usually try to hide themselves with their own arms while they poured tears onto the floor and leaned against the wall like they'd collapse without its support.

"What happened?" I asked. I could hear that my voice was full of practiced sympathy, but I didn't actually feel it. The last time I'd interacted with Miri, she'd tried to shame me for not pulling my weight in the community.

I watched her chest heave as she struggled to breathe.

"Can you tell me what happened?"

"My life . . ." she said. "It's—it's . . . over."

"I'm sure that's not true," I said. I reached out to her. Even though she couldn't actually see me, she somehow sensed my arm, and leaned hers toward me so it could be held.

"Why?" she asked. "Why? I don't—I don't understand."

"Miri. I can't help if you don't tell me what's going on."

It looked like Miri was trying to tell me. She pulled her arm away from her eyes and took some deep breaths. But after a few moments, she just shook her head and continued her journey down the hall, picking up pace as she went.

Sooner or later, I'd need to know what was going on so I could help solve the problem. So I decided to do some investigating, and went the opposite direction, the way she'd come. I took the little half flight of stairs that went down to the cafetorium.

I tossed my backpack onto one of the cafeteria tables near the front and slid into the seat next to Dassi. Dassi was in the productions because of Shira, but she never had a speaking part. Today she had Khan Academy open on a Chromebook and a notebook open in her lap. The stuff on the screen was definitely not what we'd been doing in class. Miss Simpson gave Dassi what she called "enrichment."

Mrs. Gomes was up on stage giving out directions. "Shira. Shira," she said, with her hand clamped on Shira's arm. "Listen." Mrs. Gomes was from Israel, and she spoke English with the slightest accent. You only heard it in certain words, like Shira's name, which she said with the emphasis on the second syllable: Shi-RAH. "Shira, you are the matriarch. You are a *queen*. You rule the family. You rule the village. Chin *up*. Rivka. Rivka!"

Rivka Bloom stepped forward out of the crowd of girls, but she did so cautiously. She eyed Mrs. Gomes's viselike grip warily.

"To everybody else, she may be a queen, but not to you. You are the eldest daughter. You are *strong*. You do not fear her."

Rivka feared *something*, but I didn't know if it was Shira or Mrs. Gomes.

The productions were all very similar. The protagonists were generally facing two threats: one from within, one from without. There was always an internal issue, drama *among* the Jews. And then there was an outside issue, usually non-Jews oppressing the Jews. Through their faith in God and dedication to Torah, the protagonists overcame their adversity. There was comfort in the consistency of the productions. You knew that the good people would end up happy, with their faith and family intact.

When me and Mrs. Gomes had looked through different options, I'd liked the complexity of the frayed mother-daughter relationship in this one, and the way it resolved. Rivka would repair her relationship with Shira, and together they'd save the village from the marauding gentiles.

That was, if Rivka could get up the courage to be within ten feet of Shira.

But I'd thought Shira was supposed to be the daughter, and Miri was supposed to be the mother.

Suddenly I wondered if . . . if it was me. Had *I* done it? Is that why Miri was crying?

Had someone watched my Miri video? That would mean that person's phone wasn't filtered either. But even if somebody had watched it, how would they know it was about Miri? There had to be thousands of Orthodox Miris—not to mention other *M*s: Menas and Malkas and Menuchas—all over the country. My TikTok could have been from anywhere.

"Chorus off stage," called Mrs. Gomes. "Enter when Shira starts singing. Rivka, I *love* how sad you look—so, so sad—but you need to project strength also."

"What happened?" I asked Dassi in a whisper. I was glad I didn't have to speak in my normal voice, because I didn't think I could keep it steady.

"I don't know. It was right when rehearsal was starting. Everyone was on stage except Mrs. Gomes and Miri. They were off behind the curtains, stage right. Then Miri just started crying *really* loud, and she ran off stage and out the door, and now Shira is queen."

"There isn't a queen in this one. She's just supposed to act queen-*like*."

"Shouldn't be a problem for her either way," Dassi said. "She doesn't even have to act."

I would have laughed—Dassi was funny in her deadpan

way—but I felt too sick to laugh. I was thinking about the way Mrs. Gomes had acted at JHR on Sunday, and the way Miri had shielded her face and cowered against the hallway wall, and I was suddenly terrified that somehow they were connected, to each other, to me.

I studied Dassi's face to see if she knew anything about the cause of Miri's demise. I wanted to ask her outright, to see if she'd somehow heard about the video, if she'd seen it, if somebody had mentioned it to her. But I couldn't think of a good way to ask the question without suggesting that *I* knew something about it.

I was afraid. I was scared of what I might have caused. And then I was scared that the people I wanted to take that fear away for me were the wrong people.

Before, that person had been Esti, *always* Esti. If she were here, she'd put her tiny arms around me, and hold me, and coo in my ear like I was a little girl. She would literally squeeze the fear out of me.

But now I thought of different arms. I wasn't supposed to want those arms, and it made me physically uncomfortable thinking about them. I felt like I was going to start squirming in my seat, like a little girl who didn't know what to do with her feelings.

Because I wanted to lie on Mickey's bed and stare at her ceiling while we watched TikTok videos on her phone. I wanted to watch the one where the pet parrot identifies objects made of glass and says the word "glass" repeatedly in a silly voice. I wanted our hair to splay out above us on the bed like we were wearing headdresses. I wanted her hair to intertwine with mine as we lost ourselves in the little slices of life we saw through the window of her iPhone.

Because I *really* wanted to sit in Shua's spartan basement while he read to me from ancient books. And I admitted this to myself, because I wouldn't actually *do* it: when he ran his finger over the text, I didn't want to watch a spider move along the wall. I wanted to watch his soft hands move along the page. When he straightened up to ponder a particularly interesting rabbinical observation, I wanted to lean against him. I wanted to put my head to his chest and listen to his heartbeat and see if I could hear anything else, maybe see if his self-assuredness made some kind of comforting sound. I knew that if I could create that moment, I would feel safe and secure in it.

I got up. I wanted to get out of rehearsal before Mrs. Gomes saw me and paused the whole thing to ask me about my fundraising progress. As I walked out, I composed and deleted a series of texts to Shua. I finally settled on one and hit send. 8:30 on Friday night? Just cause no1 will see me that way.

The Friday night part had nothing to do with the darkness. I just couldn't wait all the way until Saturday to see him. If I could have thought of a single reasonable excuse, I'd have called an Uber right then and paid the driver cash to speed through every traffic light and drive me directly into Shua's basement right that second.

I'd give the driver extra to compensate for the damage his car would sustain going down the stairs.

CHAPTER 25

IT WAS THE WORST SHABBOS SUPPER I could remember. The little guys kept distracting me, and I completely forgot to baste the chickens. Even the dark meat was dry. Nobody said anything about it, but I knew both my parents blamed me.

The Shabbos supper table was quiet and subdued. This was the first time I could remember not having a single guest. The dining room felt too big, like there was extra space between us. There was *literally* more space between us, but I didn't think that was why.

The Kornblatts and Cantors were supposed to be there, but I think they'd canceled last minute. I didn't exactly miss them—if I never saw Bina again, that would be fine with me.

I looked over at the place Bina would have occupied next to my mother. When we'd all started eating, and we reached the point where my father usually started a discussion, he said nothing. He just ate. We were all trying to make eye contact with him, but he returned none of it, reserving it for the too-dry chicken.

"Where's Bina?" I asked, hoping that was a safe topic.

It was not a safe topic. My father winced noticeably but said nothing.

"Can I ask what might have—"

"Not now, Yocheved. I'll thank you to leave that subject alone."

I left that subject alone. And all other subjects. So did

everybody else. The only sounds were the clinkings of silverware on plates and bowls.

My mom and I put the boys down together. We took turns reading to them. When I came back downstairs, Nachi and Abba were having a quiet discussion, probably about Torah. I paused to watch them with their heads bowed together.

I stood in the front hall and tried to decide if I needed to make an excuse. Should I say I left a book at Shira's or Dassi's? They both lived nearby. But when neither my dad nor Nachi looked up, I didn't bother. I just threw on my new puffer jacket and stepped out into the night.

CHAPTER 26

THEY SAY THAT CURIOSITY KILLED THE cat. I always figured that the cat died of curiosity because cats are just really dumb, and are probably susceptible to death by lots of innocuous things, not because there was anything inherently dangerous about curiosity.

But I was learning differently.

I took an indirect route to the Holtzmans'. I walked in the street. The street wasn't wet but it had a slick look to it, the streetlights reflecting on the dark asphalt.

I decided to make a detour.

I took a right on Lower Glanamman, and the house I was looking for was one in from the corner. It was a duplex.

Rather than use the front walk, I cut through the yard and approached from the side. I walked around the perimeter of the house. It was Bina's place, but there didn't appear to be anybody home. The rest of the house was pitch-black. I guess there *could* have been somebody home, but who spends the Sabbath in complete darkness?

I didn't know what I was trying to figure out exactly, but I completed my loop, walking along the side of the house, then across the grass to the sidewalk. The house didn't have a driveway, and there were three cars parked at the curb. I almost cried out loud when I realized that one of them was occupied.

I only noticed because there was a light in the car. But it wasn't a steady light, like a car light left on. It was a random and occasional light, like there was a firefly trapped in the vehicle. But it was the wrong season for fireflies.

There was a person just sitting in the car.

I guess it wasn't against the rules to just sit in your car on the Sabbath. But it was definitely weird. Plus, the automatic setting was usually that a car light turned on when you opened the door, and that illumination was a clear Shabbos violation.

As I stood on the sidewalk, I tried to decide which was more shocking: encountering a person just sitting in a car on the Sabbath, or that the person was Rivka Bloom.

I wanted to make sure I hadn't seen wrong, so I took a step closer. Rivka—it was definitely Rivka—brought something to her mouth. When she did, the object lit up. Rivka put the object back down and let a cloud of vapor slip out of her mouth. Then she closed her eyes and pressed her head back against the headrest.

My feet told me to move, but I didn't, and when Rivka opened her eyes again, she saw me.

The Rivka of two seconds before, the vaping Rivka, was not a girl I knew. But this Rivka was very familiar. She was terrified, and her eyes darted back and forth like she was looking for an escape route.

Cars have many exits, but she was boxed in by the laws of Shabbos. If she opened the door, it would illuminate the overhead light. She'd have to turn the car battery on to roll down a window. I think her best bet, halachically, would have been to smash one of the windows.

I was rooting for that outcome. Whatever was compelling Rivka to vape alone in a car on Shabbos, I wanted to see it possess her into bashing out a car window.

But that's not what happened.

I'd already seen Rivka violate the Sabbath when she ignited the vape and turned its light on. And I could see in her eyes that she knew I'd seen that. Still, she didn't seem to want me to watch her do it again. The vape remained out of sight. Rivka didn't reach for the door. She just sat there.

At first, she kept her eyes down at her lap, but then she brought them up to meet mine. She was mouthing words to me, but the windshield distorted her face a little, and I couldn't read them. But her eyes made it clear. She was saying, "Please." She was asking me not to tell, to keep this between us.

And I guess I could have given her some kind of assurance, one of the Gold family solemn nods.

But I didn't. I just turned and walked down the block.

CHAPTER 27

WHEN I WAS SEVEN, I BROKE my arm. I tripped on the playground and smashed it into a spinning merry-go-round. In the moment, I was pretty sure it was broken. It didn't feel like my usual, intact arm felt. We went to the emergency room and they took X-rays. The doctor projected the images for me and my mom, and they clearly showed the radial and ulnar fractures.

The doctor set the bones back in place, put a cast on the arm, and told us it would be fixed in two months.

As I opened Shua's basement hatch, I wondered if my faith was broken. It didn't feel like my usual, intact faith. But there was no X-ray I could use to be sure, or to see where the fractures were.

And if my Judaism was broken, how would I fix it? It didn't seem as simple as setting it, immobilizing it, and waiting.

"Man. Are you *okay*?" Shua asked as soon as I appeared at the bottom of the outdoor steps.

I tried to look down at myself to see if I was okay. Maybe my dress looked off-kilter, or maybe my spiritual fractures were visible.

"I think so," I offered.

"You don't look okay," he said. He'd been bent over his coffee table, but now he was sitting up straight, alert. He had his head cocked to the side, examining me through squinted eyes. And I realized he wasn't looking at my dress to see if it was ruffled. He was looking at *me*, and he could see how I felt, that something had thrown me off and I didn't know how to get back on. This was just not the look I usually got when I walked into a room. And the look felt amazing, and I felt myself breaking down, my composure crumbling like a building in one of those implosion videos where the whole thing just collapses in on itself.

I said nothing, but I stumbled over to the coffee table, threw myself down on the floor, and let myself feel the despair I'd held off on the walk over. I could feel its weight, pressing me down into Shua's musty carpet.

"What's wrong?" he asked.

He had one light on, a lamp that illuminated his bed and his coffee table, and just enough of the rest of the room that you could see your way to and from the bathroom. His face was mostly in shadow. I worried that it would be hard for him to sleep with the light so close to his bed, but I saw that it was on a Shabbos timer, so it would go off automatically.

"Everything," I said.

"Not everything," he said. "You're here with me."

"But I shouldn't be."

"Maybe. If you feel that way, maybe we should . . . not do this. Because I like to justify my decisions." He gestured at the book open on his coffee table. "I need to be able to at least argue to myself that I'm doing the right thing."

I turned over on my side, away from him.

I didn't really want to look at him but wasn't sure why. Was it because the sympathetic lines on his face would make me fall apart? Was it because if I looked at him, I'd want to do things

I knew I shouldn't do? Was it because if I ever saw Esti again, I'd have to admit that following the rules, waiting until marriage, wasn't quite as easy as I'd thought?

"Do you want to tell me what's wrong?"

"I want to, but I—I don't know."

"You don't trust me?" he asked.

Of course I trusted him. I trusted him implicitly, in a way that really scared me. I wanted to tell him everything. Not just about the TikTok videos and their potential consequences, but all the feelings that made me create them in the first place, and how I kept doing things that were wrong but felt right, and I was getting those two opposite things confused. And I wanted to tell him about the little things too, the ones that didn't even matter at all, like how the faux-fur on my new jacket kept making my hair all frizzy in the dry winter air.

But the more I told him, the closer I felt to him. And the closer I felt to him, the more I was reminded, by an instinct I couldn't shake, that I wasn't supposed to be close to him.

"Even if you don't trust me," he said, "you've got so much dirt on me. You could just blackmail me."

I sat up to face him. We were both silent.

"Who was the best student at your yeshiva?" I asked.

Shua's eyes were on the book in front of him. But he wasn't reading it. It was more like he was watching it. And I was watching him. "Probably me," he said. "The rabbis loved me, right up until they didn't."

"And your classmates? What did they think?"

"They liked me okay, I think."

I took it to mean that he was very popular, that everybody wanted to study with him. It didn't surprise me.

"And did you want to be the best?"

"Yeah," he said reluctantly.

"And did people resent you if you tried to be better than them, if you wanted to impress people, if you tried to show them how great you could be?"

"I don't understand," he said. "It's not that I don't want to answer. I just don't know what you're asking."

I was trying to make a point without saying it directly. It wasn't working. I took a deep breath and said, "It's not like that for me. You and me, we're both being asked to walk a certain path, but I feel like mine is more narrow. I'm supposed to be smart, but not *too* smart. I'm supposed to be ambitious, but I need to make sure my ambitions don't step over anybody else's. I need to have my own opinions, but not be too forceful with them. I'm supposed to be pretty, but not too pretty."

Shua looked up from his book, eyeing me. I wished I hadn't said the pretty part, because now I was wondering if he was judging my prettiness, and it was distracting me from the point I was trying to make.

"And if that's what HaShem wants from me, fine," I said. "But what if it's just what the people around me *think* HaShem wants from me? Like, the difference between those two never used to feel important. I assumed they were the same thing. If my dad said that's what HaShem said, that was good enough for me. But now I'm not sure, and it's . . . I'm not sure what the right word is. Is it bothering me? Is it tormenting me? I think it's something in the middle, but closer to torment."

"Can I show you something?" he asked, motioning first to his book, then to a spot next to him on the bed.

I said nothing. I hesitated, but then I found myself moving in the direction of his coffee table, and I did sit on the bed. Not *with* him. Just on the same horizontal surface. I didn't like that the surface was a bed. That was the most personal of padded surfaces. I tried to tell myself, and God, that, *really*, there was no difference between, say, a couch cushion and a mattress. Both had fabric on the outside, foam and/or springs inside. But I was having trouble convincing myself. I'd sat on the same couch as a boy before, and it had *not* felt like this. It had been *way* easier to breathe on the couch, and I don't remember my hands sweating this much.

"It's like when they kicked me out of the yeshiva in Jerusalem. I feel like that's when it started, but maybe it was before that. I don't know."

He was quiet for a moment. I didn't know how to respond, but he seemed comfortable with the silence. I loved that he was comfortable with silence.

"So I was breaking the filters on kids' phones. I accepted money for it—it was a service. The rabbis found out, and they called me into an office. They showed me their written policy, showed me where I'd violated it. It was a whole long thing, but it could have just been the line you see on those bumper stickers: 'Kosher phone. Kosher home.'"

"'Kosher Yid,'" I finished for him.

"I knew that might happen, so I was prepared. I literally brought books with me. I quoted Torah to them. I'll show you the exact line I showed them."

He pointed at the book, but I looked at him, not the page.

"It asks, 'Can it enter your mind that a person can go to a judge that is not alive in his days?' What it means is that—"

"You shouldn't be judged by dead people from another time."

"Yep. Now, the rabbis pointed out that they were alive, which was true. But I explained that I have to be judged in my own age. I live in a modern world. I can't be judged by the standards of an old one."

"But they judged you anyway."

"Yeah."

"I'm sorry," I said. The bed had no back support, so I leaned a little to my left, reaching my hand down to the mattress for support. It came dangerously close to Shua's. I think I felt the hair on the back of his hand just graze me, but he didn't seem to notice.

"That's not even the problem. I was ready for any punishment, except the one they gave me. You know, he probably doesn't remember, but your father taught me and Moshe something I'll always remember."

Now it felt like my dad was in *this* room, conjured by Shua's memory, and I did not appreciate his presence. I looked down at the inch of space between my hand and Shua's pants, imagining a miniature version of my rabbi dad in that space.

"He said, if your argument cannot convince your audience, then the flaw is with your argument, not with your audience."

"There's no way he said that. He's never spoken a sentence that concise."

The hint of a smile appeared on Shua's face, the first I'd seen since I came down the stone steps. "Well, no. It was part of an extended metaphor about an overturned wagon and an ox with a broken leg, but that's what I took from it. What I'm saying is, I expected the rabbis to punish me in a way that kept me close, that convinced me, that showed me the righteousness of their ways, that persuaded me that the way to be a good Jew was *their* way."

"But they kicked you out."

"I had to leave that day. My parents are furious at me. I see their anger every time I go upstairs. Only Chani treats me completely normal, and I think it's just because she doesn't want it to be awkward when I drive her places, or when she comes down here to do the laundry."

"I like it down here," I said. It was kind of a non sequitur. It was a weird thing to say. But I did envy him that he had his own space.

"Yeah?" he said, looking around like he was seeing it for the first time.

"Yeah," I said. "It's quiet." All I heard was the faint ticking of the light timer, and the sound of my own heartbeat, which was a little faster than usual. I looked at Shua's chest, watched it rise and fall, and wondered if I could hear him breathing or if I just *thought* I could. Part of me wanted to reach out and put my hand on his chest, feel him breathe. Part of me knew that was a strange thing to want, a wrong thing to want, but I felt my hand reaching out toward him anyway.

My fingers were shaking as they touched his starched shirt. Now I did hear his breath, a sharp intake. We'd both turned our heads toward each other, and our eyes were locked together like we were engaged in a staring contest. I knew I should look away, but I *really* didn't want to.

As though I was drowning, and he was a life preserver, I gripped his shirt tighter.

He leaned in toward me.

The light ticked off, plunging us into darkness.

Only God knew for sure exactly what happened next. I could only deduce from the sounds and from my own physical pain.

I leapt off the bed and started moving away from it, but the coffee table still existed in the dark, and my shin smashed into it. My leg exploded in pain. I screamed. I tumbled over the table and thudded down onto the floor. I screamed again. The carpet was thin, and when my elbow came down it felt the concrete underneath rather than the carpet on top.

Now that I was writhing on the floor, I had time to process the sounds that Shua had been making. Somehow he'd smashed the lightbulb, probably with his head, and something had whacked into the bed's metal headboard, because it was ringing like a gong, harmonizing with the moaning sounds that Shua was producing.

I was still on the floor, trying to decide which of my feelings—pain, horror, shame, amusement—I was going to let take over, when the door to the basement opened from above, and somebody stepped onto the top step.

"What are you *doing* down there?" asked Chani.

"I'm fine, thank you," Shua said.

"That doesn't answer the question."

Shua said nothing. I tried not to express my pain audibly, but it was hard. There was so much of it.

"Do you want me to wait while you invent a plausible explanation?" Chani asked.

"No. I want you to leave me alone."

There was a silence. Was it more awkward than the previous one? Or was I just *thinking* it was more awkward? Did Chani hear me call out? Did she know I was here?

Chani headed down two more steps. "You might need first aid. Remember, I'm—"

"Certified? Really? You hadn't told me."

"Should I . . . go get my kit?"

"Yeah. *Yes.* Go get your kit."

Chani's feet hustled back up the stairs through the door. A faint light came down the stairs and I could just make out Shua, kneeling next to his bed, rubbing his temple.

"That was smart," I whispered, picking myself up off the floor.

"No, well, yeah, but I think I'm actually bleeding."

"Oh," I said, in lieu of goodbye. Because I could hear Chani's feet upstairs, moving closer to the basement door, and I headed for the other basement door.

CHAPTER 28

WHEN SHABBOS ENDED ON SATURDAY NIGHT, I went straight to the bathroom. It was the first time I'd had a chance to examine my injuries. They weren't bad: just bruises, purple marks on my shin and elbow. They didn't even hurt anymore.

What hurt was the shame, from what I'd done, from what I almost did. I'd felt it all day. It was worst in the synagogue, where God felt closer, but it was also pretty bad in my living room, where my father was studying and talking about Torah with Nachi and a couple other men. The sin crawled on my skin, creeping around like something with many small legs. But the shame was subcutaneous. It was *in* me, like a bruise somewhere at my core, growing, expanding, black and purple like the marks on my leg and arm.

And, as usual these days, I had nobody to talk about any of it with. Nobody I was supposed to talk about it with. Nobody who would understand *and* keep my secret.

I pulled out my phone.

"R was seen in her car on Shabbos. Don't worry, she wasn't driving. Or, do worry, because she was vaping. But I guess the question is: Which part should we worry *about*? The violation of the laws of Shabbos? The health effects of nicotine? We do need to worry, but not about that. We need to worry about whatever it was that made her sneak out at night on Shabbos to sit in the dark in a parked car and vape alone. And we need to worry that it's *us*, that *we're* the ones who made her do that."

Rivka wasn't a hypocrite. Rivka was . . . I didn't know what Rivka was. I'd known Rivka my whole life, but I didn't *know* Rivka. The closest I'd felt to knowing her was when I was standing in the street in the dark, and I watched her press her head back against the headrest of her family's car. I'd never tried the drug that was in the vape, but I knew that feeling, the need to relieve the pressure, to release it out into the air, in vapor or video form.

I posted the video and waited for the usual feeling of release that accompanied it. But this TikTok felt different, and my usual relief started to feel more like regret. I took Rivka's "please" to mean "please don't tell anybody about this." I thought it might make my own shame go away if I shared Rivka's in a sympathetic way. But if anything, it just added to it.

But before I had a chance to take it down, the video took off. Lots of views. Lots of reactions. Just like with the other TikToks, there were a lot of similar stories, ones that were eating away at the commenters. And just like with the other posts, there were a lot of people who chastised me for sharing, for taking something private and making it public, for airing "dirty laundry."

I was just starting to process the initial comments when my phone rang. "I wanted to see if you think this is cool or creepy," Mickey said when I picked up. "I set an alert on my phone that tells me when Shabbat is over."

It was a tough call between those two, but I felt myself smiling a little, so I said, "Cool."

"Are you free? Do you want to come over?"

I arrived at Mickey's ten minutes later. Her mother greeted me at the door, but she seemed like she was in the middle of something, so she only said hi and indicated that Mickey was upstairs.

I stood in Mickey's doorway. I was a little scared to go into the room, because it appeared to contain smog. I think it was a combination of perfume and hair spray. The scent was strong enough that it stung as I breathed.

Mickey was standing in front of the mirror, applying lipstick to a fully made-up face. Her top was a one-garment scandal. It resembled a shirt, but all of the center fabric was missing. The black material went over her shoulders and a little way down her arms. The front of it covered about 60 percent of her boobs, and just about nothing else. The rest of her chest and stomach were completely bare. The only thing keeping it from opening up entirely was a single string across her sternum.

She was wearing jeans. They sat at her hips, but the buttons were undone. I could see the top of her underwear. The underwear said "ho hoes" on them and had little pictures of packaged cakes.

"Do I look cute?" she asked, turning to face me.

I had no idea how to answer that question. "Don't you think that those underwear make you seem like you're something to be eaten?" I offered. "A sugary treat?"

"Am I not though?" she asked, and popped her hip out at me. "I thought you'd be more likely to say yes if you were already here. Will you come out with me?" she asked.

"Out?" I said, like I didn't know that word.

"Out. To a party. Do you like dancing?"

I leaned against the doorframe and considered. I did like

dancing. But I wasn't sure if Mickey and I had the same idea of what dancing *was*. When I thought of dancing, I thought of spinning around with my female relatives at weddings, holding hands, rejoicing in the celebration of another Jewish covenant.

On the one hand, I needed *something* to do. I didn't want to sit around alone in my bedroom. And Mickey was the closest thing I had to a friend right now.

"Do you know how scary you are when you just stare at me and say nothing? I hope you know how terrifying it is. It's like your superpower, and you should know how powerful it is."

On the other hand, was this how it started? Grabbing Shua's shirt, going to this dancing party? Was that how you ended up at the bottom of the slippery slope, your Judaism shattered in a way that no cast could fix?

"Please?" Mickey asked. "I haven't gone out since Tess and Nick happened."

I stepped into the room and stood behind Mickey so I could look in the mirror too. I wanted to know if she wanted me to come with her because she liked spending time with me, or because she was just another person who needed my support.

"I know what you think," Mickey said.

She thought I was still focused on her outfit.

"But we should all be allowed to dress in a way that makes us feel good, that makes us feel strong. We shouldn't have to think about how it'll make other people think or react. I like my body. I think I look good. It makes me feel empowered."

"You're going to feel cold. That's how you're going to feel. Do you not worry that a guy will just . . ." I wasn't sure how to dance around this one, so I just asked. "Are you worried you'll get groped or whatever?"

Mickey didn't look offended at all. Her reflection shrugged at me in the mirror. "I think you always have to be aware of your surroundings, and not put yourself in dangerous situations. But I'm also not gonna be bullied into not wearing something because it'll be too alluring, and people just won't be able to stop themselves from jumping on me. And hey, there's nothing wrong with a little groping. Or a *lot* of groping, so long as it's consensual."

Normally, I would have had to imagine the look on my face, but I was standing in front of a mirror, so I could see it. But where I expected to look horrified, I just looked thoughtful.

I was picturing Mickey and some boy with their hands all over each other. "But, why?" I asked. "You're not going to marry the gropist. So what's the . . . goal?"

"There is no goal. It's just fun."

If the light hadn't flicked off, would I have kissed Shua? Would he have put his arms around me? Would my hand have stayed on his shirt, or embarked on further explorations? I had to admit that it might have been fun to find out. But I guess that was the thing that made Mickey's life and mine so different, the reason we still had to be careful talking to each other: Mickey thought about what was fun instead of what was right. No, that wasn't fair. She thought about what was right. She just didn't think about what God said was right.

If you lived your life that way, did that make you feel free? Or did it make you feel lost, without direction or purpose?

"I'll go," I said.

Mickey let out a little squeal and grabbed me by both arms. "This is so fun," she said. "But you can't wear that."

I looked at myself. I was wearing a long, dark, loose dress. Dark tights. Boots with a short heel, good for walking. It was not my brightest Shabbos outfit, but I hadn't been in the mood to wear something colorful.

I said nothing. I was exercising my superpower, trying to get Mickey to let me wear what I wanted.

But instead, her eyes lit up, and the beginnings of a mischievous smile appeared at the edges of her bright pink lips. "Have you ever worn jeans?" she asked. And I saw her appraising my body, looking my figure up and down. The joke was on her, because you couldn't see much of it under my dress, which was the point.

That was one of the things I liked about being Orthodox. I cared if I looked good, but I never stared at my body and wondered if it met certain standards.

But I did find myself wondering what I might look like in a pair of jeans, and if this was the right time to find out. I tried to imagine what Shua would think if I walked into his basement wearing jeans. Would he stare at my hips? Would he run to his bookshelf for a book, trying to find out for himself if it was okay for me to dress that way?

"I don't own any," I said. "And I *definitely* won't fit into yours. I know dark colors are slimming," I went on, waving my hand at my dress, "but I think my calves are wider than your thighs."

"I think my sister's about your size. Come."

I followed Mickey past the hallway bathroom to another

bedroom. It was smaller than Mickey's, and it had a *lot* of clothing. Some of the clothes were on shelves along the wall, but some were in giant plastic bags, spilling out onto the floor.

Mickey overturned one of the trash bags and started rifling through its contents. There didn't seem to be an organizational system. She was tossing around shirts, leggings, bras. Finally, she found what she was looking for, and held them up: a pair of dark blue jeans. "Try these on," she said, handing them to me.

She seemed to think I was going to do that *in front* of her.

"Fine. Use the bathroom. But take this top. You can't wear your muumuu over your jeans. It defeats the purpose."

"Which is what again?" I asked.

But Mickey only shook her head. And I figured I'd gone this far. I might as well see what it felt like.

It felt weird.

I thought it might feel like thicker tights—those were pantlike in a way. But this was different. First, the jeans were kind of hard to put on. I had to shimmy into them, but once I pulled them over my hips, they buttoned up over my stomach. The fabric was scratchy on the inside.

I took a step to the side. Then a step back. There was no swish of a skirt, or flow of a dress. Just my legs, slicing back and forth like scissors. I was a combination of horrified and giddy at the idea of going out in the world like this. I felt like I was wearing a costume, like it was Purim and I was dressing up as a gentile.

I reminded myself that Mickey was Jewish, that her mother was a rabbi. Maybe it was more like I had the lead in the musical, and I was stepping out on stage to perform my big song.

It is I, Yoyo, and this is what my legs look like.

I pulled the top she gave me over my head. I appreciated that she'd given me a whole shirt, not just part of one. The sleeves were tznius, long to the wrists. But the collar was a V-neck. It dipped down farther than a neckline should, but you could only see the very tops of my boobs. It wasn't *that* scandalous, but maybe my standards had changed, shifted just a little.

Mickey knocked on the door. I must have been staring at myself. And how could you blame me? My appearance was so unusual, it defied belief. Like, I could literally see myself and still wasn't convinced it was actually me. This was not how Yoyo Gold dressed. This was not how *Golds* dressed. This was not how a Jewish girl dressed. But then there was a Jewish girl knocking on the door who said she felt empowered this way.

I unlocked the door.

Mickey opened it. "Damn," she said. And she was doing an exaggerated raising of her eyebrows. "You look hot."

I was having trouble processing all of this. I was leaning forward, supporting myself with my hands on the edge of the sink. Part of me wanted to pull my dress right back over this outfit. But part of me wanted to go down into Shua's basement and show off my new look, to see if he had the same reaction that Mickey did.

And Mickey seemed impatient. She was typing frantically on her phone as she talked. "Cassidy is going to pick us up. She never drinks or does drugs. Do you need to be home at a certain time?"

The boys were already down, so I honestly didn't think it mattered. I could always say I fell asleep on somebody's couch or something.

"I'll take your silence to mean you do not have a curfew."

I followed Mickey down the stairs. Mickey's mom looked up from her spot on the couch. I was bracing for her to say something about my clothes, or Mickey's clothes.

But she said nothing about clothing. "Where are you off to?" she asked.

"Out," Mickey said, and she took two strides toward the door. I followed, because I didn't know what to say. I knew the rules for conversation with my friends' parents—I'd known them all for at least a decade. But Mickey's mom was an unknown entity.

Mickey opened the front door, but her mother cleared her throat. "As your mother, I have a right to know where you're going and who you're with."

Mickey gave her mom the same look of mischief she'd given me earlier. "A place," she said. "With people."

I expected her mom to get up and drag Mickey back inside. But she didn't. "Mick," she said, "we've *talked* about this. With the new congregation, you have to remember it's a small world. You have a responsibility to think carefully about who you're with, and what's—"

"You don't want me to tag the synagogue's official account in my selfies?"

"I just want you to think about the repercussions of your decisions," Mickey's mom said.

A car pulled up at the curb, and Mickey said, "We gotta go, Ma. Cassidy is here. She's one of the people with whom we will be going to the place."

"Lord," her mom said, shaking her head.

"You literally have an app that *shows* you where I am."

"But I want to *trust* you, and it's less about where you are and more about what you're doing when—"

But Mickey pulled me out the front door and closed it before I heard the end of the sentence.

"How do I get her off my back?" Mickey asked me, as we walked to the curb.

"I don't know," I said. "I manage by just doing what my dad expects, but I feel like that's not really what you're looking for."

We'd reached the car, and Mickey stopped with her hand on the passenger door. "Is that what you're doing now?" she asked. "What your dad expects?"

She said it with a big grin and it reminded me of Esti, and I couldn't help but smile back.

"Maybe I should have used the past tense," I said.

CHAPTER 29

CASSIDY WAS PLAYING MUSIC VERY LOUDLY. As soon as Mickey was in the car, she started dancing to the song, shimmying around in the passenger seat. Cassidy gave me a wave of her hand and pulled away from the curb. "You look different than in the candy TikToks," Cassidy said to me.

It was hard to hear Cassidy over the music, but I could just make out her words.

"I *feel* different," I said.

"You look cute."

"The jeans are Sarah's," Mickey explained.

By the time the song ended, we were there.

The house was a lot like Mickey's, a twin. We entered through the front door. "Kaden's parents are real chill," Cassidy explained. "They don't really pay attention to him, and they don't care if kids drink in their house. They might be out somewhere, or they might be upstairs, but they'll leave us alone."

"It's pretty sad, actually," Mickey said. "Very irresponsible."

"Our gain," said Cassidy, unconcerned. She led us through the living room and directly down into the basement.

The basement room was finished. Unlike Shua's, it was carpeted all the way across, and it contained fewer rakes. Along the walls were strung little LED lights. Mickey had similar ones in her room, and they could light up different colors.

The room was filled with kids our age. Some of the boys were wearing pants, but a couple of them were wearing gym shorts like they were going to spontaneously do basketball.

The girls were all dressed like Mickey and Cassidy. It was like they'd been given one of those math problems where it was like, "What's the smallest fence farmer Tom can use to enclose his pasture?" but the girls needed to figure out what was the smallest amount of fabric they could use to cover certain parts of their body.

Nobody was doing any math though. They were standing around drinking out of plastic cups, moving subconsciously to music from a Bluetooth speaker on the table. The table was full of liquor bottles.

I hung back a bit as Cassidy and Mickey walked toward the table. It was actually a Ping-Pong table, but the net had been removed to make room for the bottles. Mickey looked back over her shoulder at me. She grimaced. "I don't know if this stuff is kosher," she called to me.

Unless it was made from fruit or something, all liquor was kosher. I was taking chemistry: it was just grain, fermented and distilled.

I'd actually bet that Orthodox Jews did a lot more drinking than your average kids. Not *this* kind of drinking. And it was definitely more acceptable for boys to drink. But alcohol was an important part of many Jewish rituals. I knew the blessing over the wine before I'd heard of intoxication, before I knew about the liver.

The stuff on the table was not the kosher wine I was used to.

But both of the vodka bottles had hechshers on them, little symbols that indicated that they were legal. It was actually a funny distillation—pun intended—of the contradiction I was living more and more, where something could be legal in Jewish law but not secular law, or vice versa. I knew my dad would be pretty upset if he had a window into this basement, but he'd definitely be more concerned about the kosher status of the beverages—and about the jeans—than the fact that I was four years away from the legal drinking age.

I let Mickey pour me a mixture of vodka and Coke. I didn't like the taste, but I hadn't had a big supper, and pretty quickly I got a heady feeling of lightness, like the heavy things weighing me down were just the littlest bit less heavy. It was as though the sharp edges of the world were fuzzy, or padded like the corners of our living room coffee table when the boys first started walking.

Pretty quickly, I was enjoying myself.

Mickey introduced her friend Kaden. He was broader than I'd expected him to be, more muscular. He looked like he lifted weights. He was one of the guys in gym shorts. He smiled when Mickey introduced me, and looked totally at ease. He was cute.

He extended a hand.

I was thinking about how strong his handshake was when it dawned on me that I'd actually taken his hand. His hand was in my hand, and vice versa. It was a sudden and abrupt violation of a rule I'd always followed. But I'd done it without even thinking, and now I was shaking hands with a boy I'd never seen before, except in a TikTok video.

"You look different when you're not picking candy out of your teeth," he said.

It was a sudden reminder that he already knew what I looked like and had previously described me as a "sexy field hockey player." It gave his gaze a different feeling, and I wondered what he thought of me now, what he thought of this be-jeaned, non-tznius version of me. I didn't want to care what he thought, but I did.

Somebody called to Kaden from across the room, and he disappeared into the corner.

Mickey was spending a lot of the time on her phone. She was scrolling through various apps pretty frantically, but finally noticed me eyeing her. "I knew Tess wouldn't be here," she said. "But I thought Nick would be."

She was looking at Nick's social media, sleuthing to see if there was an explanation for his absence. Every so often, she looked over at the stairs, hoping, I guess, that he would suddenly be there.

"I know. I know," she said. "This is pathetic. Wasn't I just saying something about boys and self-worth? Or maybe I was just thinking it. But sometimes you can't help how you feel."

"Tell me about it," I said. Because when I put on these jeans, I thought about what Shua would think about them. And now that I'd had two cups of vodka and Coke, what I wanted to do was have more vodka and Coke, but with him. He was becoming this reference point in everything. I kind of had to pee. Did Shua have to pee right now? I'd had a lot of spinach for supper. Where did spinach rank in Shua's hierarchy of leafy green vegetables?

Mickey reached for my hand. "Let's dance," she said, pulling me into the middle of the room.

The basement was more crowded now, and people had had more alcohol, and the music was louder, and I was pretty sure the LED lights hadn't been flashing before.

The song was a hip-hop tune I didn't know. But it had a beat that was easy to move to. Mickey started moving her hips in a little circle that matched the pulse of the music.

She playfully danced over to me and brushed me on one of her little hip twirls.

Most of the dancing I saw around me involved lots of physical contact: butts against thighs, butts against butts, butts against crotches.

It felt safe to start dancing with Mickey, so I did. A song came on that I knew from TikTok, and I leaned forward and sang the lyrics to her, while she sang them to me, while we both moved our bodies to the music. It was something Esti and I used to do in her car, minus the dancing.

My worries were feeling lighter and lighter as I danced. I recognized some of the music, and Mickey and I were vibing, dancing in sync, even though we'd never danced together before.

I started to lose track of both time and place, and that felt pretty good. It was nice to not have to be hyper-vigilant, worrying about the other people around me who might need help.

At a certain point, this Nick person appeared on the stairs, like Mickey suspected he would. I didn't see his appeal. He had a dark, brooding look to him, but he also had these blond highlights in his hair. I guess they were supposed to look cool, but it really looked like he was trying to emulate a large cat species: a cheetah or leopard.

When Nick arrived, Mickey disappeared, and was replaced by Kaden. There was something about Kaden that reminded me of Shua, but I wasn't sure if it was *him*, really, or just that he was a boy and I was in his basement.

He helped me replenish my plastic cup as he replenished his. "Mickey said you were cool," he said, "clinking" his plastic cup with mine. I thought his eyes were moving up and down my body, but I was definitely feeling the effects of the alcohol, and not everything was as clear as it had been before I started drinking.

Kaden led me back to the dancing area, pulling me by the hand. I craned my neck to look around for Mickey, but I couldn't find her. And anyway, another song was on that I recognized, and liked, and Kaden wasn't a bad dancer for a boy. He had a good sense of rhythm, used his lower body rather than his upper, and managed not to spill his drink, even though it was filled to the brim.

He put his hand on my hip and I let him. I watched his fingers snake through one of my—Sarah's—belt loops. I closed my eyes and felt my body moving to the music, and felt the little bit of extra weight I was pulling around, his hand attached to my jeans in a way that should have felt like a violation, but just didn't.

I didn't feel violated when he slid his hand around to my back, or when he moved his body closer to mine, and I could smell his deodorant and see the tiny beads of sweat on his neck.

We danced like that for a while, with his hand on my lower back, his body against mine. He was warm and I could feel his pulse, which felt like it was in sync with the music, even though I knew that wasn't possible.

When I'd first started dancing, with Mickey, I'd been keenly aware of the people around me, wondering if they were looking at me, and if so, what they might think. But now I'd let all that go. My eyes were closed. I was in the dancing space of this suburban basement, but I could really have been anywhere.

There was another song I recognized, and I mouthed the lyrics into Kaden's neck. I opened my eyes to see that he was also singing along, and he flashed a little smile when he saw that I knew the words too.

Mouthing words was something you did with your mouth. And as we danced and mouthed the words, our mouths got closer until his was on mine, and mine on his, and I could feel his tongue moving in my mouth, but I wasn't sure if it was still trying to keep up with the lyrics, or if this was just how kissing worked, since this was my first time doing it.

Kaden steered us over to the couch. I only noticed when my legs found it, and I fell into a seated position. Kaden slid down next to me, and we kept kissing. I could hear his breathing, which was heavy and ragged, and feel his hands, which were clumsy and grabbing, and his lips, which were somehow both aggressive and soft. The kissing itself was a nice feeling, and so was the feeling of being wanted like that.

One of his hands was on my knee, and he started to slide it up my leg, climbing up the inside of my thigh. It sent a little electric shock through my body. Kaden felt it, and took it as encouragement, spreading his hand out, and bringing it farther up, reaching toward the buttons on my jeans.

It felt good, but that shock—even though it was a good

feeling—changed something in me. It was like a sudden reminder that the hands I wanted on me were a different boy's.

I grabbed Kaden's hand and put it back on my knee.

He paused kissing me. "Sorry," he whispered.

"It's okay," I said. "Just this, okay?"

"Yeah," he said, and he brought his mouth back to mine, but now it wasn't the same.

Ten seconds ago I'd been totally lost in the world of kissing. But now I was too aware: aware that his lips were not Shua's, aware that there were two other people on this couch. Two girls. One of them was on her phone. The other one looked sick, or too drunk, or sick because she was too drunk.

There weren't actually that many people in the room anymore, and I caught a few of them looking at me, but their faces were inscrutable because it was dark and I'd had a bunch to drink, and I looked around but I couldn't find Mickey, and I didn't know what time it was, and I knew I shouldn't be there, that I should never have come in the first place.

I pushed myself away from Kaden. He looked shocked and started to say something. It seemed apologetic. I wanted to respond, wanted to make eye contact with him, but my body was filled with a kind of panic that was brand new, and all-consuming, and I didn't have the headspace to deal with whatever he had to say.

Who *was* he, anyway? I didn't even know him.

I walked toward the stairs, my head on a swivel for Mickey. I found her upstairs in the kitchen. She was giggling. She had one hand on the fridge door. Her other hand held one of those vapes that looked almost like a pen. "Where's Cassidy?" I said.

"I want *cheese*, Yoyo," Mickey said. "But they only have those little single slices, and they aren't even *real* cheese."

"Should I just walk?" I asked.

"Nick!" Mickey shouted.

Nick was there. He'd appeared in the kitchen doorway right behind me.

"I'm cheeseless," Mickey cried. "Will you help?"

"Of course," he said, feigning deep concern. "Don't worry."

"My stuff is at your house," I said, but I didn't expect a response.

Mickey's eyes passed right over me and rested on Nick as he came around the kitchen island in her direction.

I went the other way, out into the night.

It was freezing. But my puffer jacket was at Mickey's house. So were my regular clothes. So was my purse. So was my parents' minivan, which I couldn't drive because I was drunk. I realized my phone was in the back pocket of my jeans. I guess that was one advantage of pants. Pockets. But the phone was too small and slid out too easily, and it wasn't my phone at all.

It was Mickey's sister's expired high school ID card. It must have been in there the whole time. I didn't know where my phone was.

I was about to start walking home when I realized that I didn't actually know where I was. The street looked just like all the other Colwyn or Tregaron streets, and I wasn't operating at my full navigational capacity.

I walked back into the house. At first I tried to find my phone, but I quickly gave up. I just needed to get home. I couldn't find Mickey, but I found a girl I didn't know, and she lent me her phone. The time on her screen said 2:04.

There were only two phone numbers I knew. One of them was Esti's. I dialed the other one and waited.

"Hello?" said Moshe.

"Hey, it's Yoyo. Can you give me Shua Holtzman's number?" I asked. "His new one? I sent it to you a while back."

Moshe hesitated. "Yeah, I think I have it. But . . . are you sure you want to be talking to him?"

I wasn't sure at *all*. But of the many bad solutions I could think of, that was the least bad. "Just give me his number. Please."

I put Moshe on speaker, and I punched the number into this girl's contacts as he read it out.

"Thanks," I said.

"No problem. Wait, what time is it there? And why—"

Of course *now* was the time he wanted to start thinking about the time difference.

I hung up on him and dialed Shua. He didn't pick up. I called again. Then again. He answered on the fourth try. "It's Yoyo," I said.

"Yoyo." I could picture him in his bed, his phone pressed to his ear, trying to come to terms with being awake. "Are you okay?" he asked.

"I have a flat tire," I told him.

"What are you doing driving now?"

"I don't really have a flat tire. But can you pick me up? I'm at a— Can you just pick me up? I really need a ride."

"Yeah," he said. "Of course. Of course. Where are you?"

I opened Google Maps on this girl's phone. I gave him the nearest corner, hung up, and handed the phone back to the girl.

I went back outside. I let out one gigantic breath, watching the cloud of vapor in the cold air. I walked to the stop sign at the corner and wrapped my arms around myself to try to keep warm. I stood there and felt the shame wash over me in real time. I could feel it eroding me, creating a hole through which I could feel my self-worth escaping.

Shua arrived a few minutes later. He reached across the console to open the door for me. As soon as I sat down in the passenger's seat, he opened his mouth to speak, but I cut him off. "I know I don't really have the right to ask this of you right now, but can you not ask me any questions? I know that I'm asking you a huge favor, and I woke you up in the middle of the night, and I'm asking you to sit with me alone in a car, and that's not really fair, but this is just a situation where it would be really—"

"I was just gonna say that there's a sweatshirt in the back seat if you're cold."

"Oh." I didn't deserve him. "I am cold."

He reached back and swiped a hoodie off the back seat. I unbuckled briefly to pull it on. It was big and fluffy, like a cotton-poly hug.

Shua drove me home in silence. He didn't ask me where I'd been or where my phone was or why I smelled like vodka and body odor. He didn't even really look at me, didn't openly notice my scoop-necked shirt or my jeans. When he pulled up to the curb, he said, "Do you have a key?"

My key was in my purse, back at Mickey's house. "There's one hidden in a flowerpot by the kitchen door," I said.

"Will you just, like, flash a light or something when you get inside, so I know you're safe?"

I nodded to him and closed the car door behind me. I let myself in through the kitchen door and walked through the house to the front hall. The house was silent, and I didn't want to wake anybody. I was too scared to flash a light, but I did go to the little vertical window next to the door and wave into the night. I wasn't sure if Shua saw me, but as soon I waved, I saw the car's rear lights head up the street.

I went directly to bed. I didn't even take off the jeans. I needed to hide them someplace, and under the covers felt like as good a spot as any.

As I lay in bed, I counted up the betrayals. I'd betrayed myself, and the person I'd thought I was. I'd betrayed my religion, the faith that had been the foundation of my life. I'd betrayed Shua. I knew there was something between us. Or, there *had been* something. I'd known that and I'd still kissed Kaden, pressed his body against mine, let him slide his hand up my leg.

I was still wearing Shua's sweatshirt. It smelled like him, like detergent and deodorant, but also a smell that was just *him*, one that I couldn't describe. It only made me feel worse. I wanted to take the hoodie off and burn it, but instead I held it closer to my body, buried my face into the hood and breathed through it.

Before I forgot and just drifted off, I tiptoed down to my dad's office and grabbed the old digital clock thing he kept on one of his shelves. I plugged it in next to my bed and set the approximate time and an alarm.

CHAPTER 30

I WAS THANKFUL, THE NEXT MORNING, that the backyard shed was unlocked. So I was able to get out of the house and on my old bike without anybody noticing. I wanted to get across town before anybody else was awake, so I could avoid questions about how I was home but the car wasn't.

But I wasn't sure what to do when I got to Mickey's. I couldn't just call her, because I didn't have my phone.

I knew which second-story window was Mickey's, so maybe I could throw something at it, but what? I couldn't throw a stick that far, and I thought a rock would break the window, and that would be less of an attention grabber and more an act of vandalism. While I was standing at the curb trying to figure it out, the door opened.

Mickey's mom was standing in the doorway with a mug of coffee. She gave me a little wave, and I followed her inside. She was wearing a bathrobe over pajamas, and fluffy slippers. "Coffee?" she asked. "I have paper cups."

If you kept kosher, you couldn't use a mug from a non-kosher kitchen, because it would have been washed along with who-knows-what kind of random utensils. "That would be great. Thank you."

She brought me a cup of coffee and I perched awkwardly on

the ottoman. I was in the middle of the room, like I was on display. I didn't know why I'd chosen this seat. Or why I'd accepted coffee. I didn't like coffee. It was so bitter. But I was very tired, and coffee was caffeinated.

Mickey's mom held her mug in both hands and leaned forward from her seat on the couch. The fingers of her left hand drummed on the side of the mug, like Shua's on the steering wheel. "I'm glad you're safe. Mickaela assured me that you were, and I trust her, but still it's good to see, since that responsibility falls to me."

I was safe. But no thanks to "Mickaela."

I took a sip of coffee and tried to find a comfortable way to sit.

"I hope she's not pressuring you too much," Mickey's mom said. "Mickaela is . . . strong-willed. She has strong opinions, ideas about the world. I think that's great, and I'm proud of her. But I wish she weren't struggling so much adjusting to my new position. I try to remember it must be hard for her, suddenly being in a spotlight, having people use you as some sort of reference point, especially when you're still a kid. I'm sure it's hard for you too, of course."

The coffee was a trap. I wanted out of this conversation, but the cup was still three-quarters full, and it was too hot to drink fast. "It's fine," I said. "I've had a lot of practice."

She nodded. "I'm sure that's true. I've always admired women in your community. You have to grow up so quickly. Many of you get married so young. I've seen you around town with those little boys. It's almost like they're yours."

I was creeped out by her somewhat accurate generalization, and by the fact that she'd "seen me around town." That was the kind of thing a serial killer said to his next victim. But Mickey's mom didn't look like she was about to attempt murder.

"How are you Jewish?" I asked. I hadn't meant it to come out exactly that way. I was hoping to practice more tact than she was.

But she didn't seem offended. "You're asking because I look East Asian?"

I nodded.

"My father was Jewish," she says. "My mother is Korean American."

I didn't know what to say to that.

"You've probably been taught that that doesn't make me Jewish?"

I didn't like her assumption. But she was right. I'd been taught that Jewishness was matrilineal, that you were Jewish if your mother was Jewish. Some people seemed to think that observant Jewish women weren't given enough . . . autonomy? Power? But in the observant world, women held the key to Jewishness and they alone could create Jewish life.

"In the Reform movement, I'm considered Jewish. But more than that, Judaism has been important to me my whole life," she went on. "Its traditions. My faith. They've saved me so many times."

A little while ago, I would have said, "Cool. That doesn't change God's laws." But now I didn't say it. I didn't even think it. If she felt Jewish, if Jewishness was important to her, then fine. People were allowed to have their own interpretation.

And anyway, I really wasn't in a position to pass religious judgment, given that I was sitting in her living room, hung over from a night of drinking with her daughter.

Mickey appeared on the stairs. "Hey, sleepyhead," her mom said, smiling.

"I have your phone," Mickey said to me.

I got up and followed her upstairs. When her bedroom door closed behind us, she gave me one of her mischief smiles and said, "*Soooooo*. Did you have a good time last night? Kaden says *he* did."

I gulped. She'd ditched me to get home by myself, without my phone, and all she wanted to talk about was me kissing her friend.

"Your phone was under a certain couch cushion. I wonder how it got there. It didn't go as well with me and Nick. But we kind of talked it out, and I think he and Tess are—"

"I'm just here to get my stuff."

"Oh. Uh. Okay." Mickey had my phone, my clothes, and my bag united on the floor next to her bed, and she passed them to me.

"Do you want to just hang out for a little bit, and we can go to JHR together?" Mickey asked.

"No," I said. "I'm not going to JHR today. I have too much to do." It was true that I wasn't going, but it was not true that I had other plans.

"Okay," Mickey said. "Are you . . . Are you mad?"

I definitely was. I was angry at a lot of people, including myself. But with Mickey, there was something else that was a little stronger.

I looked at the phone I'd just been reunited with. I had tons of notifications, and I took a second to scroll through them: texts from my mom, a bunch of comments on TikTok, a message from Shua.

"With you I'm just *so* disappointed," I said.

"*Disappointed*?" Mickey said. "How *old* are you? You sound like my mom."

"I went there *with* you. And then you ditched me, left me drunk and alone to get home by myself. What kind of person *does* that?"

"Are you sure you're not *trying* to sound like my mom?"

"You asked, and I'm trying to answer your question. I'm not thinking about who I 'sound like.' I was in *your* place, and I clearly needed help, and you cared more about boys and—and *cheese* than you did about me."

"Okay, okay," Mickey said, and she started to say sorry, but they weren't real apologies, because every sorry had a "but" after it. I walked toward the door, and Mickey followed me with her sorrys and buts, but she stopped about halfway down the hall.

I walked down the stairs, past the coffee cup I'd left on the end table next to the couch, and out through the door. I shoved the bike through the minivan's back hatch and hit the road.

At home, my mom was on the living room floor. She and the little guys were playing with blocks, making different colorful, elaborate structures, and then knocking down the colorful, elaborate structures.

"I fell asleep at a friend's," I said.

I expected my mom to ask which, but she didn't. She just smiled and placed a block precariously at the top of a tower. I could hear Nachi banging around in the kitchen, trying to find calories, but I just headed upstairs, where Naomi was still in bed, in her own dreamland or somebody else's.

As I walked down the hall toward the bathroom, I tried to decide whose betrayal of me was more painful, Mickey's or mine? I took out my phone and answered the question just as I hit record.

"Y was seen drinking at a party with a group of gentile kids. It was dark and crowded, but that didn't keep HaShem from seeing. In her non-tznius clothes, Y was observed kissing a boy she didn't even know, letting him touch her all over her body. What would her father think? Let's make sure he doesn't find out. So we'll all keep our lips sealed, even if Y didn't."

I did my usual blurring and voice alterations. I posted the video. Even though she'd never see it, it felt like an apology to Rivka. And if the other videos were a way to express my anger, this one was a way to express my shame.

I got in the shower. This way, if the TikTok didn't work, I could wash the shame off with soap and hot water.

CHAPTER 31

AFTER MY SHOWER, I TEXTED CHANI and asked if she would do the JHR spreadsheet. She seemed like a good candidate, and it suggested to her that I wouldn't be there, which would send an indirect message to Shua.

She said okay, and I sent her the template.

Downstairs, the boys were still building. They invited me to help them put the finishing touches on a military base they were putting together. Yitzy immediately destroyed it with his foot and started announcing casualties, calling out victims by name. The Cohen family had been particularly hard-hit. It was a little disturbing, but mostly hilarious.

Nachi was still banging around in the kitchen. The rapid opening and closing of cabinets was starting to sound more and more desperate. And Yoni was chewing on the collar of his shirt as though he wished it were food. I figured if I wasn't going to do JHR, I might as well make myself useful.

I piled up a stack of our reusable bags, headed back out to the car, and drove to the Colwyn Kosher Grocery.

There were a bunch of things we needed, but I was mostly looking for stuff I knew the boys wanted. What was fueling me right now was the mental image of their joy when I presented them with treats: ice cream bars for the boys, date paste energy bars for Nachi.

The date paste bars are exactly as bad as they sound. Nachi agreed that they had abhorrent "taste, texture, appearance, and consistency," but he liked them anyway because they were *very* caloric, so after he ate one he could go as many as fifteen minutes before he had to eat something else.

I grabbed one of the little carts and started up the snack aisle, looking for things that would please my siblings. The market had a kind of festive atmosphere today, and it was nice to be a part of it. The first two women I passed, my mom's friend Tikva Siegel and her sister Amalia, smiled at me and paused to ask me which family members I was shopping for, and to compliment me on my father's sermon from the previous day.

But then, when I was about to turn the aisle onto the one that contained the date bars, I heard two hushed voices talking. Something about them stopped me in my tracks. And it wasn't just because it was giving me flashbacks to Bina.

I paused and pretended to examine a bag of Bissli snacks.

"Have you seen the latest one?" one voice said. I didn't hear the response, but the first voice chimed back in, "Yeah, yeah. Just this morning. Something about a Jewish girl kissing a gentile boy at a party."

I froze. My whole body was frozen except my hand. I went mostly numb, but I knew my hand was shaking, because I could see it rattling the snack bag. I tried to get the rattling under control so I could hear the rest of the conversation.

"Can you *imagine*?" said the second voice.

"Mmhmm," said the first girl.

"I literally can't."

"I'm trying to think, like, if that was me and Eema and Abba found out. Or what if it was *you* and your husband *watched* that video?"

Based on their voices, they sounded about my age, give or take a few years. I thought I recognized one of them, but I wasn't sure. This one shifted her tone. "Who do you think it is?" she asked.

That question sent a deep chill through me. It implied that they might know that person, which implied that they knew the video was about somebody from *here*. I ran my TikToks over to myself in my mind. Had I ever mentioned a specific place? I didn't think so. But maybe I hadn't been careful enough. I figured nobody I knew even *had* TikTok, so maybe I'd let my guard down?

How long was a normal amount of time to be standing at the end of a grocery aisle? There had to be a point at which it was suspicious. I had no idea how long I'd been here. I turned the cart a little, so I could see partway down the aisle where the girls were talking. They were standing right in front of the date bars.

One of them reached out and grabbed a box of something, put it in her cart. They turned together and walked up the aisle, away from me. They were walking side by side, one with a cart, one with a basket.

The girl on the left was Elisheva Moritz, Miri's older sister. The other one was another Moritz girl. She'd graduated a couple years ago. I couldn't remember her name, but I could picture her in school. I remembered having a conversation with her in this same market, about the ills of deceptive food packaging. She'd married recently, so she had a new last name: Lieb or Liebowitz or Gottlieb. She looked different now, and not just because of the new last name. She appeared to be pregnant. She had one hand on her cart, the other on her belly, which was not the way non-pregnant people grocery shopped.

Before I had time to think about it, I surged up the aisle, trying to stay within listening range. I swiped a couple boxes of date paste bars into my cart as I slid by.

"It has to be somebody we know," Elisheva was saying. "It gives me a creepy feeling, like I'm being watched, like somebody's secretly listening to my conversations."

"It's sickening," said the sister. "It's awful that somebody would broadcast something so . . . personal." She stopped and swiveled her head around, and I busied myself reading the ingredients of the date bars. It was mostly dates.

"I can't tell in the videos," Elisheva said, "but it's probably somebody young, right? Could be somebody in my class, somebody at school."

They reached the end of the aisle and turned right. The non-Elisheva sister paused at a display of pasta. She started pushing boxes aside, looking for one in the back. "Of course. Of course," the sister said. "I guess Rabbi Gold was right when he said we should use phone filters. Yisroel and I have been talking about it, and we know *our* kids will have filters on *their* phones."

I scoffed, but only in my head. It was a silent scoffing.

Except that both girls looked up, surprised to see me. The sister almost dropped her pasta box.

I'd scoffed out loud. I pretended the scoff was just part of a coughing fit. It was a dual-pronged strategy: a cover for my audible scoffing, and a repellent. Most people didn't want to stand in close proximity to somebody exhibiting signs of disease.

But both girls smiled at me, like they'd been actively hoping I would appear, just then, in a fit of feigned tussis. "Yoyo," Elisheva exclaimed. "So good to see you. How *are* you?" She'd seen me two days ago at school and hadn't said a word. Maybe she was showing off for her sister, showing how well she knew Rabbi Gold's daughter.

"Fine," I said.

"Great," said Elisheva. "You know my sister Malka?"

"Of course," I said. "How are you?"

"Fine," said Malka.

Malka was still holding a box of ziti in her hand. "How's Moshe?" she asked. I was putting pieces together. Her husband, Yisroel—who agreed about their fetus having a filtered phone—was older than my brother, but had hung around with Moshe and Shua, on the periphery.

"Last I heard, he had a flat tire, but I think it's fixed now." The small talk I used to do so easily felt forced and difficult.

"Yisroel, my husband, talks about him all the time. They're still *so* close."

There was no way they were still close. They probably hadn't talked in a year. I made my face do the smile thing. "Great," I said. "I should finish my shopping," I continued. I pulled out my phone and pretended to check the time. "My younger brother Nachi hasn't eaten in . . . almost half an hour now, and you know how teenage boys are. I sometimes think we should just tie a feedbag around his neck."

They both narrowed their eyes at me.

"That's what they do for horses," I explained. I was hoping that my concern for my brother would outweigh the fact that I'd compared him to a horse. But that didn't appear to be the case. Malka dropped the box into her basket and tried to smile at me, but instead she was just staring, puzzled.

My phone buzzed. It was Shua. Why weren't you at JHR? he asked.

I composed the response in my head immediately: Because I'm in love with you, but I kissed another boy, and I couldn't bear to face you.

Uh-oh.

No.

"Are you okay, Yoyo?" Elisheva asked. She reached out a concerned hand, which found my arm, because I was frozen in place.

A grocery store was really not the place to realize you were in love. I wasn't sure exactly where the correct place was, but it probably didn't have so much fluorescent lighting.

It was such a sudden realization that I felt like I should make an announcement. I should have called it out in the store: "I'm in love with Yehoshua Holtzman." Or I should have texted it to somebody. Or I should have made a TikTok about it, standing there with Elisheva Moritz's hand on my arm. I could have asked her to act as some kind of verifying witness, like a notary signing off on an official document.

Instead I just announced it to myself, repeated it over and over in my own head. It was like a new sweater I was trying on for the first time, turning this way and that to see how it felt, how it fit.

I owed Esti an apology. I needed to say sorry for mocking her when she'd told me Ari was her bashert. I hadn't understood how you could know such a thing. I'd been taught that that was a decision reserved for God, that if you *fell* into love, it was because you were naive, your faith weak, your reverence for God incomplete.

But I'd fallen in love with Shua. I'd tumbled right down love's slope into its basement.

Which was one of the reasons my sudden realization was so upsetting, because just like I'd betrayed my faith by falling in love with Shua, I'd betrayed Shua. I'd let my evil inclination take over, and I'd let Kaden kiss me.

No. That wasn't honest enough. I hadn't just "let him kiss me." I'd kissed *him*.

I double-checked my phone to make sure I'd only sent that response in my head. Then I put my phone back in my bag, shook off Elisheva's hand, and hurried to get the ice cream to the boys before it melted.

CHAPTER 32

SHUA DIDN'T HEAR ME COMING DOWN the stairs because there was music playing. I didn't recognize the music, but I recognized its type. It was something Israeli, and probably Chasidic, because the singer was using Ashkenazi Hebrew, lots of "oys" and "yoys." Like most Jewish music, it was in a minor key, and it had a sad, lilting melody.

Shua's appearance was notable for two reasons.

First, he was standing in the middle of his room, straddling the line between the concrete and the carpet. And he was swaying both forward and back and side to side, like he was praying.

Second, he was naked. Or, not naked. He was wearing a white undershirt with a translucent tzitzis on top. On his bottom, he had on boxer briefs. They didn't leave much to the imagination. My imagination started right up and filled in the blanks.

I should have gone right back up the stairs. I should have cleared my throat, announced my presence, closed my eyes until he was dressed.

I'd tried to figure out, as I walked there, what exactly I was coming there for. Did I want to confess my love? That didn't seem right, since I barely wanted to confess it to myself. Was it to apologize for kissing Kaden? It would be hard to do that without admitting to him that I'd kissed Kaden, which would also involve telling him who Kaden was and how I knew him. Did I just want emotional support?

Because the feelings I was having about Shua were not emotionally supportive.

If I were a different type of girl in this situation, standing there feeling this way, filled with a need to touch him, to wrap my arms around him, to run my hand down his chest, his back, to melt in his arms like an ice cream bar, I wouldn't have questioned it. I'd have just let that feeling stay and hang out. I'd have stood there, feeling it actively. I'd have let it fill me to overflowing, until I had to act on it. But I just couldn't. Outside of the party basement, in a long skirt, with the absence of mind-altering substances, with Jewish music playing, it was just . . . wrong.

And that's why I wasn't some secular girl, and why I wasn't in Las Vegas so I could be saved from becoming one.

So I was shocked when, instead of closing my eyes, alerting Shua to my presence, and waiting for him to dress, I walked over to him.

Shua noticed me at the last second. He glanced over his shoulder, saw me, turned toward me. He looked like a deer in the headlights: surprised, confused. Like a deer in the headlights, he froze.

I accelerated into him.

I pressed my head against his chest and wrapped my arms around him. I just wanted to listen to him before he pushed me away.

But he didn't push me away. I listened to his heart pound as he wrapped his arms around me. It occurred to me that I should push *him* away, but then it unoccurred to me.

Shua was stronger than he looked.

I'd felt like I was untethered, unmoored, drifting. But he was holding me in place. He had me.

He bent his head forward. He buried his nose in my hair, and I could feel him breathing. I could feel it when he mumbled, "I texted you."

"I know."

"You didn't reply."

"I know."

"Is it all right if I'm . . . vulnerable with you?"

I wasn't sure exactly how much more vulnerable he *could* be. He was hugging me while not wearing pants.

But I was down to find out.

"Yeah," I said.

"Every Sunday, I make some kind of excuse to drive Chani to JHR, because I get to see you for, like, five seconds. And unless you come down here, those five seconds are the highlight of my week. When you weren't there today, and then you didn't reply to my text, I thought . . . I don't even know what I thought. I *couldn't* think. I just came back here and—"

He was cut off very suddenly. He tried to keep talking, but could not.

This was a small sample size—you could argue that the evidence was just anecdotal—but it was impossible to talk when somebody else's tongue was in your mouth.

I was living out a scene I would have skipped in a video or book, our bodies pressed together, his hands roving all over my body like excited insects, my fingers scraping through his dense, coarse hair.

I knocked off his kippah.

We both paused and opened our eyes. The kippah was on the floor, cast aside. Even in my current . . . state . . . I was aware of its symbolic significance. "Are you looking at your kippah, thinking about its symbolic significance?" I asked. "Are you thinking that it's there to show us what we've done, that we've cast it aside as we've cast aside everything that we were taught and believed?"

Shua took a step away from me. He reached down and grabbed his kippah.

I straightened my clothes, tugging on my sleeves, my skirt, willing them to be longer. I felt panicked and exposed. The room was so open. I looked around like I was trying to find something to hide behind. But there wasn't anything.

I glanced at Shua's tzitzis, its tassels hanging limp at his side. They were supposed to remind the wearer of God's commandments. If I kept staring at them, I couldn't help but think of all of the rules we'd just broken. I could feel them in my body, like the fractures in my metaphysical bones. This time, I could feel the breaks, and I figured any X-ray would show them.

Shua put his kippah back on his head.

And that should have been the end of it. I should have taken the stairs, and he should have gone back to his bed.

"We shouldn't have done that," he said.

"No. We shouldn't have."

"You should go."

"I should."

"I should put my pants on," he said, eyeing them.

"You should. Yeah," I said.

The pants hung over the foot of his bed. But when he walked to his bed, I didn't walk to the stairs. I followed him, and he didn't end up at the end of his bed. He sat down right in the middle and pulled me toward him, and kissed me again.

The way this felt, my hands on his back, him nuzzling my neck, only underlined what I'd realized when Kaden ran his hand up my leg: hands weren't just hands. Kaden's were the wrong ones, and Shua's were the right ones. This was exactly what was written, what it was supposed to feel like when you came together with your other half: a completeness of the soul. It really did feel like there was a part of me missing, and now I was holding it in my hands.

Except that it was not supposed to happen like this, and not now.

I pulled away again. I took a moment and tried to concentrate on the ceiling, following its winding cracks toward the bare bulb hanging from the center of the room, wondering if it mattered in which order we did our soul reunion, before or after marriage. But that was like asking if it mattered whether you did a burial before or after death. Of *course* it mattered.

This was all . . . a lot. Part of it was that my body kept distracting my mind from the actual thinking process. And then part of it was that you just couldn't process a big moment while it was happening.

"What are we going to do?" I asked.

Shua turned and looked me in the eye, but then I saw his eyes wandering down my body. "I don't know," he said. "But we need some kind of intervention. Because if we just keep lying here, I'm going to . . . I'm going to want to do some things that—"

"I meant what are we going to do about the things we've *already* done. Is there something in your books that says that what we've done is okay?"

Shua took a hand off of me and used it to cover his eyes in what appeared to be an attempt at sensory deprivation. "No. There's nothing like that. But HaShem is forgiving," he said. "I believe that. He loves us. We messed up. But we can do better from now on. We can ask for forgiveness, and he will give it to us."

"If we do that, will we mean it?" I asked. *I* needed to ask forgiveness for what I did with Kaden. I needed to ask forgiveness of God, and of Shua. But how could I ask forgiveness for this if I was still doing it?

"I don't know," he said. "I don't know. We'll have to try."

So we tried. I sat up in bed and shook out my hair. I pulled my hair band off my wrist and put my hair back up in a ponytail. But then he sat up too, and we made accidental eye contact which led to accidental mouth contact, which continued for a long enough period of time that it was clear to everybody—me, Shua, God, the spiders on the wall—that it wasn't accidental at all.

A little while later, once we'd racked up a few more violations of Jewish law, there was the slamming of a car door, and then some footsteps upstairs. It was a call back to reality, a reminder that Shua's basement room was not a timeless world in which other people did not exist. In fact, it wasn't even fully Shua's. "Chani usually does the laundry when she gets back from JHR," Shua said.

"I should help my mom deal with the boys' unstructured time."

I stood by the basement door and straightened my clothes.

They were already straight, but I felt like anybody who looked at me would see what I'd done, and I was shaking myself like love was something I could just throw off, like a wet dog shaking water from its fur.

"Look both ways before you go up through the hatch," Shua said. "Sometimes Chani takes more than one trip to the car."

I didn't think I'd ever left Shua's while it was still light outside. The brightness was shocking, and I felt exposed. To get away from the Holtzman windows, I cut through the neighbors' yard. There was a child watching me from a downstairs window. I waved to her. She waved back. She was a little Jewish girl. It was like waving at my former self, a different, more innocent, better version of the person I was now.

CHAPTER 33

I WAS TRYING TO CONCENTRATE ON a graph on Desmos. It was complex in a beautiful way, intertwining lines of green, red, and blue. Two years ago, Miss Simpson had promised us we'd find trig functions beautiful, and she was right. They were one of the complexities of life that reaffirmed your awe of God: special ratios that were at once about circles, triangles, and waves. Shua had showed me in Torah commentary where the medieval rabbis talked about pi, in awe of the fact that it was somehow both beautiful and literally impossible to comprehend.

The thought of Shua distracted me from the graph. My mind was slipping back to the weekend, and I found I was staring off into space.

Except the space I was staring into was the doorway. And the doorway was open, and Rabbi Levin was there, clearing his throat. "Miss Simpson, may I borrow Hadassah Roth and Miriam Moritz? Hadassah, Miriam, please come with us." At first I'd only noticed Rabbi Levin, but now I saw that behind him stood Mrs. Gomes and Shira. Shira looked enraged. Mrs. Gomes looked bereft. Rabbi Levin looked soft-eyed and sad.

Dassi always experienced angst when she and math were forcibly separated, but the distress on her face went beyond the usual. Miri also looked concerned. The two of them rose and followed the doorway threesome out into the hall.

The class devolved. Miss Simpson said the rest of us could leave. Leah and Chani packed up and scooted out the door. I wanted to finish my assignment, but I'd accidentally closed my Desmos tab. My graph was lost, and I didn't want to have to input the functions again.

Watching Chani leave the room made me think of Shua, and what I'd done, the line I'd crossed.

I was the same me. But I should have felt different. I should have felt repentant. And I did feel that way, somewhere deep in me, somewhere buried. But in the front of my mind, I didn't. I was just . . . thinking about Shua. I texted him: Thinking of you.

Same, he said. Too much.

The earth had rotated an entire one time since I'd seen him last, and I didn't know how many more rotations I could do.

I was lost in my texts with Shua, but the door was still open, and I started to hear raised voices down the hall where Rabbi Levin had his office. And then Dassi appeared in the doorway and said, "Yoyo, we need you. I think Miri is gonna gouge Shira's eyes out, and Shira's gonna make Rabbi Levin cry *his* eyes out, and nobody will have eyes, so, *please*."

I left my bag and followed Dassi into Rabbi Levin's office. Miri was crying again, shaking with sobs. Shira had her anger laser eyes turned up to 10—that's the highest they go—and was shaking with rage. Mrs. Gomes was standing between them, like she was concerned they might actually fight each other, like those girls who beat each other up in school hallways on TikTok.

"Rebbe," Miri sobbed, "it's not about me. It's *not*."

"Did somebody plant the receipt in your bag, then?" Shira asked.

"Probably *you*," Miri snarled.

Rabbi Levin was the only one sitting down. He looked up at me from the chair behind his desk. "Yocheved, have you seen this video?"

"Which one?"

"Don't make me watch it again," Miri said.

The rabbi reached out for Miri's phone. Miri turned her body, trying to shield it from him. But Dassi stepped in, grabbed Miri's phone, and passed it to the rabbi.

I heard my distorted voice playing from the phone speaker. I was talking about "M" at the McDonald's.

I was shocked. I could feel my legs start to give way, and I reached out for the doorjamb to steady myself. I didn't know which was more shocking: hearing my own distorted voice in Rabbi Levin's office or realizing that Miri had an unfiltered phone.

So did Miri's sisters, and who knows who else. I guess people *said* they wanted phones to be kosher, but not *their* phones. Everybody thought they were the only one uniquely equipped to filter through the filth.

"So?" Rabbi Levin said, looking me straight in the eye.

The Torah was pretty clear about lying. You shouldn't lie, it said. I knew it was wrong, lying. Just like I'd decided to walk out of Shua's basement instead of into his arms, I decided I would tell Rabbi Levin the truth.

"Yocheved. Have you seen that video?" Rabbi Levin asked.

"No. No, I haven't," I replied.

"Who do you think made it?" he asked.

I know that my father was the higher community authority, but he wasn't in the room. So Rabbi Levin seemed to defer to me, like I should be the arbitrator here. What did he go to rabbinical school for, if not to learn how to arbitrate?

"I don't know, Rebbe."

"*I* know," Miri said, glaring at Shira, and I think I understood what was going on:

It had come to Miri's attention that the reason she'd lost her part in the production was that there was a video about her eating at McDonald's. She'd decided that Shira made the video to sabotage her. And, to be honest, knowing Shira, I was a little surprised she *hadn't* done that.

"Innocent until proven guilty," Shira said.

I was impressed that Shira had got that much out of US government class, given how seldom she paid attention.

I could say that it *was* Shira. I could throw her under the bus by saying that she *had* been making up stories about Miri. Then I could back the bus up over her and suggest that she'd also been spreading rumors about other people: B, A, R, Y. I could wash my hands of the whole thing. But I'd just told Rabbi Levin that I hadn't seen the M video, so I couldn't now say that I'd seen the others. Plus, the videos meant something to me. They made me feel better. I felt less alone when people thanked me for making them. They connected me to other people who thought like me, and they also allowed me to share my small world with a larger one.

Shira had her backpack slung over one shoulder, her phone

poking out of the small pocket. I grabbed the phone and unlocked it. I went to download TikTok, but a message popped up, her filter jumping in to save the day. *She* at least had her filter set up. I turned the phone to Rabbi Levin, who took off his glasses so he could see the screen. He registered the impossibility of Shira's complicity.

"Miriam?" Rabbi Levin said, turning her way.

"I *told* you this would happen, Rebbe," Miri said, growing desperate. "I *told* you those three would cover for each other. She must have another device. Search her bag."

Shira started emptying her bag onto the floor. "That's not necessary," Rabbi Levin said, but Shira was, as always, committed. She dropped a phone charger, candy wrappers, hair ties, a used tissue, a bunch of receipts. There were no schoolbooks, but there was a siddur, a prayer book. With each item Shira removed, Miri produced more tears, as though Shira was turning some kind of faucet, opening it all the way.

"You three may leave," Rabbi Levin said, looking at Shira, Dassi, and me. "Thank you, Mrs. Gomes. Miriam, I wish I understood why you were doing this."

"Who do you think Y is, Rebbe? There are only two Ys in the school."

Shira paused reconstituting her bag to laugh out loud at Miri's suggestion that I could be Y. "If Yoyo kissed a boy, your next trip to McDonald's is on me, Miri."

"Shira!" Mrs. Gomes said, aghast.

"We'll each have the triple treif burger. We can do drive through, and then just eat on our way to Gehinnom."

"I've never been there!" Miri shouted. "*You* just can't handle—"

"Oh *please*, Miri."

"You're jealous and . . . and . . . evil," Miri shouted.

Maybe I'd been wrong about the physical violence. Miri looked like she had enough potential energy that if she didn't do *something* kinetic, she was going to explode.

"Silence!" Rabbi Levin shouted.

There was sudden and complete silence, at least inside the office. But now we could hear voices out in the hall. A decent-sized crowd had formed outside, and I could see faces trying to peer in.

Rabbi Levin got up and ushered everybody but Miri out of the office. Mrs. Gomes immediately started doing damage control, trying to shush people, telling them that "nothing" was going on. But she also told them that it was none of their business, which implied that there was something after all.

People turned from Mrs. Gomes to us, looking for an explanation. Only one of us spoke. It was Shira. "If I were Yael Reznikov, I'd start preparing an alibi."

I stumbled back into Miss Simpson's room to get my bag. She was packing up the room, moving papers around, slipping them into folders and binders.

I paused, one hand on my backpack strap, and watched her. Miss Simpson was different from all of our other teachers. She was non-Jewish and mixed race, and lived some kind of life totally disconnected from ours, except for the hours she spent teaching us advanced STEM. I always thought of her in terms of calculus and chemistry. But now I suddenly wondered about her life, where and how she lived.

She looked up.

"Do you have a question, Yoyo?"

"Yeah," I said. "If you post something on Insta or TikTok or whatever, can somebody tell where you posted it from?"

"Not a classic Yoyo question. Okay. Well. Usually on those apps there's a setting where you can choose whether you're sharing your location."

"Thanks," I said, shouldering my bag.

I was thankful she'd had the answer to my question, but not thankful for the answer itself. Because as I walked out the door, I pulled up TikTok, and even before I looked through the settings, I knew what I'd find.

You didn't need to be some kind of computer hacker to figure out that my videos were posted from Colwyn.

CHAPTER 34

I DECIDED TO TRAIN NACHI TO help his little brothers through their bedtime routine. I considered Naomi first, but she was willful and stubborn, and I didn't feel like negotiating with her. Nachi lacked guile. He was easily malleable. If my mom and I gave him clear instructions, he would bend into whatever shape we asked him to.

The problem was that my mom thought it was a bad idea.

Her first argument was that we should not distract Nachi from Torah study with domestic activities. I countered this by pointing out that the things we were distracting him from were not Torah. Her second argument was that Nachi, being male, lacked the natural nurturing instincts that we women had. I countered this by pointing out that washing, reading, and prayer were all things that Nachi knew how to do. So then she turned to her third argument, which was that Nachi simply could not be trained.

"They train elephants for the circus," I told her.

"I'm not an elephant," Nachi said. He was in the room with us for the whole conversation. Ideally, he wanted to avoid the extra responsibility without losing his dignity. But I was going to make sure he had to choose one or the other.

"I don't think they *do* train elephants anymore," my mother said. "I think they decided it was cruel and inhumane."

"Are you suggesting it would be inhumane to make Nachi brush Yoni's teeth?"

"Yes, but I'm not sure which of them it would be inhumane for." My mom laughed. "Fine. Nachi, do as your sister says."

"Doesn't he *always*?" I asked, giving him a triumphant grin, which he did not return. I reached out and pinched his cheeks like he was a baby.

As Nachi followed me upstairs, I tried to comfort him. "Elephants are surprisingly sophisticated," I explained to him. "They mourn their dead. They can use tools, even."

"Why are you doing this?" he asked.

There was a bigger reason. It had seemed impossible just a month before, but what if I wasn't there anymore? What if I tried to live some kind of totally different life? Or what if I just needed a change? And Nachi might have understood those questions, but I decided to go for the simplest explanation: "I need to go out sometimes," I said. "So I want you to step up. Plus, you love your brothers."

"I don't know. They aren't actually very—"

"You *love* your brothers, Nachi."

Naomi came in during the washing-up. I thought maybe she wanted to use the bathroom, but she just stood there in the doorway, watching the three boys. Maybe I should have asked her first after all.

"Am I doing this right?" Nachi asked, one hand palming Yitzy's head like a basketball, the other holding a toothbrush.

I was going to answer, but Naomi beat me to it. "It doesn't matter," she said. "Every one of those teeth is going to fall out no matter what you do."

Yitzy turned to the mirror, concerned at a toothless future, since Naomi had not teased the idea of adult teeth. But Nachi was comforted by her fatalism, and without any hesitation, he drove the toothbrush into Yitzy's distressed face.

When Nachi led the boys toward their bedroom, Naomi followed them, and I went the other way, toward the stairs.

I was at Shua's basement door by eight thirty, which gave me about two hours before I needed to be in my own bed.

I opened the door slowly.

He was studying, bent over his book, rocking slowly forward and back. I didn't make any kind of sound to announce myself, but he looked up and saw me. Just as I'd expected, I was filled with various urges that were strong enough to overpower the rational Yoyo that existed outside of this basement. It was all I could do not to run to him. It was really pretty embarrassing. I guess that was one advantage of your love being forbidden: you didn't have to humiliate yourself in public. Shua was the only one who saw me trying to get to him, flailing through the dark basement like one of those salmons flopping around in an Alaskan river.

And he didn't seem to find the behavior embarrassing. He got off his bed so fast he knocked the book onto the floor.

Here's another reason I felt like we were meant for each other: our heights were such that when I physically threw myself at him, my chin rested perfectly on his shoulder. We fit like puzzle pieces, and I nuzzled his neck while he nuzzled through my hair.

Pressed together in the middle of his room, I asked, "Have you been asking for forgiveness?"

"No, because I just . . . don't mean it."

We did a lot of kissing, and a good deal of what Mickey might have called consensual groping, which was, just as she'd suggested, pretty fun. But if I ever talked to Mickey again, I meant to tell her that it was more fun when you cared about your groper or gropee. Because when I was kissing Kaden, it was fun, because kissing was just a fun activity if you didn't think about it too hard. But when I kissed Shua, I wasn't doing it because it was fun. I was doing it because I needed to, because I needed to express how I felt about him. And I could tell by the way he kissed me back, the way he ran his fingers through my hair, the way he drummed his fingers on my lower back, that he felt the same way about me.

I didn't know if it was because Kaden—and what I'd done with him—had leapt into my mind, or because the scene in Rabbi Levin's office still felt so fresh, but when my self-imposed curfew was getting closer, and I looked at the door, it was like I could see the things I'd done sneaking into the room to inhabit the basement with us.

Shua was showing me all of my worth, but somehow I still felt worthless. Because even the way he was showing it to me was wrong, or I'd been taught that it was wrong.

I got up to use the bathroom, and when I came back toward the bed, I sat on the floor, staring at the discarded holy text, the one Shua'd kicked over on his way into my arms. I picked it up and placed it back on the little shtender.

Even separated from him, I could still feel Shua's lips on mine. I could feel his hands where they'd touched me. They were like impressions, like the ones that remained when you lifted your head from a memory foam pillow. They were like dark shadows he left behind on my body. Except the feeling didn't fit with the memory of three minutes ago, because when his hands were actually there, it felt incredible.

"I really messed up," I said. "This is not how I meant for it to be."

He was sitting on the edge of the bed, looking past me at the dark shadows by the washer and dryer. "Me either. I know. It's not only on you."

"Maybe *this* isn't. But this isn't the only thing."

Shua chuckled, but it wasn't a real laugh. There was no humor in it. "This isn't enough?"

"It is. There's just more. There's a lot. And—I don't know. It's like every little thing was fine. Every step I took felt like the right step at the time. But then I didn't end up where I wanted to. And I should have known. I *did* know. I was told over and over, but it took all of these steps to figure it out myself."

"I'm sorry," Shua said, "but I don't really understand. You're being a little light on the details."

"I know."

"You can talk to me. You can tell me anything."

"No. I can't. Look, I'm not trying to burden you. I just don't know who I am right now, or if I like that person."

"Yoyo. Tell me: Why did Rabbi Akiva's twelve thousand pairs of students die? Why did they perish all at once?"

Shua was shifting gears, straight from make-out gear to study gear. It was a sudden shift, but I tried to follow him there. This was an easy one any kid I'd grown up with could answer. "They all died together because they did not respect each other. They were not united. They did not love their fellows as they loved themselves."

"Good. Rabbi Akiva then declared that the most important principle of the Torah is to love your fellow as you love yourself."

"Well, I'm killing it, then. I love basically everybody a lot more than I love myself right now."

"That's what I'm *saying*. That's the problem. In *order* to love others, you have to love yourself *first*. In order to accept others, you have to accept yourself. In order to care for others, you have to care for yourself. I would never question how much you care about others, but you also need to care for you. Cut yourself slack. We're all just human. Even you. And if you don't want to do it because I'm telling you, do it because the Torah tells you to."

I checked the time. "I should go."

Shua looked down at his feet and scratched at the side of his face. It was a look of shame. It reflected the way I felt. "I'm sorry," he said.

"Me too."

"I could lock the door."

I tried to picture that, him locking me out for my own good. But I didn't think it would work. "I'll just bang on the door with all of my might. Then we'll be in the same situation, but your whole family will know about us, and I'll have a broken hand." I headed toward the door. "I think hand fractures can be particularly problematic. The hand has lots of tiny little bones."

"I'd open the door on the first knock, anyway."

CHAPTER 35

SHABBOS MORNING, SATURDAY, I SAW SHUA somewhere other than his JHR car or our underground dates. Though those weren't really dates. I'd still never been on a date. I'd just kissed two boys in their respective basements. Maybe someday I'd kiss somebody *up*stairs. Or outside. Hopefully that person would be Shua Holtzman. Hopefully I'd kiss him every day, both inside and outside, and in places that weren't quite either, like those pavilions at the county park that have ceilings but no walls.

When Esti had first left, shul was weird. Shira and Dassi and I didn't know how to act. We were driving like a car with three wheels. But now we'd established a new routine. We went together as a three-wheeled vehicle *to* the synagogue, but afterward, they went one way and I went another.

Shua hadn't been coming to shul. He didn't want people to ask questions about why he was home from Israel. But he was there today. It was usually hard to pick out individuals among all of the black hats and suits in the men's section, but now I felt like I would recognize Shua anywhere, at any distance. You could have thrown me into space, and right before I suffocated from the lack of atmosphere, I'd have looked back at earth and picked out Shua just based on the way he stood.

At one point, he turned and looked up in my direction, and

without thinking I started to wave at him. I had to reach out and pretend like I was going to pat Dassi on the shoulder.

On the surface, everything was normal. We prayed. We read the weekly parsha. It was exactly like every other Shabbos morning, for everybody else. But I didn't experience it the same way I always experienced it.

I experienced it through Shua. I watched him pray, wondering why he was here all of a sudden. Probably to start his repentance, I told myself, to stand before God and start his journey back to him.

I should have been doing the same thing, but instead I just watched him do it, hoping he wasn't doing the thing I thought he was.

"Yoyo? Hey. You coming?"

I was the only one left in our row, except for Shira and Dassi. I was just standing there, alone, staring at the spot where Shua had been.

Dassi waved a beckoning hand at me. In a daze, I followed them out.

There was a kiddush in the hall across from the sanctuary. I grabbed a little cake from the table and started looking around for my people. I wanted to get out of the synagogue as soon as possible.

Shua was in the room. It was tough to be in the same room with him and not be *with* him. It was made worse by the person he was talking to: my father.

Shua was talking in an animated way, gesturing about something with his hands. My father was nodding in the thoughtful way he does when somebody has made a good point. The end of his beard swayed a little out of sync with his nodding head.

I found Nachi with the boys and informed them that I was walking home. I grabbed Yoni and Yitzy by their hands and looked around for Naomi. I found her with my mother and gathered them both. I was like a cowgirl, rounding up the herd.

I had everyone gathered and walking toward the doors when Shira and Dassi reappeared. "Where are you off to?" Shira asked.

"Home," I said, indicating all of my companions who also lived there.

"Can we come over?" Shira asked. "It's been too long. I know things have been different and everything, but . . ."

I didn't really want to spend time with them. All of the things we used to talk about—school, the production, boys—felt unimportant, except for the last one which felt *too* important. I just wanted to lie in bed, alone, and think about Shua. "Why don't I meet you at the Roths'?" I asked.

"We'd rather come to your place," Shira said. "It's so much closer."

"I don't know. I've got—"

"Of *course* you can come over," my mother said. "Yoyo made her famous salmon."

"Ooooooh," said Dassi. "With the teriyaki? That stuff is fire."

Dassi smiled at me, but I didn't smile back. I didn't understand what was going on.

At my house, we ate in silence. They both complimented me on the salmon. Dassi shared an idle thought about the last chemistry lab we did, and told me about Shira's frustrations with Rivka's tentative singing at rehearsals.

Shira excused herself to go to the bathroom. There was one in the hall by the front door. She poked her head in there, and then turned around and went upstairs to use the other one.

I figured we might use these dishes again today, so I took them to the sink and washed them. I was rinsing the last plate when Shira came back down. She didn't even enter the kitchen. She just poked her head into the room and said, "Ready?"

"Yeah," said Dassi, and they started walking toward the front door.

I put the dish on the drying rack and followed. I should have been relieved that they were leaving already. But it didn't make sense to walk all the way here only to have a few bites of salmon and leave, even if the salmon was fire, which it was, especially with the zucchini-and-onion side I'd made, which was soft and oily in the best way.

CHAPTER 36

AS SOON AS SHABBOS WAS OVER, I informed my parents that I was taking the car, and I went to Shua's. I didn't even wait to hear my mom's protests.

I parked around the corner from the Holtzmans' and took the stairs two at a time. Shua wasn't even pretending to study. There was no book on his shtender. He was just sitting there staring at the door, like a zoo animal who knew his keeper was about to show up with food.

It was kind of a gross simile, because it implied that I was either Shua's keeper or his food. But honestly, I would have been happy to be either, so long as I could spend a couple hours in his enclosure with him.

Actually, I *really* liked that idea. Because when I'd seen Shua at shul that day, it reminded me that he existed outside of this space. And I didn't want a free range Shua. I wanted a Shua that was *mine*. And this basement was the only place he could be mine. Out in the world, I couldn't hold his hand, put my palm on his face, share mischievous eye contact. I could only do that down here, where nobody could see us.

He was too ambitious to stay down here. He wanted to study, learn, be part of a community. And in order to do that, he'd have to emerge, and go out into the world. In a year or two, he'd be a *man* man, and I'd have to share him, and I didn't want to.

I closed my eyes and pressed my head against his chest. I curled up small so he could wrap his arms around my whole body. We hadn't even kissed. We were just lying here, curled up in his twin bed like little mammals in a small burrow.

"It was nice to see you at shul today," I said. "No, actually it was—"

"Torture," he said, finishing my sentence.

"Yeah. When I said 'nice,' I meant torturous."

"Yeah," he said. When we snuggled, he did this thing where he twirled my hair with his finger, like they were the fringes of his tzitzis. It felt nice, the usual meaning of nice. "It was nice to see you with your family, though. You're such a good big sister."

Most people, when they said this, what they really meant was: You'll make a good mother. You'll do a great job raising seven or eight children of Israel. But Shua wasn't most people, and he just left it at that, complimenting me on the thing I was now, not the thing he hoped I might be, if he even hoped that at all.

There was a cool breeze that swept through the room. That was not a normal thing that happened in rooms, but I'd gotten used to it. Somehow I'd gotten used to all of this: sitting alone in a room with a boy, touching him, kissing him, sharing my feelings with him. I looked at the steep basement steps, and thought of them as the slope, wondering how I'd fallen down it so quickly.

CHAPTER 37

ON MY WALK BACK TO THE car, the sky was clear and I could see the stars. I was in a kind of dream state, a state of love in which everything felt unreal. I wondered at this world, the love world full of contradictions. The things I was doing were wrong, but they felt right. The night was cold but felt warm. The stars were light-years away, but I felt like I was walking among them.

When I got to the car, the dreamworld got even dreamier, because there was a version of Shira Birnbaum standing at the car door. There was a moment when I really *did* think it was a dream. She was wrapped up in a wispy coat that didn't look fully solid, and I wondered for a second if she was an apparition of some kind, maybe a manifestation of my guilty religious conscience.

But it wasn't a dream, obviously. It was just Shira.

I fumbled around for the car fob.

"I thought you would be surprised," she said. She was leaning against the car, back against the passenger door, feet on the curb, giving me a look that was a mix of confusion and scorn.

"I'm *very* surprised. I'm just not expressing it that well."

"Can you give me your phone?" she asked.

Even though I knew this was the real Shira, it still felt unreal when she reached into my bag—just like I'd reached into hers in Rabbi Levin's office—and extracted my phone.

She held it in one hand as she spoke. "I thought it best to do this in person. I didn't want anything recorded or written down."

"How did you know my car was—"

"I know everything," she said. "I know it's you."

This was a moment I should have imagined, a calamity I could have—should have—anticipated. Still, I didn't know how to react. I was unprepared. I just stood there, frozen, while Shira showed me my own TikTok account. It displayed the videos I'd posted. My last one was still doing pretty well. I also noticed I had one unread DM.

"Should we sit in the car?" Shira asked. She looked up and down the street. There were a couple walkers coming our way, and a car from the other direction.

I unlocked the minivan and got in. I put my foot on the brake and pressed the start button.

"No," Shira said.

"We can have heat this way," I explained. I adjusted the dials so when the engine warmed we'd get heat at our feet. "How did you figure it out?" I asked.

"I didn't. Dassi did. She said something about hacking into Wi-Fi and cross-referencing IP-somethings, but in the end she just recognized your bathroom."

This dream had turned into a nightmare really quickly.

"Don't worry," Shira said. "I won't tell anyone."

I breathed a sigh of relief. I imagined what her telling would look like. Nobody at school would talk to me. It would destroy my parents, mostly my father. You couldn't be the rabbi in charge of kosher phones when your daughter was using her unfiltered phone to spread rumors about people she was supposed to care about. Nobody would look at me the same. It would be traced back to Shua, who would be indicted again for the same crime, and he'd be relegated to an even deeper basement, one without a door of any kind.

"Thanks, Shira," I said.

"I have a condition," she said.

Of course Shira had a condition. It was just like Shira to have a condition, and to tell you about it *after* she promised to keep your secret. "I can talk to Mrs. Gomes about whatever you want, if there's somebody you want in a certain role, or if you want your name printed—"

"I don't care about the stupid production." I could see that she had unlocked my phone and was scrolling through it. "You can't see Shua Holtzman anymore," she said. She said it quietly, but it was clear.

I didn't say anything. I didn't react.

"Hey, Yoyo. You look like I showed you a corpse or something."

I'd actually be fine if she'd showed me a corpse. Corpses were probably interesting.

But I must have been making some kind of expression. One of anguish, probably. But I couldn't really feel my facial muscles, so I wasn't sure.

"It's just a boy," Shira said.

He's not just a boy, I thought. That's what I wanted to tell Shira, about all of the ways he wasn't just a boy. But she wouldn't understand, and it probably wouldn't help anyway.

"You'll stop seeing him," Shira said, and she flashed my phone screen at me, showing me my text exchange with Shua. "None of this is appropriate."

I could hear my voice cracking and breaking as I tried to speak, but I forced myself to get the words out: "If you just don't tell anybody for now—like, just wait until I talk to my parents about it—it won't be a big deal. It happens all the time. Kids do some stuff, but if they wait and start *officially* dating later, people forget and—"

"I know," Shira said. "Doesn't make it right."

"So then—"

"Yeah, here's the thing. I'm going to date Shua. You knew that. I've told you that. Nobody will find out about what he's done with you. He'll fix his image and your father will help arrange an engagement for us—he's always liked me, I think, your dad."

I once saw a story online about a guy who got impaled. He was working at a construction site and a giant beam went right through his chest. It didn't kill him. But he just had this giant beam in his chest, going through his body. They couldn't remove it, because then he'd start losing tons of blood, so they just had to leave it there. I don't know what ultimately happened to him. I assume he just had to live the rest of his life with a steel beam going through his chest.

As I'd have to do from then on.

My beam—the one Shira had just driven through me—was figurative, but I was sure it hurt just as much.

Because the choice I had was literal, and literally impossible to make. It was a choice between Shua and my family, Shua and my entire world.

"How do you know he'll—"

"I know his secrets too."

"You're a bitch," I told her.

"Do you kiss Shua with that mouth?" she asked me.

I wanted to attack Shira. I could lock the car doors and just dive at her, hit and tear at her until I was exhausted. I'd seen a lot of fights on TikTok. The successful girls always went straight for the other girl's hair.

But I was not going to fight Shira. It wouldn't do any good. I was as angry at Shira as I'd ever been at another person. More, actually. This was unprecedented fury. But still, I was also a little angry at myself, and as I sat in the driver's seat, as the heat finally started to warm my stockinged legs, that part grew, until I was all rage, but I no longer knew exactly who the anger was for.

"We're not friends anymore," I told Shira.

"We haven't been friends since Esti," she said. "You haven't been available to anybody since then."

"Get out of my car."

"You mean Rabbi Gold's car?" Shira put my phone on the console and got out of the minivan.

I drummed on the steering wheel. The drumming made me think of Shua, and I balled up my fingers and started pounding the wheel with my fist, so hard I was worried the airbag would deploy.

CHAPTER 38

WHEN I GOT HOME, MY MOM tried to talk to me, but I went directly to my room. She called my phone, but I ignored it. I waited to hear her feet on the steps or in the hall, but I never did.

I lay in bed and tried to distract myself with TikTok. I scrolled through my feed. I watched this parrot I followed identify the colors of different sheets of paper. I watched French people compete to see who could make the stretchiest cheese. The stretchiest cheese was *really really* stretchy. But then there was a video of an Orthodox girl talking about tehillim, and the ways in which they uplifted her soul. And I locked my phone screen and stared at the wall instead.

I remembered I had an unread DM, so I reluctantly unlocked my phone and opened TikTok one more time.

When I saw who it was from, I was glad I was lying down.

It was Esti.

The first message said the same thing lots of creepy guys said when they slid into my DMs: Hey cutie. She included a peach emoji.

I knew it was Esti. Her account had a picture of her, her short hair with a purple streak in it. I guess anybody could make an account with a picture of Esti, but the messages were just *so* Esti. And anyway, I just knew it was her. Even if "Hey cutie" had been the only message, I would have known. I could always feel when it was Esti messaging me, and even though it had been a while, it felt like it always did. It was like a smell from when you were little. It immediately transported you back to wherever you first experienced it.

Her messages continued.

You're brave, she said.

But dude, if you want to be all
secret don't share your location.
Especially when your bathroom tile is so unique.
I can't believe you hooked up with a gentile boy
and then ratted yourself out on TikTok.
You must have been drunk af.
I wish I'd been there.
OMG.
Good Shabbos.

I read each of the messages ten or fifteen times. I had trouble understanding the last one, but then I looked at the time stamp on it, and on all the rest of them. They were sent in the middle of the night on Friday.

Maybe Esti was traveling some place where it wasn't the Sabbath. I brought up a map of the world time zones. I calculated that if, and only if, she was in French Polynesia, it wouldn't have been Shabbos. I imagined it was beautiful there, in French Polynesia, but that's not where Esti was.

Esti was in Las Vegas, and she'd DM'd me on Shabbos.

My heart started racing all over again. There was some horror in there, but a thrill also.

It was hard to explain, but breaking the Sabbath felt like the ultimate departure. Eat some unkosher food, fine. Kiss your secret boyfriend in a basement, fine. Spread rumors about people on an app you weren't supposed to have, fine. Those were violations of religious law, sure. But if you kept your phone on and DM'd somebody on Shabbos, that was a dismissal of the whole thing. That was an announcement that you were just not observing anymore, that you were embarking on a new life entirely.

You were still Jewish. There were all kinds of ways to be Jewish. But Orthodox life revolves around observing Shabbos. If you stop observing it, you're just . . . not Orthodox anymore. You're something else. You're living a different life. And you might have to live it with other people, because you won't belong with the old ones anymore, at least not in the same way.

It was scary to think about.

I wondered what made Esti do it.

You're brave too, I sent.

I thought I was going to get a quick reply. It was like I could feel Esti through the phone screen. It felt like she was right next to me but also not right next to me. Like she was very close but not quite tangible.

But there was no quick reply. There was no reply at all.

I'd meant the things I'd said to Esti, back when I reprimanded her for her choices. But I'd turned out to be the exact type of hypocrite I was trying to call out. Maybe she wouldn't forgive me. And when I decided what to do with Shira's blackmail, there would be *somebody* who didn't forgive me: my friends, my family, Shua. Maybe I wouldn't forgive *myself* no matter what I decided.

I could feel myself start to cry. This time it was not the kind that shook my body. It was the silent kind that appeared out of nowhere and flowed continuously like a river in spring. I put my head in my hands. "I'm sorry," I said aloud, to God. I figured now was as good a time as any to try talking to him again. "I know I failed your test. I know I did. I'm not saying I deserve anything better. I just want you to know how much it hurts. And I get that maybe it's supposed to. But it just hurts *so* much, and I don't know if I can handle it. I just—"

I heard the clearing of a throat. I spread my fingers just enough to see through a gap between them. As was often the case, I'd forgotten about the existence of my roommate, Naomi.

I assumed she was going to scold me—like she had the last time I'd cried—for distracting her from her all-important book. But she didn't. Without even reaching for her bookmark, she closed the novel and tossed it onto the floor. "I know you're talking to HaShem, not to me. But I'm more likely to respond."

I just looked at her. She was looking me straight in the eyes in a way she hadn't in years.

"I guess somebody figured it out."

It took me a minute, but I understood. "You too? *How?* Are you on *TikTok?*"

Naomi threw her arms up like it was a stupid question. "Of *course?* Where do you think I get my book recs? Some old bag at the library?"

That's exactly what I'd thought.

Naomi sat up on her bed and leaned forward, resting her chin on her hand. "And who do you think I talk about the books with when I finish them?"

I said nothing.

"*Nobody?* Like I'm a bearded recluse in a cave, mumbling to herself in the dark?"

With her leaning toward me, I could see she did have one chin hair that could use plucking, but I wouldn't have called it a beard.

"You think I'm just this . . . silent, lonely person?"

The hits just kept on coming.

"You don't know me," she said. It was blunt, biting. It was just like I would have said it.

"I guess," I mumbled. "But it's—it's not like you come out and make yourself *known*."

"I used to." Naomi lay back on her bed and looked up at the ceiling. I followed her eyes. The ceiling was a slightly different color from the wall, and I couldn't believe this was the first time I'd noticed it. "I feel like I *tried*," Naomi continued. "But all that stuff you do—cooking and babysitting and talking to Abba's guests about . . . See? I don't even know what to talk to them about. It comes naturally to you, but it's *hard* for me, and I feel like I tried, but you and Eema thought it was easier to just do it yourself than to try to do it with me."

First I wondered how much of that was true. But I quickly decided that the answer was probably all of it. So I moved on to wondering how much of it was my fault. I wanted to wonder it out loud, so Naomi could hear, but I was having trouble getting words out. Instead I expressed myself by crying harder.

I gave up on words and waved at Naomi, beckoning. When she didn't move, I caught my breath and got two words out. "Come here," I said.

She got up slowly and slinked over to my bed. I made room for her. She didn't nuzzle. She didn't snuggle. She didn't hold me, but she let herself be held. She let me stroke her hair like she was a little girl who'd had a bad day at school. "You're my sister," I told her. And I repeated it to myself. Maybe I'd lose Esti and Shua, and the respect of my classmates. I'd try not to, but maybe there was nothing I could do about it. "We have our whole lives to know each other. We'll get there, yeah?"

"Yeah," Naomi said.

"How did you get around your phone filter?" I asked her.

"I didn't," she replied. "I just bought a second phone, same one I got for Nachi. It looks just like our regular ones, and I got cases of the same color."

I temporarily took my arm back. "Wait, *Nachi* has another phone?"

"How do you think he watches porn?"

"He *doesn't* watch—"

"Of course he does. I guess it's not as noticeable these days, since I got him earbuds."

"HaShem yishmor," I said. "That's . . ." But I wasn't sure what it was. It was almost unbelievable, that *three* of Rabbi Gold's kids had unfiltered phones. I did believe it, but just barely. "Okay. I—I don't even know what to— Let's talk about something else. *Anything* else. Tell me about the book you've been reading."

So she did. There were some witches. Their powers derived from an old tree. I couldn't figure out if it was one singular tree, or a species of trees. But the tree was under threat. It was some kind of climate allegory. Naomi was really excited about it. She went off on a whole tangent about the connections between the arboricultural magic system in the book and different Jewish plant-based healing practices in the Torah, like the cedar and hyssop in *Vayikra*.

That was about the point when I started to feel myself drifting off, into a dreamworld, a real one this time. I'd leave this waking world to Naomi and her book social media, and Nachi and his pornography, and the town of Colwyn and the calamities I'd made for myself that would wait through the night and greet me tomorrow with vigor and enthusiasm.

CHAPTER 39

ON SUNDAY I TOOK THE CAR in the morning like I was going to JHR, but I drove to the Holtzmans' instead. On the way over, I didn't think about Mickey, but I did think about Mrs. Dvornik, and if she'd ever been in love, and if she'd spent her life—or part of it—with her love, and not in a way where she had to hide it.

Shua was asleep when I got there, and I let him go on sleeping. He was a heavy sleeper.

I watched his chest rise and fall, and thought about Shira's blackmail. Giving in to it was definitely the easy path. If I just let her have what she wanted, nobody would know I'd made the videos. Nobody would know that the rabbi's daughter had unkoshered her phone and spread rumors about her own community. My father wouldn't know how far I'd fallen down the slippery slope.

All of that would be saved, but Shua would be lost.

He blinked himself awake and saw me. He smiled, and I noted for the first time that one of his front teeth was a little longer than the other. It only made me like his smile more.

Shua kissed me. Then he got up and went to the bathroom. I took a book off his shelf and passed the time reading.

He came back, got dressed, and grabbed his tefillin bag.

I was still reading when I found him standing over me. "Can you just wait outside, like, in the stairwell, while I pray?"

"Of course."

I sat out on the cold stairwell, on the concrete, scrolling through my phone. I balled up my skirt so my butt didn't feel as cold.

I could picture Shua praying, swaying up and down, maybe side to side, with his siddur in front of him. I wanted to watch him, but I understood why he wanted to pray alone.

If I let Shira win, I'd also save Shua. He could slowly move himself back into the community and be whatever part of it he wanted to be.

If he stopped seeing me, would it hurt him as much as it would hurt me?

I spent the rest of the afternoon on Shua's bed, talking. Or, he talked. I didn't say anything. I just lay there, thinking about what I was going to do. I was relieved that I was facing away from him, that when I opened my eyes, I saw the washer and dryer, and not Shua's face. It was the only way I could hold it together.

I left when Chani got back from JHR, and we heard her feet moving toward the basement door, on their way to do laundry.

CHAPTER 40

"YOYO," MISS SIMPSON SAID TO ME. "If you're sick, you're supposed to stay home. I know everybody used to just 'power through,' but that's the only good thing to come out of the pandemic. We can practice self-care."

I wasn't sick. I guess I just looked sick. I'd done some sniffling. My eyes were probably red. I definitely felt tired, even though I'd slept plenty.

"Math will be here," Miss Simpson reminded me.

I looked around the small classroom to see if anybody else knew why I looked sick. But everybody else had her nose in her notebook. Except for Dassi. Her look was knowing, but flat. She'd already taken a side.

After class, I was still sitting in my seat, again. It wasn't that I wanted to stay here. It was that I didn't want to go to the other available places. Still, I knew Miss Simpson would lock up the room when she left, so I slowly slid my books into my bag.

As I walked down the hallway toward my locker, Shira got my attention. She and Dassi were standing at Shira's locker, rifling through it, pulling stuff out onto the hallway floor. It was a destructive activity, but she was doing it with a kind of jauntiness.

She motioned for me to come over. I only complied because I didn't want her to raise her voice.

I didn't understand how a person could be so cruel but project this kind of carefree lightness. "Tomorrow," she said. "Tomorrow I will tell everybody. Does your father go to that five thirty minyan?"

I'd heard my brother sit around with his friends and discuss what they would eat for their last meal if they were on death row. It seemed like a morbid conversation, but they enjoyed it. Nachi always chose something I made. He said I should be honored by this. I pointed out that in this scenario, I'd serve him this meal knowing that he was about to be killed. "You won't hear me scream," he reassured me, as if that was the part I was worried about. "One of the injections immobilizes you so you can't make any noise, or even struggle."

"Rivka really isn't very bright, is she?" Shira asked.

It seemed like a complete non sequitur. But then it dawned on me: the locker Shira was rummaging through wasn't Shira's. It was Rivka's.

"Like, after the TikTok, wouldn't you keep this *anywhere* else?" Shira was holding up Rivka's vape.

Shira closed the door, leaving the guts of Rivka's locker spilled out on the floor. She walked purposefully toward the cafetorium, with Dassi in tow.

"Shira," I said. "Don't. Don't do this to Rivka."

Shira didn't turn or look back. She just kept walking. "I'm not doing this to Rivka," she called. "*You're* doing this to Rivka."

Inside the cafetorium doors, I watched, frozen.

Dassi interrupted rehearsal to run interference, talking to Mrs. Gomes.

Shira called Rivka to the side and showed her the vape. I don't even know if they exchanged words. Rivka grabbed it, tucked it under her sweater, and hurried out of the room.

A few minutes later, the room started to clear out, until it was just me and Mrs. Gomes. I watched the theater teacher make her way slowly from the stage to where I sat in the back. Each of her footsteps echoed in the empty space.

I wanted to be somewhere else but hadn't moved. I didn't want to have to speak to anybody on the way out. I didn't want to run into Shira, or Dassi, or Rivka. I didn't want to walk home in the open air, exposed to the world. I didn't want to go home, period.

Mrs. Gomes sat down next to me. She was a feisty woman, but she looked defeated. "Yoyo, I need to ask you a favor."

I didn't say anything. I didn't move.

"I need you to fix this problem. This whole thing has turned something that's supposed to be joyful, celebratory, to . . . nothing. It's nothing right now. You and I, we can't fundraise for a production that won't happen. Can you talk to the girls and try to settle this down? You know they listen to you."

I knew they used to.

"I'm not the right person to do that," I said quietly.

"You *are* though. You've always been exactly the right person. I've always admired that quality in you."

"Not anymore."

"You're telling me what I do and do not admire?"

"I'm saying . . . I'm saying that if you still admire me, you won't much longer. And you'll understand why I'm the last person who can fix this. And it's not just because I haven't sold a single program ad, and I don't intend to, and I haven't thought about how we'll do tickets, because I don't want to be part of the 'we,' or I don't *feel* like I'm part of the 'we.' I—I'm not even going to come to the production this year. And I should have told you all that—the parts I knew anyway—a while ago, and I'm sorry."

Mrs. Gomes stared out at the empty stage, at the big empty room. "Yes, you *really* should have told me that earlier. But we'll . . . Well, I— Honestly, I don't know what we'll do. That's disappointing, Yoyo."

"I know," I said.

Would it be any consolation if I told her how disappointed *I* was in me? I didn't think so, so I left her alone in the empty cafetorium.

I walked home alone, thinking about last meals, last words. Just in case I wouldn't get a chance later, I took out my phone and sent a message. I sent the same message to two people, to Esti and Shua: I love you.

I'd never actually told Shua I loved him. But I did. And I needed to tell him.

CHAPTER 41

"**WHAT IS THE MEANING OF THIS?**" the prominent rabbi Yosef Herschel Gold asked his eldest daughter, Yocheved.

As usual on a weekday, we all ate at different times. My father was the last to do so. I lay in wait, ambushed him, and dragged him and my mother into the living room. My mother I *literally* dragged, pulling her by the sleeve. My father followed reluctantly, his eyes wandering around, his mouth grumbling things like, "What's going on here?" and "I have things to do" and "That soup was wonderfully flavored."

There were ways in which it was harder to wrangle them into the room than it was with the little ones. I couldn't just tell them there would be chocolate in the living room, or that I'd let them play a game on the iPad.

Nachi was already there when we came in. Now he was still there, his hand submerged to the elbow in a bag of potato chips. I'd have preferred him not to be there, but I felt like my parents were uneasy enough already, and I'd put them over the edge if I ordered Nachi out of the room.

He did get up and move from the couch to the loveseat. My parents took the couch. I took the old, worn, leather chair. It used to be in my father's office, but when it was no longer fit for official visitors, he moved it down here. It didn't match the decor, and my mom and I had asked him to remove it, or give it away, or set it on fire, but he did none of those things, and now I was seated in it.

"Okay," I began. "Here's the deal. I'm going to say something that's really difficult to say, and I know you won't react to it positively, but I want you to tell me you'll wait until I've said everything I need to say, without interr—"

"Are you *okay*, Yoyo?" my mom asked.

I took an ostentatiously deep breath. "Eema. Do you see how you've already interrupted me, during the very part of the speech where I *specifically* asked you *not* to interrupt me?"

"Don't talk to your mother like that," my father said.

"Like *what*?"

"Without the respect she deserves," my father said. "'When a person honors their—'"

"I think Eema and I can figure that honor stuff out between the two of—"

"It's unusual for you. But again you speak of your mother with a lack of the proper—"

"Stop!" I said. I clapped my hands at the same time, like a preschool teacher trying to get everybody to pay attention for one second. It worked. "I've been making videos, spreading rumors about people in our community, posting them on the internet."

My phone buzzed. It was Naomi. Don't do this, she said.

But it was too late, because I'd already started, and because I'd already made up my mind.

I got another text. It was Shua. I love you too, Yoyo Gold.

"What are you saying?" my father asked.

"There's a girl who's been making videos about her friends and other people doing stuff they shouldn't do, and that girl is me. I unfiltered my phone, and I've been making the videos in the bathroom, and posting them online."

"This I cannot believe. Did you know this, Chaya?" he asked my mother.

She looked pretty distressed. Her eyes were wide and she was picking at her headscarf. She managed to shake her head.

There was a long silence. It slid comfortably into the top three of my life's most uncomfortable silences. The only sound was the persistent rustling of Nachi's hand in its crinkly bag.

"How could something like this have happened?" my father asked my mother. "In the very home you've made."

"*I've* made?" my mother said.

"You always treated her as an equal, left the girl to her own devices, to grow up without the kind of strong maternal figure our son Moshe had."

Now my mom looked angry. I'd seen her angry plenty of times, but I'd *never* seen her angry at my father. If that anger existed, if it was expressed, it was private.

"Oh, *I* left her? Where were you?"

"Performing my duties to the—"

"Community? Congregation? What about the family? Is shalom bayis not the *most* important?"

"Shalom bayis, shalom bayis. We've had shalom bayis. Have we not had peace between us? Has our daughter not known peace?"

"Does the law not say a man must teach his children? Teach them Torah? Teach them a trade? Teach them to swim?"

My father stood. He pointed a finger at my mother. "I *did* teach her to swim."

"No," my mother said, with a shake of her head. "*I* did. You taught your *son*, Moshe, then decided you'd done your duty, and went back to your—"

"I taught *myself* to swim," I said. "Now stop, both of you."

They quieted for a moment. The only sound was Nachi, licking his fingers with a series of sucking sounds. I walked over to his seat, ripped the chip bag out of his hand, mushed it into his face, and pushed him toward the door.

I walked back over to my parents.

I wanted to be like my dad in this one way: expressions of anger were unbecoming of me, of *us*, he always said. And the man did walk the walk. He was furious right now, but you wouldn't know it. No matter how angry he became, he could maintain a veneer of calm, one that made you feel childish and hysterical by comparison.

I tried to match his stoicism, his restraint.

But I failed, and when they started arguing again, I jumped in between them. "Stop. Stop! You raised me to be resilient, to be mature, to take care of things myself. You didn't hold my hand through the world." Even as I tried to hold it back, I could feel my voice rising into a shouting rant I couldn't control. "I taught *myself* to change a tire, because it's a useful skill. I taught *myself* to swim because swimming looked cool and if Moshe could do it, *anyone* could. And *I* made this decision all on my own, because I didn't like the way people weren't honest with each other, the way people are more worried about people *knowing* stuff about them than they are about that stuff in the first place, and I was angry at myself that I couldn't live up to people's expectations, and I was angry at *you* and the community who held me to a standard I couldn't meet, and I—"

"Who knows about this?" my father asked.

"No! That's *not* the question. Please, *please* don't let that be the question. Don't you see you're proving my—"

"Who knows about this?" he asked again, and this time there was an edge in his tone that made me answer.

"I wanted to tell you first."

My mother paced in the space between me and my dad, like she was trying to protect one of us from the other. But when she looked back and forth between us, she appeared to have equal fury for us each.

"You'll tell nobody else," my father said. He considered this the end of the conversation and started to move toward the doorway.

"No. I'm going to tell everybody," I said. Or Shira would. But actually, I'd decided. I would tell everybody no matter what Shira did.

He stopped in his tracks, spun around, leaned toward me, and extended a single finger. "The law says, 'He who engages in rechilus has committed a sin equal to those for which a Jew must expect death.'"

"I know *exactly* what the law says," I snarled back. "And I don't care."

As I said it, I wondered if it was true. Did I actually not care what the law said? Maybe I just didn't care about his specific interpretation of the law. And maybe I didn't need Jewish law in the complete and total way my father did.

"Should I expect death?" I asked. "If so, I'd like the time to put my affairs in order."

"No," my mother said. "Of *course* not. Yosef, Yocheved is grounded. She is not permitted to drive. She will walk to and from school with Naomi. I'll send a message to Rabbi Levin and have him meet with her."

"No," my father said. "I'll speak to Rabbi Levin. We need to talk about all the girls' phones anyway."

My father got up and left the room. My mother followed.

People underestimate small children. People do this because small children don't know anything and they struggle to wipe their own butts. But little kids are hyperaware of household tension.

Yoni and Yitzy were sitting at the bottom of the steps, staring at us with looks of grave concern.

I must have looked distressed, because when I made eye contact with them, they leapt up and ran over to me. They hugged my legs.

Now that his sons weren't blocking his way, my father headed for the stairs. My mother followed a moment later, shaking her head, but at which one of us I wasn't sure.

"It's okay," I said to the boys. "It's fine. It'll be fine. Should we read a book together?"

Neither of them said anything, but they let me lead them up to their room. They just wanted their world to feel normal, and this felt normal, them lying on their sides in their beds, me on the floor with a book.

Just as I was opening the book, Naomi came into the room and sat down on the floor next to me. "I wish you hadn't done that," she said quietly, as though the boys wouldn't hear.

"I had to," I said. For Shua, or for me—it didn't matter. "You don't understand."

"*You* don't understand. You don't understand how much we need you."

I didn't know which way she meant it. Was it my peers who needed my TikToks? Or was it my siblings who needed their sister? I guess it could have been both.

I'd done a pretty good job getting through a tough evening, right up to this point. But Naomi had broken me. I was falling apart here on the floor, breaking into little pieces like so many tiny Legos. I'd get embedded in the carpet and people would step on me in the night.

When my voice quavered, Naomi grabbed the book and picked up the reading. For somebody who spent so much time reading, she was pretty bad at reading aloud.

CHAPTER 42

I EXPECTED SCHOOL TO BE WORSE than it was. From an objective perspective, it was horrible. It included all of the things a girl might dread about school.

Everybody knew. They were talking behind my back, but right in front of me. I heard Shira downplay her ten-year friendship with me. How could she help it if, when she was five, our moms had arranged for us to play together? *She* couldn't have been expected to see this coming. She was only five. "I'm a good judge of middos," she explained, "But, well . . ."

At lunch, nobody would sit with me. Well, Naomi sat with me, but that was a lot like sitting alone.

"How are the tree witches?" I asked.

"All dead," she said. And those were the only two words she spoke during our entire forty-minute lunch period.

Still, I was happy she was sitting with me. It wasn't like she was spending social capital to do it—she existed outside of the social system—but it was nice to sit across from her.

At home, Naomi did me another favor. I had to walk home from school with her, which meant I couldn't go to Shua's. I hadn't even told her about him, but she seemed to just understand that I needed space. So instead of reading in bed, she read on the couch downstairs.

I lay in bed and talked to Shua on the phone. He'd seen one of my videos, the one about Miri that went viral. That didn't surprise me.

He didn't know that I was the one who made it—he'd never seen my bathroom. But he didn't seem surprised when I told him. He didn't seem to have much reaction to any of it. Maybe it was just that I'd gotten used to reading his body language, which wasn't possible on the phone. But he was the same as always. He was quiet, and sweet, and thoughtful, and funny in his understated way.

A routine developed for the rest of the week. I went through school alone, my eyes only on my schoolwork. I watched Naomi read during lunch. I came home and did my homework and called Shua. I wanted to scroll through social media, but my dad had the filter reinstalled on my phone.

I got a little anxious on Friday morning. It was one thing to be shunned at school, or to seclude yourself in your room, but Shabbos would be a whole other animal. Would I cook with my mom? Would I help the boys wash and get into their nice clothes? Would I play board games with my family like everything was normal?

But I never found out.

When I got home from school, I received Esti's text. She'd never replied to my I love you from the other day, but now she had:

```
Love you too.
Meet me at Tanigawa. 7:00 pm.
Please please please.
I'm only here 2nite.
I was staying with cousins in the city, was supposed
to go home yesterday.
```

```
Flight got canceled.
Please.
```

I closed the door to my room and took a seat on my bed. I ran my fingers along the lines of the quilted bedspread.

Tanigawa appeared to be a ski resort in Japan. But it was also a sushi restaurant in Center City Philadelphia. I assumed Esti wanted me to meet her at the latter.

There was an urgency in the texts, the way she'd split them up, the way she'd sent the fourth *please* in its own message.

I yearned to see her, but I was boxed in by Shabbos.

I used Google to calculate the walking distance. If I left now, I wouldn't make it in time. I checked the train schedule, but even if I was going to break Shabbos, the trains stopped running too early to get me home. I went to see what it would feel like to hold the car fob in my hand, but I remembered that my mom had taken it.

I could only think of one other option.

CHAPTER 43

"YOU *CALLED* ME?" MICKEY SAID WHEN she picked up. "Are you done being disappointed in me? Because I have some news about Mrs. Dvornik's grandkids that you're going to be *really* interested to hear."

"There's no way that's true," I said.

"Correct. You will not be interested. But I'll tell you anyway. You see, after Sacha started that job with the 'computer company,' he—"

"Mickey."

"Yeah?"

"I don't have time for this," I said. Naomi attempted to open the door, but I waved her back into the hallway. "Are you free tonight?"

"Well, first I have to go to Friday services. And then Marisol is having people over, but I've been talking to this kid Jaden and I'm trying to see if he'll invite me out."

"Will you come get sushi with me in Center City? I need to meet up with a . . . friend. But I don't have another way to get there. Please. You owe me."

"I *don't* owe you. But I'll do it anyway. My mom will probably let me skip services if I tell her it's just this week. You do know what day it is, right? Or did your paper calendar decompose or something?"

"I know what day it is."

"What time should I pick you up?"

"Don't pick me up. I'll show up at your place at five thirty."

I let Naomi back into the room, went to my closet, and stuffed a couple things in a bag. I put my purse in the bag too.

"Will you help Eema chop vegetables?" I asked Naomi.

Naomi slid over to the edge of her bed. "Is that safe?" she asked.

"You'll both have knives, so if Eema comes after you, you can defend yourself."

Naomi nodded and followed me out of the room. "Where are you going?"

"I'll be back," I said.

At the bottom of the stairs, Naomi went off to the kitchen, and I left the house. I still had an hour and a half before I needed to be at Mickey's, so I just wandered through Colwyn. I avoided the downtown strip where lots of people would recognize me, and judge me, and talk about me just like the girls did at school. I walked mostly through the residential area. The only non-house thing I passed was the public library, where there were huge crowds of moms and kids checking out big stacks of books for Shabbos.

One side of the library was all windows, and I stood and watched for a minute. There were two little girls, clearly sisters, lying on the floor, their long hair spread all around them. Their collective hair was all frizzy from the static electricity, and some of it appeared to hover in mid-air. They had one book open, held by the sister on the right, and they were both reading, silently but together. Every so often the sister on the left reached up and turned the page.

Naomi and I had been those sisters, on that same library carpet. Actually, it was a different carpet—they'd recently replaced it. But even if we couldn't get back to the same carpet, I wondered if that closeness—the kind where you turned each other's pages—was something we could return to.

I watched the girls for a while. Their mother came to retrieve them. They helped her carry the books. When they disappeared, I stayed, watching the spot on the floor where they'd been reading.

CHAPTER 44

MICKEY GREETED ME AT THE DOOR. "Shabbat shalom," she said. And then she disappeared into the kitchen. There were candles lit on their kitchen table. I could see them from the living room. "Challah?" Mickey called.

I looked around the house. It had the warm, peaceful feeling of a house on Shabbos, except that the TV was on at low volume.

I followed Mickey's voice.

In the kitchen, there was a challah on the counter. It was beautifully braided. Mickey was standing by the fridge, drinking milk directly from the plastic carton. When we made eye contact, I saw that she had questions. But she was polite enough not to ask them. Instead, she offered me the milk carton. I declined.

"Are you wearing that?" Mickey asked.

"I'll change in the car. I brought your sister's jeans."

"Your jeans," Mickey corrected me as we walked to the car.

I don't think I'd ever been in Philly after dark. I lived twenty minutes away, but I could count my visits to the city on one hand.

What jumped out at me were all the lights. The brake lights of cars on the highway as we crawled through traffic. The skyscrapers, each of their windows lit, even though their offices were empty for the weekend. The lights pouring out of everybody's phones on the sidewalk, as they walked and scrolled, talked and texted, stood on the corner tracking the progress of their Uber, which pulled up to the curb, its hazard lights flashing.

Mickey found a parking spot on the street. "I'm going to parallel park this thing on the first try, and I expect enthusiastic applause." She handed me her phone so I could document the feat. "Note that the car is old and has no backup camera. The level of difficulty is insane. I'm like Simone Biles when she did the double pike vault, just taller."

I was impressed, and I did applaud.

Out in the bright night, Mickey walked with purpose like she knew exactly where she was going. I walked self-consciously, like people would notice that I felt weird here, that I didn't quite fit in, like they'd somehow know I was doing something I never expected to do. At the same time, it was strange to walk somewhere nobody knew me. When people approached me, they didn't look up. There was no recognition.

The restaurant looked just like the ones in Colwyn. There was a sushi counter on the right, a line of booths along the wall on the left. Esti was seated in the back one, facing the door. Next to her in the booth was a giant suitcase. Her head was bent forward, and she was scrolling on her phone. There was a glint of something on her face, and I realized she had a big ring in her left nostril. She had her legs crossed. She was wearing jeans. They were baggy, and there was a giant hole in one of the knees.

"Yoyo," Mickey whispered. "We can't just stand in the doorway forever. We can stay. We can go. You had to know it wasn't a kosher restaurant."

I hadn't realized how much I'd missed Esti's nostrils. I hadn't realized how much I'd missed her kneecaps. I wished I could see the other one.

I *knew* I'd missed her, obviously. It just wasn't clear until just now in the doorway—where, Mickey continued to tell me, I was not to remain any longer—just how big the absence of this tiny person was.

Mickey identified Esti when Esti started to wave frantically at us. When we got to the booth, I introduced Mickey and we sat down.

A waitress brought us water, just in time. I was trying to talk to Esti—I had *so* much I wanted to say. But she was not making it possible.

"Esti," I said, "you *have* to stop crying."

"Nope. I refuse," she said.

"Then at least you have to hydrate." I pushed her water glass closer to her hand. Eventually, she wrapped her fingers around it and drank.

We waited in silence for Esti to finish crying. It took a while, but eventually she was done. No more tears. She did still have a lot of snot on her face, though. There was one long tendril of it, hanging down over her upper lip. "Tissue?" Mickey asked, holding a napkin across the table toward Esti.

Esti looked at it, then wiped the snot on her shirt instead. "Why do you think God created sleeves?"

I let out a little giggle. Bare kneecap jeans nose ring Esti was the same Esti. They were all the same Esti. They were all my Esti.

It took a while to get to the real stuff. There was a feeling-out period, where we just read the menu, and ordered and talked about whether that streamer was telling the truth about that actress he just broke up with, and how cute it was when that pet parrot asked his owner for pistachios.

When the waitress brought the food, Mickey started eating, but I just stared at the spicy tuna roll. I knew it wasn't kosher, but it looked *just* like the many kosher spicy tuna rolls I'd eaten.

Esti read the look. "That's the thing about sushi," she said. "It's not cooked, and there's no meat or dairy, so it's pretty easy. It's the perfect gateway drug. It's the marijuana of treif. Next thing you know you're washing down your pulled pork sandwich with a milkshake."

"You're lactose intolerant," I reminded her, picking up a piece of treif sushi with my chopsticks.

"I've still never tried pork," Esti said. "But I did have a cheeseburger, which was pretty good. And I had sex," she said excitedly. "It was painful. Wouldn't really recommend it. The cheeseburger was better."

"Wait," I said. "With Ari?"

"No. Ari? I haven't spoken to Ari since I left."

"You said you loved him, though. You got sent away when you didn't even—"

"*Sent away?*" Esti said. She put her last piece of sashimi back down on her plate. "Did your dad tell you he *sent* me away?"

I guess he hadn't said that explicitly. But if he hadn't sent her, then Esti had just . . . left me? Without saying goodbye?

Esti watched me with a look of pain as I came to that realization.

The waitress cleared our plates.

"I made out with Ari a few times in that field down near Route 31. It wasn't what I thought it would be, and the last time we were there, he kept trying to pull me down into the grass, but I didn't want to get all scratchy. I just wanted to kiss him, and feel close to him, you know? Well, I guess you wouldn't know."

"No. I know," I said.

"So after I dropped him off the last time," Esti continued, but then she stopped suddenly, as she registered what I'd said. "Wait. You *know*? You have to tell me—"

"I'll tell you, I'll tell you. After."

"Okay. Fine." Esti gave me a look as she pulled some ice water through her straw, but she continued with her story. "After I dropped him off, that last time, I just sat in the car, and I started . . . Well, I—I started hitting my head against the window. I know what you're going to say: hit your head against the *steering wheel*, Esti, since that's not made of glass. But I tried that, and it kept honking the horn. I was so . . . angry, just *furious*, because I couldn't control my own feelings, and I couldn't stop doing things I shouldn't, and I couldn't just make myself be who I wanted to be. I couldn't make myself like you, basically."

"You were fine," I said. "You were . . . you."

"Maybe. But I didn't know it yet. I couldn't figure that out in Colwyn. I'd been talking to my dad—and your dad—about the boarding school for a while, but I decided it was time. I needed something different. And I'm *so* sorry I didn't tell you. I wanted to. I just knew if I did, if I went to tell you, I'd change my mind on the spot. And then when I got there, I wasn't allowed to call."

"I understand," I said. "I think I do. Maybe it's like, you had to step away from something you cared about, because that was the right thing for *you*."

"It's funny," Esti explained, as she reached across the table to excise a bit of Mickey's mochi cake. "The school is on the edge of the city. It feels like, just, desert. But at night you can see the lights of the strip, and it has opposite effects on people. Some girls see them and they immediately turn around, and go deeper into their faith. And then some girls see the lights and go toward them and get fake IDs and go out dancing, and get back just in time for class."

I didn't need to ask which one of those Esti was. But in case I had my doubts, she dug into her clutch and pulled out an ID that had her face on it, but said that she was a twenty-two-year-old from Utah named Grace Titan.

I used to have trouble believing that Esti was the age she was. She always looked young. But actually, now, with all of the eyeliner and the nose ring, she almost looked her age.

I turned the card over, twirling it in my fingers. "I'm sorry," I said to her. "I should have—"

"No," Esti said, taking her card back. "I'm sorry. Well, I'm not sorry I left, but I'm sorry I did it the way I did. I just needed space. I needed to . . . I don't know. You cast a big shadow in Colwyn, and I worried if I didn't just leave, I'd never get out of it."

"I cast a different shadow now," I said.

"And it didn't seem right to—I don't know—keep dragging you down."

"You never dragged me down. You dragged me lots of places, but down was never one of them."

Esti put her card back in her clutch and got up. "Where to?"

Mickey found us a coffee shop, where we sat and talked and laughed for another hour. I burned my tongue on hot chocolate while I tried to tell Esti about everything she'd missed: the TikToks, Mickey, Kaden, Shua.

"I wish I'd been there," Esti said. "I want to see *all* of that."

But the irony was, if she *had* been there, she probably wouldn't have seen any of it. The way I felt talking to Esti about it now . . . If I'd had her here the whole time, I don't think any of that stuff would have happened. I wouldn't have needed it to.

Esti called an Uber to take her to the airport.

"Come visit over Pesach," she said. "Most girls go home, so the dorms will be empty. If you let me know in advance, I'm sure I can make you a member of the Titan family. We can be the first Mormon Jewish sisters. It'll be a Titanic good time. Get it? Titan. Titanic?"

That was the moment that Esti's Uber pulled up, and the driver came out to help her get her bag into the trunk. I knew I should say something, but I didn't. I reverted back to the person who just stared and said nothing as Esti's car pulled away.

"As heartwarming as that was," Mickey eventually said, "there's a limit to how long I'm willing to just stand here on the curb. Also, full disclosure, Jaden has just sent me a very graphic message that I'd really like to respond to *in person*, so—"

I just started walking in the direction I thought her car was located.

CHAPTER 45

GOOGLE SAID THERE WAS NIGHT CONSTRUCTION on I-76, so we took the east river drive along the Schuylkill, and then wound through parts of the Wissahickon. Mickey was respectful and let me have my quiet. She didn't even play music, just drove in silence.

I kept my eyes closed, watching Esti on the insides of my eyelids, which was why I didn't see it coming. I just felt the car suddenly brake, and then I heard the initial impact.

My eyes opened just in time to see the deer hit the windshield. Mickey screamed and so did the tires. I wasn't exactly sure how she did it given that there was a large animal blocking her view, but Mickey managed to pull the car onto the shoulder.

Somehow, the deer was not dead. As I reached for my seat belt release button, the animal writhed in its glass trap. Its eyes were wide, and they flitted in different directions, randomly. I stumbled out of the car, partly just to avoid looking at the deer. It made me appreciate kosher slaughter, the quick slash to the throat. This was not how anything should die.

"Are you okay?" I asked Mickey. I wasn't looking at her. I was looking at the dark trees at the side of the road. But I could feel her standing on the shoulder next to me.

"Yeah."

Mickey called her mom to tell her what happened. Then she

called a tow truck. By the time it arrived, the deer was dead. Its eyes no longer flitted. They stared at nothing.

I looked at the tow truck, and then at my phone. The time told me I needed to get home. There was a certain point at which my family would decide there was an emergency. Then, even on Shabbos, they'd use the phone. They'd call me. Clearly they knew I was out, but they didn't know that I'd been in a car. For all they knew, I was at a friend's house, observing the Sabbath, just like them.

I was about to get in the tow truck when my phone rang.

It was too late. It had already been too long. But it wasn't my family calling. It was Shua. "Hello?" I said.

"Are you okay? Are you safe? Where are you?"

"I don't know where I am."

"I can't play games right now. Nachi came to our house. Little dude is going door to door asking for you. I think your sister is doing the other side of the neighborhood. Where are you? I'll pick you up."

I legit didn't know where I was. But I looked at Mickey, and the older bearded dude who was finishing attaching Mickey's mom's car to his truck, and I knew I shouldn't let her drive alone with this guy. I read the address of the tow place off the side of the truck.

Mickey called her mom and told her she was getting a ride home.

Shua was waiting for us when we got there, drumming his fingers on the wheel. We said nothing until Mickey disappeared into her house.

Then we still said nothing. He started driving again. I figured he was going to drop me at home, but he sped right by my street. "You can't go home dressed like that," he explained.

I looked down. I was still wearing my jeans and form-fitting shirt. I could keep my jacket zipped up, but there was no way to hide my pants.

My regular clothes were still in Mickey's car.

I *could* go home like this, in jeans. The question was, did I want to?

Shua pulled up by his house. "I'm going to go in the front door," he said. "I'll find a skirt for you and meet you downstairs."

I headed down the outside steps and waited for him. I sat down on his bed and tried to calm my heart rate. I tried not to think about the deer's eyes. Instead I thought of Esti, who was currently somewhere in the sky over the middle of the country, maybe thinking of me like I was thinking of her.

Shua came downstairs. In his usual thoughtful way, he'd brought tights with the skirt.

"Thanks," I said.

I hesitated, with the tights in one hand, and found myself staring at the bathroom, where I could change with the door closed. But I was in a hurry, so I pulled off the jeans and tossed them aside. I told myself not to, but I paused to see if Shua was watching. He was. He was staring . . . quite intently. But then he closed his eyes and said, "Please." And it was not a "please stay half-naked so I can keep staring at your legs" please.

I pulled the tights up, then the skirt.

I needed to go. I needed to get home so Nachi could stop

knocking doors like the gentiles when they go trick-or-treating. But I didn't want to.

I walked to the bed to say goodbye. I bent down to kiss Shua. But he didn't move to kiss me back. He didn't look at me. I'd bent my face down right in front of his, but he was looking through me.

I stood back up and headed toward the door.

"Yoyo," he said. "Wait. Can you just— I don't need to know where you were, what you were doing, why you were dressed that way. I don't even think I need to know who that other guy is or—"

"Was," I said.

"Whatever. Like I said, I guess I want to know all that stuff, but I don't need to."

I was tired. Physically tired. I took a seat on the last of his concrete stairs and looked across the basement at him. "What do you need then?" I asked.

"I need to know if this was . . . a one-time thing."

It was a weird question coming from him, because since we'd said our kissing and groping was a one-time thing, we'd kissed dozens of times, and groped almost as many.

I looked for irony in the lines of Shua's face, in his dark eyes, but I didn't see any.

"I mean, we've done all kinds of—"

"I know exactly what we've done," he said, "and exactly how many times. But this is—this is Shabbos. This is—you know it's different. And anyway, we can't just keep doing all that. We need to . . . I guess I'm just saying . . . I'm saying. Crap." He looked like he was in pain, and he was looking down at his own body like he was trying to find the source of it.

If whatever he was trying to say was hurting him, I wondered what it would do to me.

"Okay okay. I'll just say this. Yoyo, I'm never going to go out on a Friday night. I'm not gonna stay down here alone. I want to live my life in a Jewish community, in *this* Jewish community. If you and I are going to continue to— I don't know—see each other, I want to step back, as much as I can. I should move back upstairs, and if you want to come over, we can sit in the living room together and talk to Chani about— I don't know. She's really such a boring person, but we'll find something. When you graduate, if you still want to, we can ask your dad if we can date. And, look, I'm not going to tell you what to do, but *I* can't be the one . . . sneaking you out of your pants. Yoyo? Are you listening? Of course you're listening. You're always listening. You're just . . . being you."

Was I being me? I wish he'd been more specific, included a full description of what exactly comprised *me*, because I wasn't sure I could describe it myself.

I considered his initial question. Was this a one-time thing, my Friday night trip to non-kosher sushi? I thought so. In that moment, I wanted it to be. But could I look Shua in the eye and tell him it was so?

I could barely look at him at *all* right now.

He was probably right about the step back—he was right about a lot of things. And what had I said to Esti? It was about her, about stepping away from something she loved because that was the best thing for her.

But maybe now it was true about me.

I finally met Shua's eyes. I looked at him, and his bed, and his bookshelf, and the book open on his shtender. I had so many questions, but none of them seemed like they were for him. And I wondered if we'd answered all of the questions we could answer together, in his basement, with his library. I looked up behind me at the concrete stairs and wondered if the remaining questions were ones I had to answer for myself, all alone in the cold night air.

"I think you're right," I said. "This time I wish you were wrong. But, yeah, you're right. And I'm gonna go. I need to go home."

He didn't say goodbye. He nodded like he was agreeing with me, but he had his head in his hands, so I wasn't sure.

I walked up the stairs and into the night.

CHAPTER 46

OUT ON THE SIDEWALK, I HAD that dreamy feeling again, like I had the night I'd found Shira waiting for me at the minivan. It wasn't dream-like exactly, just a feeling of unreality.

I walked with my eyes closed.

I pictured Esti in Las Vegas. In my mind's eye, I saw her in a short dress, drinking something fluorescent-looking from a plastic cup. She was in a dark room with flashing lights, dancing with a boy, and the two of them were making peace signs with their fingers.

Then I pictured her in the desert, like I first had when I learned where she'd gone. But this time I didn't picture her wandering. And she wasn't alone. I was there too. We were together. We were together in the desert at night, looking out across an expanse of scrub and sand. In the distance there were city lights. Esti started to walk toward the lights.

In Colwyn, I opened my eyes and stopped walking.

I turned around. I could still see the Holtzman house.

I looked back at the outside basement stairs. I took a moment to remember their musty smell, the sensation of the concrete through the soles of my shoes, the faint creak of the hatch's metal hinges, the way I felt when I descended: that paradox of complete safety and thrilling abandon.

I wanted—needed—to remember that place, because I'd probably never be there again.

CHAPTER 47

"I'LL DO BETTER," I SAID, BY way of greeting. "And I'll do whatever I have to do to get there."

My father stood in the doorway. He looked . . . something. Angry? Furious? Livid? He opened his mouth to speak. "Yocheved, are—"

"I'll shape up. I will. But I want it to be clear that I'm not going to do it for you."

"Are you—"

"You can tell me what you think, but you can't tell me what *is*. And if that's not good enough then—I don't know—we've reached a breaking point."

I was still outside, and he was still inside, but my father reached out across the threshold and touched me on the shoulder. He seized my upper arm and just squeezed. We Golds weren't good at expressing ourselves through touch, and I wasn't really sure what this one meant. He had his eyes closed, like he was just holding my arm to reassure himself of its existence. "Are you okay?" he asked. His eyes were moist, and he was blinking rapidly. "*Please* tell me you're okay."

"Yeah," I said. "I'm okay."

My mother sped into the foyer, sliding across the tile floor in her socks. "Baruch HaShem," she said. "Where *were* you?"

"I don't want to tell you," I said. "I *will* tell you, but not now.

If you don't ask, I promise that I'll tell you someday. And it won't *ever* happen again. But only with the condition that you don't ask."

My mom nodded. "Okay. Okay. I'm going to text Nachi and Naomi," she said, "so they can come back home."

Even though she'd announced she was going to do it, it was a little frightening to see my mother use her phone on Shabbos.

My father looked like he was going to speak, but I brushed past him and headed back to the kitchen. If he wanted to talk to me, he could summon me officially.

The thing about sushi is that it's the best thing. But it does have the one downside: it's not that filling. And I found I was starving.

I loaded a plate with roast chicken, vegetables, and a pilaf my mom and I had been experimenting with. I stood at the counter and thought about Shua. A secret basement boyfriend was unsustainable. So I thought about what a real future would look like, with an official boyfriend, then fiancé, then husband. A few days ago—maybe even a few hours ago—my thoughts of the future were almost exclusively about being allowed to touch him, to hold him, to be with him in public, to be an official part of his life. And vice versa.

But in the actual future, with a partner, there would probably be a lot of this: cooking for him, loading stuff onto plates for him. I could hear Mickey in my head calling it sexist. And maybe it was, if I was forced to do it. But there weren't that many times in life where you got to feel like you really mattered to people, and you got to feel that way when you fed them. Cooking for somebody I loved didn't feel like a chore, so long as it was what I wanted to do.

Nachi came in the front door and went upstairs. I didn't see him, but I could tell it was him by the way he walked. Naomi followed a few minutes later. She came into the kitchen. "I found Yoyo," she announced. "She's in the kitchen."

My mom shushed her from the living room, cautioning her not to wake the boys. Naomi rolled her eyes.

"So?" Naomi said.

"Shua found me," I replied.

I thought I saw Naomi smile a little. "How many ways did you mean that?" she asked, leaning against the counter.

"Just the one, I think."

"Don't do that again," she said. "Don't just . . . leave," and she waved her hand at the kitchen window. It must have been tough for her to be outside at night, especially when she couldn't use her phone to light up her book.

When she left the room, I suddenly wondered how many ways she'd meant *her* statement.

I stood at the counter, just listening to the house.

I wasn't allowed to write a to-do list on Shabbos, but I made a mental one. I wanted more clementines. I wanted my mom to buy two cans of beer so I could try a new stew recipe—the alcohol burned off in the cooking process. I wanted to tell Shua that he was right about stepping back, and it would be better if we didn't see each other for a while. I wanted to tell Esti that, so long as she didn't need an immediate answer, I'd consider visiting over Pesach. But we'd have to set some ground rules, and those rules wouldn't have any room for a fake ID.

CHAPTER 48

I THOUGHT ABOUT BEING LATE INTENTIONALLY. Now that Chani did the organizing, I could show up at the last minute. But of course I was right on time.

Some things don't change.

I was allowed to have the minivan for JHR, and I pulled it into the parking lot just as Shua was pulling up in his. I thought about staying in the car and waiting for him to pull away, so I didn't have to see him. But I'd read that tapering was a good way to avoid withdrawal symptoms if you were breaking a habit. Also, I wanted to be brave.

So I got out of my car, and when Chani got out of theirs, I gave a vague wave, one that could have been for Shua, but also could have been for Chani.

Shua gave a nod and drove away.

As I walked in with Chani, I got a text. Was that as hard for you as it was for me? he asked.

Don't text and drive, I replied.

It'll get better, he sent.

As I was composing a reply, he sent more messages:

I think

But maybe not

It can't get worse

Don't reply to these messages. That will make it worse.

....

In the warehouse, it was pretty clear that everybody knew everything. It wasn't surprising. If everybody at school knew, it was only a matter of time until everybody in the community knew.

I thought everybody would ignore me. Or I thought they'd be openly hostile to me. And I got both of those things. I think all of the girls my age felt a certain amount of betrayal, which I understood. And there were older women who judged me, either for the things I'd done, or the fact that I'd exposed them to the world. But there were also women, people I rarely spoke to, who came up and greeted me, asked me how I was doing. They didn't say anything about the videos themselves, but they gave me warm, knowing smiles, nods of the head.

They were all just gestures. They were cryptic. But I felt like I understood them. They were the equivalent of the "Shkoyach" DM I'd got from the palm tree girl, silent messages that said, "I get it." And there would always be people who didn't understand, who never would, but hopefully I could focus on the ones who "got it."

I took my usual spot next to Mickey. Shira was staring at me. I could feel it. I knew she was trying to get my attention, so I kept my eyes down. I thought that was the best way to keep from smiling.

There were so many things that had broken or fallen apart. But I had taken away Shira's leverage, and I knew that if our eyes met, I'd start gloating about it. And that wouldn't be becoming of me.

Mickey and I did our deliveries pretty quietly. We talked about the car accident and the deer, but not much else. She spent a lot of the ride on her phone, texting. Before we picked Chani up back at the warehouse, Mickey asked, "Are we still friends?"

I wasn't sure that we'd ever been friends, exactly. I liked Mickey.

I admired the way she didn't let other people's expectations get in the way of her own interests. But sometimes she took her self-interest too far, so I wasn't sure I could trust her. And trust seemed like an important part of friendship.

"Do you want to be?" I asked.

"Yeah," she said.

"Can I give you some constructive criticism?"

"Sure."

"Don't ditch me for some boy," I said. "I don't care if you don't want to feel responsible for the girls at the synagogue or to your mom—that's your own thing. But I do care if you're responsible for your friends. And if your code of friendship includes ignoring your friend because a boy sends you a 'graphic message,' you should look for a new one."

"A new code or a new friend?"

"Both."

Mickey thought for a second, then nodded. "So you're saying I should *not* give you the full play-by-play of my time with Jaden last night?"

"That's exactly what I'm saying."

"Okay. Was it hard to see Esti again?" she asked.

"It was so hard, and also so easy."

"Hard and easy are opposites, Yoyo."

"Yeah, I know." So I explained to her how it was both of those things, and Mickey listened.

CHAPTER 49

AT HOME, MY MOM WAS IN the kitchen. On the counter she had two baking pans out and all of the standard baking ingredients, plus the bottle of lemon juice that's shaped like a giant lemon. She was clearly making my favorite: lemon bars. Sour and sweet is just a phenomenal flavor contrast, and should probably be the basis for most foods.

Normally she would have stepped over and opened up a space for me to help, but she didn't, because it was clear she was making the lemon bars for me. She pulled out a half-cup measure from the drawer, then doubled back toward the fridge.

"I just came in to give you the key fob back," I said.

"Don't. Keep it," she replied, her eyes scanning the inside of the fridge. "Just don't tell your father." Then she did some muttering to herself, and the muttering became a laugh, a kind of guilty chuckle: "I really should have checked the spreadsheet. I would have known we didn't have enough eggs for this."

"I'll go to the store," I said. "We need a whole bunch of stuff."

"You don't have to."

"I still have the fob," I noted.

She closed the fridge and turned back toward me. "You know you used to *beg* me to let you do the grocery shopping?"

"I remember," I said.

"You were barely a bat mitzvah. You made that big spreadsheet, and then you would ask me to *drop* you off at the store and pick you up afterwards."

That last part I didn't remember. But it sounded plausible.

She walked back to the counter and leaned over in my direction. "When did it change?" she asked me.

I hung my bag on the back of a kitchen chair. "I guess it changed when it started being . . . expected."

"If it was a burden, you could have *told* me, Yoyo."

"I didn't . . . I didn't *know* it was a burden. I only just figured that out. It took a lot for me to figure that out."

My mom nodded. "It's funny how different your own kids can be. When Moshe was little, and I gave him food, he just ate it. Same with Nachi, Naomi, Yoni, Yitzy. All of them. Do you know what happened when I gave food to little Yoyo?"

Little Yoyo wasn't somebody I had access to, at least not right now. I just shook my head.

"Little Yoyo immediately looked around for somebody to share it with. I'm talking about when you were, like, three. I'd give you a single cookie and you'd break it in two and try to give half of it to Nachi, who had no teeth and had never had anything but milk or formula."

That sounded adorable, but it was weird to think of yourself that way. "I don't know what you're trying to say," I admitted.

"I think I'm . . . I think I'm just making excuses for myself."

"You didn't do anything wrong," I said.

"Or maybe I'm apologizing. I'm sorry I took that quality for granted. Because of course I know that feeling too. When something becomes *expected*, it changes, no matter how much you like that something."

I wasn't sure what to say. It wasn't exactly an apology so I couldn't just say I forgave her. I took a half step sideways toward her and she did the same toward me. And we just leaned on each other in a way that felt supportive and nice.

"What you did, I want you to know that I understand where it was coming from. I really do. And your father . . . Well, he knows he was too focused on the congregation, on the community, not enough on us, on you. He knows that."

"Then why doesn't he say that?" I asked.

"Oh, you know why he doesn't just say that."

And she was right. I did. He didn't just say that because he wasn't the type of person who just said stuff. Some time, maybe a week from now, maybe two months, maybe five years, he'd call me into his office and tell me a parable about an ancient Jew who stole his neighbor's goat but paid him back with years' worth of goat cheese, and his peace offering would be buried somewhere in that story, and I'd just have to find it there.

I went upstairs to my bedroom. I knocked on the half-open door, and Naomi looked up from her book. "Want to come grocery shopping?"

"Sure," she said. She got up and peered at the window. "Do I need a jacket?"

"Probably," I said. "It's not that cold, but it's windy."

Downstairs, Nachi was in the living room, sitting on the floor, looking over some homework. He'd just got back from basketball, and his face was bright red. "We're going grocery shopping," I told him.

"Okay," he said. "We need corn chips. Can you get the 'family sized' bag? 'Family' is the size that I like."

"You can pick out whatever bag you want."

"Wait," Naomi said. She had just appeared behind me with her jacket on. "We're bringing Nachi? Why?"

"Yeah. Why?" said Nachi. "Don't bring me."

"He doesn't want to be brought," Naomi said. "And just . . . look at him. He's, like, *wet*. It's like he's been out in the rain, but it's *all* his own sweat. It's disgusting."

"It's ideal," I explained. "He'll act as a repellent. Nobody will talk to us this way."

First I thought we'd go to Walmart, because we wouldn't know as many people there, and because they had the corn chip bags for the biggest families. But I found that I was driving to the Colwyn Kosher Grocery.

And I was wrong. People did talk to us. Nachi didn't repel anybody. Mrs. Jacobs asked Nachi about how his game was, and how her grandson Dovid had played. Nachi told her that it was a practice, but that Dovid had played pretty well.

"No surprise," she said. "He's so talented."

When Mrs. Jacobs walked away, Nachi whispered to us, "Dovid is the worst basketball player I've ever seen. We're on the same team, but sometimes I steal the ball from him and lay it up myself, because I know he'll miss."

We all giggled. We giggled our way up the snack aisle, then along the row of freezers in the back, where we debated whether the little guys had the dexterity necessary to operate the tiny folding spoons that came with the miniature ice cream tubs that were on sale.

When we got back in the car with the groceries, I didn't start the engine. I took out my phone and shared the grocery spreadsheet with Nachi and Naomi. "Menachem," I began, then paused. I wasn't sure I'd ever called him by his full name. It certainly got his attention. "Menachem, you know best what we do and do not have, so you will update this spreadsheet based on need. Eema will do the essentials, but you will do the snacks. If you don't understand how it works, I will help you, but only if I see that you are making an effort. Questions?"

"What was wrong with the system that we had?"

"Menachem. Have you noticed your body has been going through changes?" I asked him.

Nachi's eyes were suddenly wide, and he was looking down at himself. Most of the sweat had dried, but his shirt was splotched here and there with its residue. "I don't feel comfortable—"

"Of course you don't feel comfortable. Changes aren't supposed to be comfortable. But they happen whether you want them to or not. Your body is changing, and I need your maturity to develop in congruence therewith."

I started the car.

Nachi looked at me, but I had my eyes on the reverse camera, so he turned to Naomi. "She's asking you to grow up," Naomi explained. "Well, not really asking."

When I pulled the car into the driveway, I handed Naomi the fob. "Make sure to rotate stock based on expiration date, and hide the ice cream in the back of the freezer so the boys get to have some before Abba eats it all."

Naomi nodded and slung a couple bags over her shoulders.

"And Eema's making lemon bars if you want to help," I added.

"I don't know," she said. "I almost cut off my own foot on Friday, when you went AWOL and I did *all* of the chopping. Chopping is not a safe activity, Yoyo. Nobody should chop anything. If HaShem saw fit to make celery a certain size, maybe we're meant to leave it that way."

"Eema's baking, so let's hope there isn't celery."

"All right. Cool. I'm in."

"Actually," I said, opening the front door for her, so she could slide through with the bags hanging off both of her shoulders. "I like baking."

She paused in the foyer to look at me. "Are you *sure?*"

"I'm sure," I said.

When the lemon bars were in the oven, I went upstairs. I had a calculus test coming up, and I didn't feel comfortable texting Dassi for help. I needed at least two hours of studying, which meant I needed about four hours of time, to account for the two hours I'd waste thinking about Shua.

CHAPTER 50

I'D TOLD MRS. GOMES THAT I wasn't going to attend the production, but I figured one more lie couldn't hurt.

I didn't want to help set up the cafetorium, organize younger girls as ushers, set up the ticket booth in the lobby, sell tickets, and make polite conversation with everybody and their mother—who would also be there.

But just going, as an audience member, that didn't sound bad.

Part of me feared that, without me doing all of that stuff, there wouldn't *be* a production. But as it approached, nobody talked about postponement or cancelation or anything.

On the phone, I told Mickey about the plot. I explained that the mother and daughter couldn't get along, and the whole community was divided, taking sides, but this Jewish army officer helped the mom and daughter repair their relationship, and then the three of them kept the non-Jewish mob from hurting the Jews.

"Tell me more about this army officer," Mickey said. "What do he and the eldest daughter get up to?"

"Nothing. There's no romance."

"Oh."

"And the army officer is played by a girl, and that's the point. The whole thing is about not *needing* boys."

"You're not selling this well," Mickey said.

I let out an exasperated laugh. "I've tried on all your hats. Now it's time for you to try on mine."

"Listen," Mickey said. "I assume I'm going to have to dress differently at this thing, but I'm not wearing a hat. Don't you *dare* try to make me wear a hat."

"It's a figurative hat, Mickaela. And just *think* how happy your mom will be when she hears how Jewish your night out is gonna be."

"That's a *great* point," Mickey said.

My plan was to pick up Mickey before I picked up Naomi and my mom. It made no sense logistically, since the latter two lived at my house, but I felt like Mickey needed supervision getting ready. I brought her one of Naomi's high-collared shirts, and a couple different skirts to try.

"You know I would go with you even if it didn't make my mom happy, right?" she said, as she pulled the skirt over her leggings and did a little turn in front of her mirror.

"I know," I said. "If I didn't know that, I wouldn't have invited you."

I don't know why exactly, but when I got to the event itself, I expected to have to introduce Mickey to everybody, to explain who she was and why she was there. It wasn't that strangers weren't welcome. Any woman or girl was more than welcome. It was just a pretty tight-knit community, and we didn't have a lot of outsiders come to our events.

But then all of these women, and some of my classmates, were greeting Mickey by name, and I remembered that she'd been at JHR every Sunday, even ones when I didn't show up. There was this strange dynamic where some people didn't know how they wanted to act around me. It was like they were trying to figure out how I fit now—which I guess was the same thing I was doing—and were more comfortable around Mickey.

I noticed a bunch of production-related things that I would have done better. The ticket situation was confusing, and it was set up in a way that made no sense in terms of the flow of people through the space. There were very few ads in the program, so I wasn't really sure what the budget situation was. And I didn't think the advertisers themselves would be pleased with the way their ads were laid out.

Those little details bothered me, but there was a comfort in knowing that these things did get done without me.

My mom sat up front with Naomi like she always did, but I didn't want to be in the first row, where the literal spotlight would occasionally fall on me. I loitered in the lobby with Mickey, and we took seats in the back right before the curtain went up.

You could tell why Mrs. Gomes had originally cast Miri as the lead. Shira was capable: she could hit the correct notes and deliver the right lines with their proper facial expressions. But it all felt . . . too calculated. She could play the part, but she couldn't lose herself in the role.

I wondered if other people saw it the way I did, if they saw through her. But if they did, they'd didn't show it. The applause during her curtain call was thunderous.

"Leah wasn't a very convincing boy," Mickey said, as we walked back out of the cafetorium.

"Yeah?" I said. "That was your big takeaway?"

"Yep," she said. "I spent the whole time thinking about how her boobs were too big for the part."

But I knew that wasn't true. Because Mickey had laughed a bunch of times, and she'd grabbed on to my arm when the dastardly gentile almost ran Miri through with a sword, and at the end she'd blamed her tears on allergies, but her "allergic" reaction to the bittersweet ending cleared right up when the house lights came on.

There were snacks laid out on tables, and as we walked toward them, I wanted to say something, something like, "See how great that was? *See?* You don't need to get your self-worth by impressing boys. You don't need men for your empowerment. Boys don't have to be this focal point in everything." But that was the kind of speech you made on stage, in the production itself, not in the lobby afterward. So instead I said, "I wish I actually liked rugelach," and Mickey didn't respond because her mouth was full of it.

Naomi found us, and we talked about who had the best performances, and whether we thought the costumes actually fit the supposed time period. The thespians themselves were starting to filter out of the cafetorium, so it made it easier to assess. Whether the costumes fit nineteenth-century Ukraine was hard to say, but they definitely didn't fit today. The actors stuck out as they moved through the lobby.

I was standing at the far end of a long table. I saw Shira and Dassi appear at the other end. I could see them in my peripheral vision. The snacks were a pretense. Neither of them reached for anything, and I could sense them looking back and forth between me and the food.

At first, I thought I'd refuse eye contact, like I had at JHR. But I changed my mind. I turned to face them and made direct eye contact. Shira put on a smile, the same one she'd pasted on for her curtain call. The two of them started around the table in my direction, but I shook my head at them. They stopped and pretended to be interested in the little cookies arranged on the plastic tray next to them.

I turned to Mickey, hoping she'd seen the way I'd shut them down. But she was talking with Naomi. "Shall we?" I asked them. "Naomi, do you want to see if Eema is ready to leave?"

Naomi turned to go find her.

"We'll be outside," I said. I wanted to get out of the lobby, away from the crowd.

Mickey and I started our walk around the edge of the room toward the big double doors. Over my shoulder, I could see somebody following us, weaving through the crowd. When I saw who it was, my heart sank, and it did a bunch of other things too.

It was hard enough without the little reminders, and Chani Holtzman was a *big* reminder.

She caught up to us right at the doors. I had a grip on the handle.

Her costume makeup was starting to streak, and she sounded out of breath. "Yoyo," she said. "I—I need you to fix something for me."

I could feel my eyes narrowing. At this point, who would ask me to fix their problems? And even if they wanted to, I was trying to get out of that game. I needed to work through my own questions before I answered them for other people.

"It's Shua," she said.

A shock went through me. "Shua?" I asked.

"My brother."

"Right. Yeah. I know him."

"I *know* you do. That's why I'm— Listen. He's . . . not himself. No, that's not strong enough. I need to convey the full gravity of the situation. He's falling apart. He looks horrible. He never sleeps and I don't think he's eating. And he *keeps* trying to talk to me about obscure Torah commentary, and when I tell him that I don't care, he begs me to just *pretend* to listen anyway, because he can't 'bear to feel so alone.' And I guess I *would* stay and listen, but he's starting to smell. I don't think he's, like, bathing."

Obviously, I wanted to feed this unwashed Shua while we talked about Torah. But we'd agreed about this, the separation. I'd told myself I'd never go down those stairs again. And Shua had told me not to return his texts. I'd composed a message to him about every five minutes since he'd told me that, and I was proud of myself for never sending them. Every time I didn't send one, it got the littlest bit easier, and I told myself that sometime soon I wouldn't even have to compose them anymore.

But as I looked at Chani, as I strengthened my grip on the door handle, I could feel my resolve weakening. Had I been wrong when I agreed with Shua about the step back? Had I been wrong when I told myself I needed to figure stuff out alone?

"Just come over on Shabbos. We can all sit in the living room. If you don't want to do it for him, do it for me."

No. I hadn't been wrong. Just naive to think the pain would be tolerable.

"Okay. Okay," I said. I didn't know if it was the right thing to do, but *if* I was going to do it, I was going to do it for *me*.

I got a text from Naomi. `Me and Eema will get a ride with the Meisels.`

I pulled the door open, and waved Mickey toward it. She went out into the night. I took a moment and tried to compose myself before I followed.

Mickey was facing me when I came through the door. She looked almost disapproving. "You should see yourself right now," she said, shaking her head at me.

I looked down to see if I looked unusual.

"I've never seen you this happy. It's like you're glowing. You're *very* bright. Like, I should be wearing sunglasses if I'm going to keep looking at you."

"Let's get to the car," I said. And I started walking to the parking lot, but it didn't feel like walking. It was like I was floating, being carried like a princess by invisible creatures, up on one of those litters.

"Sounds like you've got a nice date with your boy," Mickey said. "Sounds pretty . . . empowering."

"Shut up," I told her, as I unlocked the car. "If you take this away from me, I'll make you walk home."

As I got in the driver's seat, I took out my phone. I opened up my conversation with Shua. I'd composed so many messages to him, but the last one I'd actually sent told him not to text and drive. So I left the car off, took a deep calming breath, and started typing out a message.

I knew this floating feeling wouldn't last forever, but it was still there after I pressed send, and I was happy to ride it out as long as I could.

MY DEEPEST AND SINCEREST THANKS TO THE FOLLOWING PEOPLE:

My brilliant editor: Talia Benamy.

My amazing agent: Rena Rossner.

The wonderful people at Philomel and Penguin Young Readers: Jill Santopolo, Want Chyi, Lily Qian, Ellice Lee, Kaitlin Yang, Abigail Powers, Sola Akinlana, Gaby Corzo, Ginny Dominguez, Lathea Mondesir, Carmela Iaria, Venessa Carson, Summer Ogata, Trevor Ingerson, Felicity Vallence and the digital marketing team, and Deb Polansky and the entire sales team.

My awesome friends (who are also talented critics and collaborators): Roz Warren, Rob Volansky, Michael Deagler, and Brad Gibson.

DISCUSSION GUIDE

1. Yoyo practices Orthodox Judaism, while Mickey practices Reform Judaism. What do you know about Judaism and Jewish culture, whether from your own life or from someone else? Are the Jewish customs and traditions that you're familiar with similar to or different from Yoyo's and Mickey's? Are there other parts of Judaism that you're curious to know more about?

2. Yoyo's life is heavily influenced by her community's religious and cultural traditions. Do you have religious or cultural traditions that are important to your family or community? If so, how do you feel about them?

3. How are the expectations for Yoyo affected by the fact that she is the oldest girl in the family? How does she respond to those expectations? Have you had any expectations placed on you by your family based on gender, birth order, or anything else? How have you handled those expectations?

4. Shabbos, the Jewish day of rest, helps Yoyo reset and decompress every week. Are there regular activities or traditions that help provide structure in your life?

5. Yoyo finds great meaning in her faith, but at times she finds it restricting. Is it possible for Yoyo to enjoy the benefits of being part of her community without feeling overwhelmed by its rules?

6. Yoyo lives in the same community as her friends Shira and Dassi, but they experience it differently. How and why is Yoyo's experience different?

7. Yoyo and Mickey become friends despite their different interpretations of their faith. Why might relationships between people of different backgrounds be important or meaningful?

8. Yoyo finds what she perceives as hypocrisy throughout her community. She decides it's important to expose this hypocrisy to the world. Do you agree with her approach? Why or why not?

9. Social media provides Yoyo with a connection to the larger world outside of her community, but it also causes her quite a few problems. Is the connection that social media provides worth it for her? Do you find yourself experiencing both sides of social media, meaningful connection but also potential harm?

10. In Yoyo's community, many people express their Jewish identity through their dress. For example, Yoyo wears skirts because of tradition and modesty. How does your own clothing—or your accessories—show the world who you are?

11. Yoyo gets herself in trouble by questioning some of her community's beliefs. Is there a "right" or "correct" way to go about challenging the beliefs of your family or community?

12. Even though he's not in school, Shua keeps studying because he feels "stuck," and he thinks studying will help him get through it. Have you ever felt stuck with some part of your life? How did you figure out a way forward?

13. On page 156, Yoyo says that her faith is broken. How does she go about repairing it?

14. Yoyo's relationship with her family, community, and religion evolve throughout the novel. Do you think she ends up in the right place? How do you see her future?

WINNER OF **THE WILLIAM C. MORRIS AWARD**

LONGLISTED FOR **THE NATIONAL BOOK AWARD**

A *PUBLISHERS WEEKLY* BEST BOOK OF 2022

A *KIRKUS REVIEWS* BEST BOOK OF 2022

A **NEW YORK PUBLIC LIBRARY** BEST BOOK OF 2022

A *TABLET* BEST JEWISH CHILDREN'S BOOK OF 2022

A **BUZZFEED** BEST YA BOOK OF 2022

A **JUNIOR LIBRARY GUILD** SELECTION

A **YALSA 2023** BEST FICTION FOR YOUNG ADULTS TOP TEN BOOK

PRAISE FOR
THE LIFE AND CRIMES OF
HOODIE ROSEN

"Bold, brave, and brutally honest,
it holds a permanent piece of my heart."
—DAHLIA ADLER,
AUTHOR OF *COOL FOR THE SUMMER*

"A deeply authentic story about the terror and glory of encountering the outside world without sacrificing who you are—and who you want to be. It's touching, tragic, and as Jewish as your bubbe's cholent."
—GAVRIEL SAVIT,
NEW YORK TIMES BESTSELLING AUTHOR OF *ANNA AND THE SWALLOW MAN*

"Blum gives the common but often-dismissed spiritual journey of many teens the respect it deserves in this witty, profound look at cross-cultural friendship, courageous honesty, and how a willingness to truly see and love our neighbors can change an entire community."
—VESPER STAMPER,
NATIONAL BOOK AWARD–NOMINATED AUTHOR OF *WHAT THE NIGHT SINGS*

"A refreshingly human look at the day-to-day nuances of Orthodox Judaism and the terror of modern antisemitism. I laughed, I gasped, I craved kosher Starburst. Two thumbs-up from this nice Jewish girl!"
—TYLER FEDER,
SYDNEY TAYLOR AWARD–WINNING AUTHOR OF *DANCING AT THE PITY PARTY*

"Isaac Blum has the rare talent of telling searing, visceral truths in a witty, funny, punchy way... *The Life and Crimes of Hoodie Rosen* is a vital voice in Jewish YA canon."
—KATHERINE LOCKE,
SYDNEY TAYLOR HONOR AUTHOR OF *THE GIRL WITH THE RED BALLOON*

★ "Funny, smart, moving, courageous, and so timely it almost hurts."
—*KIRKUS REVIEWS*, STARRED REVIEW

★ "Blum tackles themes of acceptance and community [in] this impressively drawn story."
—*PUBLISHERS WEEKLY*, STARRED REVIEW

★ "A sharply written coming-of-age story whose protagonist, like any teen, is figuring out where he fits in, under circumstances that are thought-provoking and at times heart-wrenching."
—*THE HORN BOOK MAGAZINE*, STARRED REVIEW

ALSO BY ISAAC BLUM

THE LIFE AND CRIMES OF HOODIE ROSEN

PRAISE FOR **THE JUDGMENT OF YOYO GOLD**

★ "Blum's depiction of a teenage Orthodox Jewish girl is remarkable in its precision and authenticity, along with the depth he gives Yoyo as she experiences life outside her community and contemplates her future. Convincing and appealing." —***Booklist***, starred review

★ "Each potential hot-button issue is handled with delicacy and nuance . . . The characters have dimension and agency, and Yoyo models a level of integrity that feels both genuine and aspirational." —***The Horn Book Magazine***, starred review

"A deeply modern and moving YA novel set in a tightly closed community, this book is a near-perfect exploration of teen self-discovery." —**NPR**

"A nuanced novel about finding oneself amid the perceived constraints and comforts of one's environment." —***Publishers Weekly***

"A kosher coming-of-age story with a bissel of romance." —***Kirkus Reviews***

"Witty, perceptive Yoyo Gold leaps off the page and straight into your heart. You'll cheer her on as she fights for her best friend and her right to express herself. Readers of all ages will relate to Yoyo's struggle to find her place in a world she loves but finds limiting, with people she loves, who sometimes don't understand her."
—**Lori Banov Kaufmann**, National Jewish Book Award–winning author of *Rebel Daughter*

"Earnest and passionate, and yet perfectly flawed, Yoyo and Shua will enthrall readers as they search for truth in their insulated community. Blum again portrays the Orthodox Jewish world with sensitivity and understanding while exploding tropes and finding humor in even the most heart-wrenching moments. Yoyo and Shua's chemistry is electric and will keep readers turning the pages and hoping for more." —**Leah Scheier**, Sydney Taylor Honor author of *The Last Words We Said*

"Isaac Blum's specialty is colliding worlds and seeing how the Venn diagram forms. Yoyo Gold has to pass through disillusionment with her known world in order to realize what she really wants. Somewhere in the intersection of past expectations and future hopes, she finds the elusive path forward."
—**Vesper Stamper**, National Book Award–nominated author of *What the Night Sings*

"*The Judgment of Yoyo Gold* showcases the power of following your heart and doing what's right in the face of community pressure. With a funny, biting, realistically teenage protagonist and packed with loving social critique, this book is for anyone who's ever got tired of swallowing their righteous anger."
—**Sacha Lamb**, Sydney Taylor Award–winning author of *When the Angels Left the Old Country*